THE ROMANCE OF VILLON

The series in which this book is included is called *Le Roman des Grandes Existences*, and is designed to present in imaginative form the biographies of celebrated figures of the past.

already published

BALZAC
by René Benjamin

THE ROMANCE OF VILLON
by Francis Carco

to be published Spring 1928

THE TRUE ADVENTURE OF CHRISTOPHER COLUMBUS
by Marius André

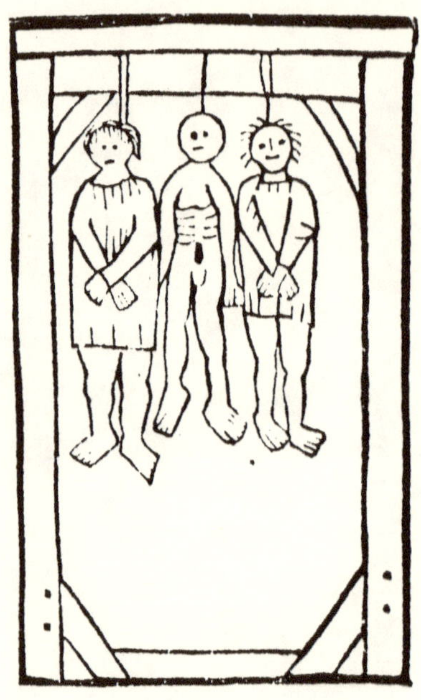

Epitaphe dudit Villon
Freres humains qui apres nous vivez
Nayez les cueurs contre nous endurcis
Car se pitie de nous povrez auez
Dieu en aura plustost de vous mercis
Vous nous voiez cy atachez cinq six
Quãt de la char q̃ trop auõs nourrie
Elle est pieca deuouree et pourrie
et nous les os deuenõs cẽdres a pouldre
De nostre mal personne ne sen rie
Mais pries dieu que tous nous vueil
l'absoul[illegible] g m.

Les Pendus. First Edition of the Grant Testament *published at Paris by Pierre Levet in 1489*

THE ROMANCE OF VILLON

BY
FRANCIS CARCO

TRANSLATED
BY
HAMISH MILES

ALFRED A. KNOPF NEW YORK & LONDON 1927

Published September, 1927
Second Printing, October, 1927

TO
PIERRE CHAMPION

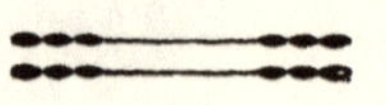

ILLUSTRATIONS

ACKNOWLEDGMENT

The illustrations reproduced in this volume are all taken from François Villon, Sa Vie et Son Temps, *by Pierre Champion, by the kind permission of the publishers, Honoré Champion et Cie.*

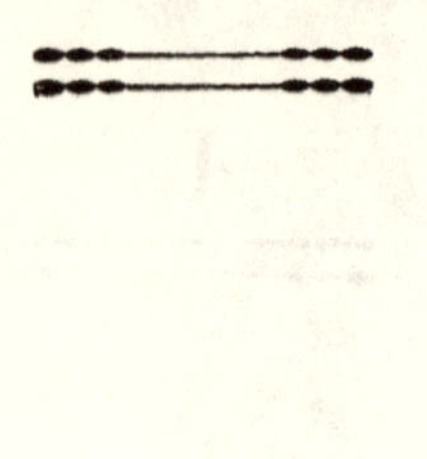

I

1

Towards the evening of a very long October day, a milky, torpid day, a damp wind sprang up and breathed down upon Paris. It came from the west. And immediately the weathercocks on top of the houses swung round their vanes in one and the same direction, and the Seine darkened and rolled beneath its bridges a yellowish, ruffled flood.

It was still light.

Hard by the Châtelet stood a knot of loungers in front of its heavy, squat door, watching an escort of soldiery which, debouching from the Petit Pont, was arriving on horseback. The iron-shod hoofs clattered and echoed on the paved way. And the inquisitive onlookers made signs to each other as the sergeants passed by, recognizing them under their hoods and following them with their gaze, until, the spectacle attracting other idlers, there soon appeared on the little square, flanked on the right by the three tall towers of the prison and on the left by the gateway of the Grande Boucherie, a crowd that talked in whispers and kept asking who were the malefactors thus brought in.

"They're vagabond clerks," said one citizen, standing in the front row. "A good haul."

"Vagabonds and coiners," added his neighbour.

"Yes," went on the first, with self-satisfaction in his tone. "You see where evil courses lead to."

And with outstretched finger he pointed to where eight or ten rogues were being led along on foot by the sergeants in the middle of the escort. One of them, apparently called Jaquet Legrant, was hailed two or three times by persons in the crowd who could not be seen.

"What has he done?" asked the citizen.

"Keep it close!" a voice cried out. "Keep it close, Jaquet! No blabbing!"

But Jaquet no doubt heard nothing, for he did not turn his head, moving on like the others, with his hands bound behind his back.

Then a burst of laughter was heard, and someone said gaily: "It's better here than over the way!"

"You're right!" exclaimed the citizen. "I'm with you there."

"The sight of it's quite enough," came the answer. "As for learning about that otherwise, God protect me from it and leave me my two legs. . . ."

The speaker was a scholar or clerk of about seventeen, insignificant, dark, and mischievous-looking. His name was François de Montcorbier. He lived in the rue Saint-Jacques with his uncle, Master Guillaume de Villon, the chaplain of Saint-Benoît le Bétourné, who had brought him up and lodged him in a little room of his house, styled that of the Porte Rouge, adjoining the church, amidst coffers, a dresser, a table, a wash-basin, wooden stools, and stout books. The bed, beneath its curtains, was narrow and hard. But Master Guillaume willed it so, judging that a young lad should not be made too comfortable. The street, with all its hazards, was enough, and François knew it, lying there on that bed, often in all his clothes, and appreciated it at its full worth, with thoughts only for the diversions that awaited him outside, and yawned the long day through more than he gave himself to his studies.

The truth was that at the hour when François de Montcorbier joined his friends again, one felt life to be better. The day's work done, everyone was coming and going peacefully, between the working-benches and, on the Pont au Change, those windows where the scriveners and their clerks, very late, by candlelight even, were blackening their sheets of paper. The vesper-bells were ringing, and men, women, girls, citizens and merchants greeted each other, stood still and exchanged a word or two, and the little children going off to fetch wine or mustard passed by with their pots, singing as they went. Inside the houses the skilful housewives were making ready the meals. Odours of lard or vegetables floated by, and when the night watchmen took their scattered way through the various quarters, calling out their second round, folk slowly turned from each other to go on to their own homes.

These were the elders. The young men, who had their eyes on the serving-maids, were never in a hurry to separate. For the most part they knew each other, and formed merry groups, chasing the girls, laughing, talking very loud, and putting their pleasure before everything. Amongst these turbulent spirits, Régnier de Montigny, sprung of a noble family of Bourges, made an attractive figure. He had naturally a taking air to him, in his garments of fine stuff and slashed sleeves. With a cap of velvet on his head, and his feet shod in long, elegant shoes that left his heels uncovered, he idled the day and night away, free and without a care. His comrades envied him, even the richest of them, for Montigny, who had little money, laughed at it. François de Montcorbier had more than once heard Montigny explain how matters are arranged when the moment comes for paying, and the penniless scholar that François was, in his poor gown, was filled with admiration that such a personage should dally with his friendship.

Every evening the two young men met each other in the rue de la Juiverie, and while they walked along, a third companion, coming over to meet them, greeted them.

"There you are!" he said. "I was looking for you."

Colin de Cayeux he was called. He was the son of a locksmith of the Saint-Benoît quarter. Low on his legs, but well planted, and with big strong hands, he had a way of eyeing the girls which made them turn and look round. And Colin, better than anyone, knew what the wenches and shop-girls of Paris are worth; when François wanted to talk of them sometimes, he bade him be silent.

"Be quiet," Colin ordered him. "You're at the age

to be made a fool of. Eh? To get to know all about that game, you need time and practice."

"Is that all?"

"You must also," replied Colin in his hard voice, "make clear division betwixt the bad and the good."

"And what is the good?" asked François.

Colin looked at him.

"The hard cash," he affirmed.

"Hard cash?"

"Yes, you rake it in, youngster."

"And the bad?"

Colin shrugged his shoulders, spat in front of him, and then gave vent to a low chuckle.

He had, from time to time, very odd ways of talking; but Montigny also seemed to practise these, and that left François speechless with surprise. For example, it was fixed in his mind that justice — between them — enjoyed the name of "the navy" or "the wheel." To trick justice was "whitening the wheel." And when Colin swore that he would never yield to "being white," François heartily approved of him, for he himself had no intention either of letting himself be played with. Already in his ideas, which he drew scarcely at all out of books, young François willingly admitted that what one does not have, one takes; but he lacked experience, and fear held him back. Under all his knowing airs he was naturally a coward, and uneasy, not very sure of himself. Everything alarmed him — and women especially. If one of them replied to his mute gaze in too direct a manner, he blushed. And then he was furious at being put out in that way.

"Do you know, I like the look of you?" Colin rallied him. "But one must wait."

"Wait?" answered François, with humour. "I see that only too well."

He saw, in the first place, that, lodging with his uncle, he was not in the least free to go out at night as he would have liked. Weak as Master Guillaume de Villon was, he allowed no trifling in this regard. To dine away from home, François had to have his consent, and had to be back at nine o'clock, for Master Guillaume then shut his door and locked it; and he came out to open it himself. This being so, how was this watch and ward to be circumvented? François gave it up. In the second place, it was to his uncle that he had to recite his lessons in the morning before going to the rue du Fouarre to attend the class with the scholars.

"And so," François lamented, when Montigny asked him the way Master Guillaume taught him, "getting Donatus and the *Doctrinale* by heart! I don't get much pleasure out of that!"

"But you'll pass and have your degree!" said Colin.

"Ha, I could do without that!"

And forthwith Colin declared that François did not know what he was saying, seeing that the advantages of every order are attached to the titles of the University. Yet he, who had no fine acquaintances, was a clerk.

"And why?"

"You'll find out some day, perhaps," declared Colin, showing his tonsure. "What does the most caitiff clerk do? He appeals to his bishop, and while you'll see other men dying, and dying a mighty tragic death, your clerk very often lives on in his freedom. — That's well worth some weariness now. . . ."

And he went on talking, and gave instances.

"Colin's telling the plain truth!" opined Montigny.

But François was thinking of pleasure.

. . . .

That evening, as soon as he set eyes on François, Régnier proposed to him to make a party for dinner, and then to join Colin in a certain place he knew of.

"We shall go and ask your uncle," said Régnier.

And he burst out laughing.

"What have I done," asked François timidly, "to make you laugh like that?"

"Stop," answered Régnier with a mysterious air. "Where we are to meet together this night, I swear you will do it."

"But what?" said the scholar. "What am I to do?"

"No," said his companion.

And taking the scholar by the arm, he drew him towards the Pont Saint-Michel, turned leftwards, and reached the Porte Rouge without having given any clearer explanation of his utterances.

Régnier de Montigny had the knack of making a good impression, and of winning his suit every time. In the eyes of the chaplain, his kinship in the church of Saint-Benoît itself with Étienne de Montigny was of instant help to him.

"Master Guillaume," he saluted him courteously, "I come to bring you my greetings."

And bowing as he doffed his hat, Régnier adroitly told a story of how he had received from one of his sisters a large pie and some game, and how, if the chaplain had no objections, he would like to share them with François.

"We shall be alone," he said. "I give you my word for that."

"But the truth remains," said Master Guillaume at once, for he was taken unexpectedly by this proposal, "that François will have no heart for his studies on the morrow."

"Oh, but I will!" cried François.

Master Guillaume made a grimace.

"Listen to that!" he exclaimed. "You see how afraid he is of not having my consent!"

"I'm afraid for my own sake as well," rejoined Montigny with a smile, and nudged François to bid him keep quiet. "Will you refuse me?"

Then, ceasing to smile and looking ingenuously at Master Guillaume, he waited, without adding another word, for him to make his decision.

"Well, there you are," said the chaplain then, touched by Montigny's discretion and agreeable manners. "If I accept for François, will you bring him back again?"

"Yes, yes. At eleven o'clock," said the scholar. "One needs time to sup at one's ease."

"Come, come!"

"What are you afraid of?" asked Montigny in calm tones. "Of some untoward meetings in the streets?"

"Exactly," answered Master Guillaume. "They are only too frequent."

"Not at all. The streets are quite safe if you keep your path without quarrelling with anyone," said Montigny. "Come, Master Guillaume, don't be apprehensive on our account. — Even if the hour of return were delayed, nothing irksome can befall, nothing at all. . . ."

And so saying, Régnier saluted the chaplain with the utmost courtesy, and the latter, taking François into a corner, handed over the key of the great door and made sundry recommendations.

The dinner was very modest, for it cost Montigny nothing, as he ordered it to be chalked up to his account, but the wines that went with it were excellently chosen. François drank more than a big pot of them, and Montigny, pushing him on to it, feigned his admiration.

"At your age," he said, "I didn't drink so much as that."

"It's good, you know."

"I know," answered Montigny.

When they came out, the curfew had sounded at Notre-Dame, but the other churches of Paris, which only set their bells a-clanging an hour later, were beginning their din.

"Go to the devil!" said Montigny.

He led François round to another tavern, and there too the reckoning was marked up on the slate. Régnier, who was no higgler, ordered ambrosia, and François felt himself aglow. What wine! Never had he tasted better: it enchanted him, it made him talkative, merry, exuberant. Until nine o'clock they drank like this. Then the landlord had to bolt his shutters, and out in the street, as the bell of the Sorbonne rang its short peals: "Ah!" François murmured, "how that pleases me! Ding! Ding! Dong! Ring louder. 'Tisn't for me you're calling to-night. I hear, and I don't hear. Ding! Ding!"

"This way," said Régnier.

From time to time the wind carried the sounds away so far that you could not have believed yourself down in the rue Saint-Jacques where this bell was ringing. The signs creaked on their great iron standards, and clashed against one another. It was the wind assaulting them with great gusts. The wind howled and complained, and although François knew that at the last stroke of the curfew all lights must be put out, yet he had the idea that it was through the violence of the wind that he saw them, one by one, going out.

The candles, in fact, were dying inside the houses, and the night appeared so much the blacker, so much the more opaque.

"Bear to your left," said Montigny, "and give me your hand. . . ."

"Where are you?" asked François.

He took the hand of the elder man and, gripping it fearfully, he moved forward into a thick darkness which was unpleasant to him and made him turn round at the slightest noise.

"What's the matter?" asked Montigny. "Are you afraid?"

"No," said François.

"You're lying. I can feel your hand trembling."

"There!" whispered François suddenly, shielding himself up against his companion.

Montigny listened, and the oaths of some drunkard in difficulties amongst the benches rose up in their fury.

"God above! A pretty voice!" exclaimed Montigny. "I should like to know who fashioned it so well. Hi! D'you hear me?"

At the same time he felt around, groping in the dark, and found amusement in the adventure.

"What need," he queried, "to throw oneself into such a pickle! Help me if I'm to help you, my friend! I know nothing about you."

"I am Jehan le Loup," said a man then, hoisting himself painfully on his legs and waving a lantern which one could not see, but could hear striking against the benches. And he repeated: "Jehan le Loup — le Loup — I have been chasing the wind."

"And the wind's pushed him over!" laughed François.

"Ay," answered the drunkard, who remained

invisible, but whose presence could be divined by a powerful smell. "When a man drinks — in a gale of wind — he tumbles."

"But where are you going?" asked Montigny.

"I be off," declared Jehan le Loup, still banging with his lantern in the darkness, "by the rue de la-a-a-Harpe."

"Come on then," ordered Montigny. "We're for there too."

François was astonished. This Jehan le Loup he knew quite well: his usual functions were measuring salt and preventing people from flinging out ordure along the river-banks; could he be so drunk as this? He kept on wondering about it. What strange discoveries one could make at night-time! Just fancy! Jehan le Loup! François could no longer be afraid of him now, when he met him of an evening, making his round under his drooping cloth cap and prowling beside the Seine.

Montigny stopped.

"On with you! Forward march!" he cried to the drunkard.

And as the latter made no reply: "What are you up to?" asked Montigny. "What ——?"

"Psssss," said Jehan le Loup gravely.

And one could hear it indeed, for the liquid ran forth as he moved forward, wetting the paving-stones, dropping noisily from his clouts, and not stopping.

2

All night long there came nothing but surprises of the same sort, for after Jehan le Loup, whom they left behind them to get over to the rue de Mâcon, the two friends ran against other strange personages with whom Montigny had talk. They grew excited without one's being able to distinguish them; then the wind bore them off, and Montigny recited some verses which François heard for the first time.

"*And these be friends whom winds bear off . . .*" he declaimed as he walked.

"Yes," observed the scholar. "But not the same ones, and not the same wind either. — This line pleases me." And pressing his companion's hand, he asked: "Do you not know other verses?"

Montigny did not reply, and François, to grave it on his memory, kept repeating that strange line —

"*Ce sont amis que vent emporte*" —

and felt a sudden sadness mingled with exaltation take hold of his senses, when suddenly a door was half opened, and Colin appeared.

"Colin!"

"Eh!" said the locksmith's son. "Come in, right away. What is it?"

"It's Régnier," explained François.

Régnier pushed François forward, and went through into the narrow chamber, where Colin and three women who seemed to be awaiting them gave them excited welcome.

"Guillemette!" called Régnier. "Come and kiss me!"

Guillemette had risen.

"Ah," she said, flinging herself on Montigny's neck, "here's somebody who loses no time."

"And whom shall I have?" cried one of the other girls, going over to François and taking him by the waist.

They all burst out laughing at once, and then Colin de Cayeux, pouring out drink, declared: "He is for you, Marion, but don't you go frightening him. He'd leave you and be off——"

"What do you know about it?" replied François, feeling his face grow red, and throwing a vexed glance at Colin. "Me? Me run off?"

"There, there! don't take offence!"

"Have you ever seen me take to my heels yet?"

"Right!" approved Montigny. "He who looks, finds. Well, for the present, let's be drinking.—François, you're talking of gold, and Cayeux too. But look there instead and see what Marion wants of you."

"Oh!" said Marion, with a tender inflection of her voice, "I only want to have my pleasure."

And drawing François closer, she planted on his lips a kiss that dispensed him from the need of any answer.

She was a dark girl, rather strongly built, with round, firm breasts, and very expert with her caresses, for whosoever should ask of them. Whoever wanted to have her had her. Keen for gain with her clients, she gave herself conveniently, by the fire, at her own house, without thought during her commerce of anything but exploiting people. All day, behind the casement of her room, she watched for them, and enticed them with a winking eye; but the night was her own, and the strange creature then became a different woman, facile and disinterested. Colin and Montigny could have said so. They had known her, both of them, for a long time back, and that is why they had agreed in choosing her for their young friend.

"Yours, François!" said Montigny slyly.

The festivity began. Round the table, on the coffers whereon the embracing couples took their places, the girls laughed and drank each time that anyone gave the signal. They emptied their glasses at one gulp, and then with little cries and a thousand enticements pressed against the three youths, who ate between whiles and made ready their strength. Marion was seated on François's knee, embracing him. He let himself be kissed, and only returned the kisses when she gave him leave; for with this very young lad her pleasure lay in seeing him being troubled, with her flattering him the while. In vain did he seize her lips with his: she kept them pressed for a good moment, and then suddenly gave forth a long caress that made his head swim. François was losing his senses. His hands, which Marion playfully caught hold of sometimes to prevent them from making free where they were instinctively moving, were burning. He was hot. He trembled as it were with a fever, and when his companion insisted on his taking a little solid food, and made him eat it, he took advantage of her being occupied to clasp her and tease her as he pleased.

"Leave me alone, will you?" said the girl. "Go on, leave me alone ——"

"Why?"

"In a moment."

"Look at the others," answered François. "I'm not a bit hungry. Marion!"

"All right, then."

And François stood up, pointing to his two comrades and the two women, in close embraces, one pair on the table, amongst the pies and the wine, the other couple on a coffer, and he pushed Marion gently towards the back of the room. She did not resist. Nay, clinging to him, and completely changed, she murmured: "Yes, come along. Perhaps you're right. The sport's best on the bed."

. . . . . .

The night was less gloomy when Montigny and Colin, with their young pupil, took leave of the three wenches and, keeping along the fronts of the houses, reached the Porte Rouge. At moments a wan light drifted into the streets, and it was speedily eclipsed by the wind that drove the clouds before it, tore down the tiles from the roofs, and struck at the swinging signs with a great clatter.

"Where is it?" said Colin, speaking low.

"Follow me," whispered François, guiding him to the lock. "Here's the key."

Montigny made him a sign to keep silence, drew him by the sleeve to make him stand aside, and watched him, leaning over Colin's shoulder.

"Doesn't he want the key?" asked François in astonishment.

Colin consigned him to the devil.

"No need of it," said Montigny, and then addressed himself to Colin, who was plunging a long hook into the lock.

"Go easy," he advised him in low tones. "To be caught opening the closed door of the honourable Master Guillaume so as not to get him out of bed — who would believe a word of that?"

Colin turned round.

"I want you to see," he declared.

"But I see all right."

"Well, then? Come nearer," said Colin, who, after a push, had silently set the door a little way ajar. "And profit by it."

"Ah!"

"François!" called Colin, who wore a very satisfied air, and held back the door lest the wind should push it to. "François! You too! Come on."

"What!" exclaimed François. "Who has opened it?"

Montigny pointed to the hook in Colin's hand and

suddenly, turning an eye down the approaches to the street, made a gesture.

"And so," said Colin slowly, "you now know the secret. Good-bye, François. Go and sleep." He put a finger on his lips. "But you've understood?"

"Yes."

"Then you must swear," went on Colin, "never to breathe a word of it."

"I swear," said François.

"Before God?"

"Oh, come along!" protested Montigny.

After a short farewell they separated, and François watched them go softly away, and turn the corner of the Mathurins. Then he slipped into his worthy uncle's dwelling, shut the door, and went upstairs to bed.

He was tired. The memory of Marion harassed him, and although utterly jaded with fatigue, he fell into a soft and stupid musing, instead of undressing. Nevertheless it was not warm, staying like that, standing between these walls, and François was aware of it when a bell rang from the neighbouring church, announcing matins, throwing out its summons in the new-born day. Other bells made answer, all shivering and almost stupefied with cold, with their even strokes, despite the wind, sounding out obstinate and insistent.

"A-a-a-ah!" yawned the scholar.

Sadly he took off his clothes, slipped under the sheets, and saw with his wide-open eyes a vague glow brightening at the top of the window. It was dawn. It lit up the room bewilderingly, and imperceptibly it spread its sinister and tarnished light over the walls. François paid no heed. He was thinking of Marion, sought for her by his side, and at the same time he called to mind Colin opening the door down there with his long hook. Doubtless he had found the hook in the workshop of his father, the locksmith. Yes. No doubt. But what reason had driven him to make use of it? This was something that François could not grasp. He didn't understand, he came back to Marion, and, slipping little by little into a heavy sleep, he mingled image with image in his mind, all meaningless now.

During the morning, taking care to avoid Master Guillaume, who scrutinized him and questioned him about his night, François was listless. He was half asleep during the grammar lesson, and he sat down to table with no trace of appetite. His sickly appearance surprised everyone, and betrayed him. He was yellow. His eyes shone with fever, and when he could not restrain a shudder — if somebody noticed it — he grumbled and shook himself. Was he going to be troubled long? He asked nothing of anyone. He, who was usually so kind with Master Guillaume, refused to answer a single question, turned away his head, and in the end, not knowing how to dissimulate his true feelings, looked away above him with an air of arrogance.

The barber Flastrier, a kinsman of sorts, who came

to visit the chaplain of Saint-Benoît in the course of the day, could not get a single word out of François. The worthy man was quite put out by it. But Master Guillaume sent François upstairs to his books in his own room, and when the youth had obeyed him, he said: "It is my own fault. I let him go out last night."

"After nine o'clock?"

"After nine o'clock."

"Ah!" said the barber, "it's not for me to judge."

"Why, yes," answered Master Guillaume. "You as much as another. I was lacking in common sense."

François, for his part, reproached himself for having betrayed his ill humour so foolishly, and was full of discontent. He opened his stout tomes, took his head between his hands, and tried his very best to muster interest in them. But the letters danced before his eyes, grew mazy on the page, and in their place there came that image of Marion which the hapless scholar could not put behind him. Where was she at this time? What was she doing? Indeed, he was ignorant, for what he knew of her and her condition he felt repugnance in admitting to himself. But what availed it to deny the evidence? Would a less dissolute woman have thus given herself in the company of other persons, and at a first meeting? It was ridiculous to think of it seriously. Absolutely. And the proof——

"François!" called a grave voice behind him.

It was Master Guillaume.

"You were studying?" he asked.

"Yes," answered François, without frowning. "To punish myself."

"My poor boy!" said the chaplain. "To punish yourself? I hardly thought that."

"It is only right that I should," protested François, who could see that his uncle was softened, and wanted to secure his pardon.

"But why?"

"Oh, you know quite well!"

Master Guillaume tossed his head.

"Listen, François," he said then. "If anyone is guilty, it is myself, and not you. Do you hear?"

"I am listening, uncle."

"Good."

"And — what is your decision?" asked the scholar, dissembling. "This is Thursday to-day."

François raised his eyes; and then, coming up to the chaplain, whom he felt to be quite disarmed, he quickly caught his hand and kissed it.

"Ah, the good-for-nothing!" exclaimed his uncle. "Go on! I ought not to have come upstairs to see you. Could anyone imagine! You'll be your own undoing, my lad, in always convincing me. You're far too clever!"

"And yet, uncle, Thursday ——"

"Well, go along then," murmured the good man. "I know. It's the day your mother expects you, and I don't want to deprive her. But at least promise me this — that you'll go straight there. Go along, now, go along. Greet her from me, son. And take her some of that pie you didn't eat at table, with my good wishes. Huguette will get it ready for you."

"Thanks, thanks!" exclaimed François. "I promise you, uncle, I'll run all the way, if need be!"

"Oh, I didn't ask as much as that," laughed Master Guillaume, laying his large hand on his nephew's head, and pressing him affectionately to himself. "But just take the shortest way, and come back in time for dinner."

"Yes, yes," answered François at once, gladly closing his books and seizing up his wretched cap.

He ran downstairs, four steps at a time, got Huguette to give him the pie for his mother, and with one bound was out of doors.

It was raining. Hurrying along the streets, François reached the bridges, crossed the water, and then, turning to the right through the crowded streets, where the horses slipped now and then on the wet paving-stones, reached the Place de Grève. Without stopping, he went on. Smells of salted foodstuffs, of wood that had been brought in for winter, of cloth and leather and wine, came forth from the shops, and François sniffed them. They put him in good humour, as also did the cries of the shopkeepers calling to the marketing housewives and attracting them to bring their custom. In the windows could be seen all kinds of merchandise hanging in nets, or hooked up pell-mell, all in abundance. You could easily have taken them, thought François. But why? Taking — when nothing was lacking at Master Guillaume's? He went his way, eyeing the people and the porters mischievously, knocking against some in his absent-mindedness, stepping aside to let others pass, and holding his pie under his arm. It was for his mother — good woman! — that he had burdened himself with it, and he carried it with every precaution. Otherwise it would have been a pie for himself! But the old woman would regale herself with it, and call down blessings on the chaplain of Saint-Benoît, who was so good to herself and her child.

"The poor dear!" said François.

He loved his mother tenderly. She lived over there at the Cordeliers, already ageing, and full of gratitude to God, in spite of her small show of earthly fortune, for having saved her son and put him in good keeping. The worthy soul lived only for him; she admired him, rejoiced over him every time she saw him, and when she managed to save a few halfpence out of her minute earnings, they were for François; and François, well content, took them.

Every Thursday, waiting for him on the step of her door, and knitting the while so as not to be standing idle, she saw him coming afar off, and at once began laughing and bobbing up and down while he made for her and threw himself into her arms.

"There you are! God be praised!" she cried out. "My little François, my darling! How prompt you are!"

And François returned her kisses and said, with

boyish pride: "Do you know, mother, I'm learning to talk Latin, and I understand it! I'm a scholar!"

"A scholar, merciful Jesu!"

She touched his gown timidly, overwhelmed and grateful, joined her hands, raised a prayer to the Holy Virgin, and suddenly, deeply moved, she sighed: "Oh, if only your father could see you!"

But he had died, still working, and poverty had long prowled about the house like those wolves of the winter of 1438 which wandered up and down and fell upon defenceless folk and tore babes to pieces. And how vivid these memories still were in the poor woman's mind!

"You used to cry," she would tell François, holding him as if in fear of that time returning. "You would call out. It was from hunger. — And I, I had nothing to give you ——"

"But Master Guillaume took me under his care," answered the scholar, "and he has taught me grammar and fed me ——"

"The good man!"

At the sight of the pie, the old woman exclaimed aloud.

"I don't want it!" she declared. "What would I do with it? A pie! No, no. I couldn't eat it!"

"Come, come," said François, "take it. I've brought you it from my uncle."

"Well, you shall take it back to him."

"He'll be offended," countered the scholar. "And I shall have had the double journey to no purpose."

"Ah, you rascal!"

"Perhaps I know what Master Guillaume said to me," he declared, placing the pie on the table. "It was with all goodwill that he sent you it. You must accept it in the same spirit."

And while he spoke he could feel his mother's gaze fastened on him and was vexed by it. The good woman shook her head.

"What's the matter?" asked François.

"You're looking pale, you are."

"You think so?"

"Yes, I do," replied the innocent creature. "You aren't ill, are you?"

"Bah!" said François airily. "It's just to tease you a little. I'm not ill. Quite the contrary. Perhaps I got chilled on my way here, but it's over now. Look ——"

And to calm the anxieties he saw in his mother's mind, he rubbed his cheeks till they were red, and broke into a forced laugh.

"There, there!" he cried quickly, but not daring to look straight in the eyes of the poor woman, who was taking his hands and drawing him towards her. "Now, do you still think I've got a poor colour?"

I

3

He went back slowly and with bowed head, jingling in his fist the few wretched halfpence that his poor mother had given him at the moment of leaving; and for the first time he found no pleasure in idling as he went. He was sad. He suffered from having had something to conceal from his worthy mother; he felt the shame of it, and an obscure annoyance too. Yet, all around François as he walked along, men and women passing or overtaking each other were throwing glances at one another, and he himself, in spite of an indefinable sense of regret, looked at the servant-maids and the girls with a gentle, modest gaze. He followed them with his eyes with no thought of evil, and, comforted by the pleasant way in which he felt himself welcomed, he automatically recovered his gaiety of heart. Was it his fault if he constantly felt the need of quizzing the maids? That was part of his nature; it was linked with the weakness he had always had for loving and being loved, for being rocked and petted. Heigh-ho! His early childhood had passed too quickly, and he saw himself, while still hardly more than a baby, being brought up by a priest who, whatever he had done, had not been able to take the place of a mother. That was the cause of everything, and gave him still his great love for his mother.

He had in him something that was infinitely tender,

something from which he had long suffered in his little room at Saint-Benoît when, during the dreary winter afternoons, pressing his forehead against the panes, he watched the children of his own age playing beside the houses. Heavens! How long and empty and insufferable the days had seemed to him! He counted how many remained till Thursday came round, for that was the day when the good woman came over to Saint-Benoît to visit him, took him with her and kissed him, and told him stories. He called these to mind. Marvellous stories they were. And immediately, in his memory, he found intact amid his recollections the colour of the sky and the houses, and perfumes rising from the garden in summer-time.

"There!" he observed, turning over these absurd thoughts. "Thus the days go by. — And why?"

No one could answer such a question, and he did not stop for an answer. Right in the midst of his distress, abruptly, by a trick of his temperament, he became alert and jaunty. He was no longer the same; he made mock of his ill humour and told himself he was out of his wits.

Perhaps he was. If not altogether that, capricious at least, turning at every puff of wind, and capable, for instance, after thinking of those days that had followed each other to no purpose, of wondering to himself: "Where have they gone? And who takes them?"

Poof! There again, he didn't know. Like those "friends whom winds bear off," it was the wind no doubt which chased off the days one by one, and then the sun shone out and the sky was blue, and between the benches in the streets the girls one met were good to look upon and smiled. Must he pout at them? François had so persistent a taste for them that the mere thought of them consoled him. Explain such sentiments as you will. He hardly troubled himself about that. To-day less than ever. To-day he was a man. He knew that game now, and, far from feeling any hypocritical humiliation in regard to Marion from knowing her to be accessible to anyone, he extracted some vanity despite himself from the very fact she was a woman of easy virtue.

However, a certain disgust came over him from his poor adventure, and he no longer left Saint-Benoît. On reflection, Marion seemed to him to be rather too common and degraded a creature, and he hated her, and swore to see no more of her; and when he met Montigny one morning, they spoke of her as if nothing were the matter.

"Poor girl," said Montigny, "she's worried, she's worried; she's asking for you."

And a little later Colin sought out François in his room and swore, in Christ's name, that such a woman ought to stay in their hold.

"For what reason?" asked François, naïvely.

Colin turned his gimlet eyes on to him.

"For the money in it. D'you understand?"

Colin began to laugh, and the scholar was troubled and lowered his face.

"What?" said Colin. "You don't dare?"

"I don't know," murmured François, who was discouraged and greatly confused by this talk. "There are means — there's the way ——"

"Others know it well enough," muttered the locksmith's son. "They've had more brass out of Marion than you've had plans or projects out of your timid brains. Aha! There's something in it!"

He shook his head.

"You need time to learn," said François sadly.

"You need to have the will first," replied Colin firmly. "The choice is yours."

"But I should like ——"

"Look at yourself," said Colin harshly, pointing to his worn robe and his shoes. "You haven't got a gallant's turn-out at all. And as for your purse, what's there? Eh? Nothing. Just wind ——"

"That's true," François had to confess.

"Well, more fool you! Do you suppose that Montigny, that wonder of grace, could have been clothed like that if it had not been for Guillemette? It's an easy matter to get things out of women: they're very accommodating. Their pleasure is in giving what the stout bourgeois bring them. Don't be a little fool."

"And you?"

"Me?" said Colin, crossing his arms with an air of satisfaction. "I instructed Montigny and made him what he is."

And he turned to pace the room with so detached an air that François felt himself convinced.

None the less he felt repugnance in following the counsels of this strange master. To demand money of Marion — that was beyond him! He could not make up his mind to that. It was still too soon.

"Too soon?" exclaimed Colin. "It's more agreeable to drink in the tavern at the expense of one's companions. So much worse for them if they take the risk, eh? They pay."

"Tush! You're talking ——"

"What?"

"I mean," exclaimed François piteously, "I mean that you aren't heeding your words and you rebuke me without listening. That's wrong. Have I the power to change my condition in a day? Just imagine! I should have to go out at night."

"Very good."

"And by what device? Here Master Guillaume keeps me. And he lies awake."

Colin was softened.

"I was anticipating you just in that very point," he answered.

François realized that his excuse was a poor one, and that if he allowed Colin to help him, there would be an end of his tranquillity. For an instant he was afraid, and then, taking a sudden decision, he stammered out: "I'll do it. I'll act as you have it in your mind I should."

At once Colin came nearer, and drew out of his pocket a ball of cobblers' wax, such as is used to take the impressions of locks for the fashioning of keys. Nothing could be easier. On the way downstairs they would both stop in front of the door and keep up their talking whilst Colin rapidly did his work. Then, the day after to-morrow, he would hand over a key to François for his own use.

"Agreed?" he asked.

François seized Colin by the arm, led him towards the staircase, and accompanied him to the door, and there what they had appointed was promptly carried out.

"Till to-night," said Colin gleefully. "You're coming?"

"At Marion's," replied the scholar. And he went upstairs again, ranged out his books, and waited until it was nearly the time when he could go out without attracting anyone's attention.

But how moved he was, how anxious and ill at ease! As he hurried along the streets, he was haunted by ridiculous ideas. He followed one street, and then another, crossed and turned back again for fear of being pursued. He saw himself already, by Colin's agency, mixed up with all kinds of adventures for which, resolute as he might be, he was in no way prepared. What adventures? He could not have defined them. This woman, in all certainty, would bring them into being. And François hesitated to ask himself. A kind of fascination drew him towards Marion, towards Colin, towards Régnier and those girls of theirs by whom they lived. Was it possible? The nearer he came to the lodging where his mistress ogled the passers-by, the more he reproached his own weakness. He was ashamed. He was hot and cold. He trembled. And when he found himself in the little room, where Marion flung herself into his arms, his first care was to shut the door in alarm and to close the shutter.

"Hi, there!" the girl reproached him. "What are you afraid of?"

He looked at her, smiled, and said very quickly: "Colin and Montigny told me you were asking for me. Is it true?"

Marion kissed him, full on the mouth. Was it true? Didn't he see it? What a question! But the girl recovered herself, and pushed François back a little: he was clasping her till she was almost choking.

"Colin has been talking to you?" she asked him.

"Yes," answered the lad.

And in a moment or two he went on: "I've a rendezvous here with him, shortly. Régnier will be coming too. Did you know?"

"No," said the girl.

"Well, there you are then," he said, put out of countenance. "I give you warning."

And with no further heed for anything he sighed, covering his mistress's face with kisses.

"I'm wretched when I am away from you, Marion — I live deprived of life, in a sort of madness and endless gloom, torturing myself ——"

"But you mustn't do that!"

"How can I?"

"And now?" asked the girl very softly, in a voice that he did not know. "And now? I want to know."

"Oh, now —" said François with fervour in his voice. "Now!"

"No more? Not at all?"

"Marion!"

Already, drawing him over to the bed, she complained of him and reproached him, kissing him and exciting him the while, with not having confidence; and he was listening to her uncomprehendingly, as if petrified, when Montigny banged at the door with urgent knocks, and Colin shouted to them to open.

"What?" protested Marion. "Is the fire burning them?"

Once in, they answered: "The fire of love, one has to ask that of you."

"As for me," went on Régnier, who seemed much heated, "it is not at all the same fury that urges *me* on."

"You've been drinking?"

"Drinking every shame," he declared. "Guillemette fools me, and I've been correcting her."

Coldly Colin explained: "Régnier surprised her with a gallant who not only doesn't give cash down, but takes it."

"No!" exclaimed François.

"And then," Colin went on, "Régnier pitched him outside, this scoundrel, without a stitch, and his clothes into the gutter. As for Guillemette, he thrashed her."

"She well deserved it," said Marion.

"Till she bled!"

"Ay!" said Régnier.

There was a moment's silence, whilst all four looked at each other, and burst in the end into loud laughter. Especially Colin. He held his ribs and, pitching into François with light slaps, forced him to enjoy the adventure and approve it as much as he was doing himself.

"You see," he flung at him, "how to behave if Marion were to play tricks on you some day! A good thrashing, there and then!"

"But there's no question of me behaving so badly," Marion threw in, overcome with genuine mirth by the tale. "What d'you say, Colin? D'you think so?"

Holding Marion by the hand, François declared: "All the same, if by some chance the case arose, I should know the remedy."

"Oh, François!" murmured the girl with delight, "would you beat me?"

"Indeed I would!"

"See? I'm a good teacher, am I not?" exclaimed Colin, who seemed to be proud of his pupil and stood rubbing his palms. "I teach him, I instruct him: there's a beginning to all things. As for the rest ——"

He winked his little eye.

"Not the slightest need for your help"; Marion cut him short.

And she turned to François, clasped him tenderly, and held up her lips to him.

"Show them," she said, her voice low with desire, "show them I tell the truth. They'll be witnesses, both of them."

"Quite enough!" said Colin thereupon, putting his rough hand on the youth's shoulder and making him step forward. "We're off now to have a drink at the 'Pomme,' and then we'll send him back."

"Yes, a drink!" came Régnier's support.

François struggled.

"Forward!" commanded Colin.

Marion called out: "Well, come back at once at least, François!"

And as Colin unblushingly asked, right in front of her, whether the scholar had anything to pay with, the girl ran over to a hiding-place, brought out a crown, and handed it with a laugh to François.

"Here," she said to him, "take it."

But François slipped away, and Colin pocketed the money.

I

4

No more was necessary. Colin, who had the crown, kept it for meeting the reckoning, and made such mock of the scholar that the latter promised inwardly to surprise his master and disarm him. The key that he gave him strengthened François in these resolutions of his. He made use of it the very first night, and ran as bold as brass to Marion's. She was not expecting him, and greeted him just as she was going out. François was in the seventh heaven. He did not notice that his mistress was hiding something from him, nor that, more than once, she had the air of spying to see whether someone were not prowling about outside round the house, or listened with an ear glued to the door, while she kept silent. Then François too had to hold his tongue. Abruptly she imposed silence on him, shielded the flame of the candle with her fingers, and stayed motionless without a word of explanation.

"It's nothing," said the lad. "What do you hear?"

Then, as if partly reassured, the girl smiled at him, and François, with the money in his mind, pressed her close. He did not know how to make himself understood. He was ashamed, and did not dare to open so awkward a subject straight off.

"Marion," he began ——

And then he stopped. But the image of Colin stuck

in his mind, and he instantly tried to come back to his project.

"What do you want?" asked Marion.

Perhaps she was accustomed to these embarrassing subjects, or perhaps François — without any practice in the game — had set about it well; but however it was, Marion guessed what was in question.

"I know," she said, "you aren't rich."

"Yes," replied François. "Why should I deny it?"

"I can see that all right," said Marion.

And sitting up closer to him, as he sat there humbly gazing at her, she said impulsively: "Poor boy! He asks where others demand."

"Who?"

"Well, Colin — and Régnier."

"Are they wrong?" replied François, feeling more at his ease. "It was Colin who gave me the idea. He feels no distress about it."

"I know," said Marion.

She was going to speak about Colin when, trembling at the shouts of a drunkard in the street, she jumped up in panic with a bound.

"Where are you off to?" asked François.

Marion pulled herself together, and then, pointing to the box where she kept the money given her, she laughed in a way that startled François.

"Oh," said he, "there's no hurry."

"Yes, there is," she said. "For at the moment it will be much better for you to leave me. It is late."

"What? Already?"

Marion came back to him, and very quickly, as if she were afraid of being caught slipping a couple of almost new crowns into the timid student's hand, she forced him, kissing him the while, to get down from the bed. Then she handed him his clothes, which he put on without a protest, and without clearly understanding why he felt sad and glad at the same time.

This odd departure astonished him, and yet François did not resist it. The money which he clenched in his hand forbade him to resist Marion, who, in her fright, was making haste. What was wrong with her? Why did she send him away like this before he had thanked her? Was she annoyed? No, not that. François turned it over in his mind. As she went on helping him to dress, the strange girl gave the impression of being more and more apprehensive, and threw such anxious glances towards the door that in the end, to calm her, he said: "There! I'll be off now."

"Quietly, then," murmured Marion. "Are you ready?"

With a great air of mystery, she half opened the door. François wanted to embrace her for one last kiss.

"No," she said hurriedly. "And take care not to tell anyone where you've come from. You'd pay for it if you did! Go on, quick!"

"Till to-morrow?"

Marion shook her head.

"What's that?" said François. "You refuse?"

"I'll let you know the day," whispered Marion, very

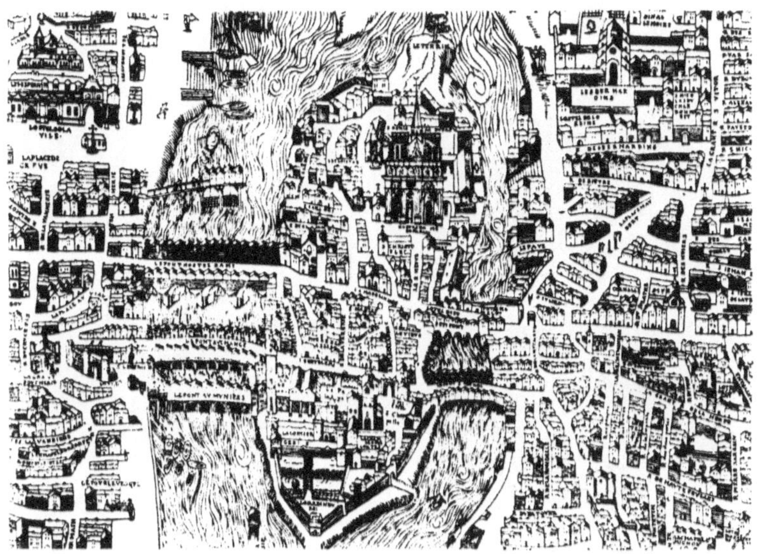

Paris in the XVI century. From a plan by Truschet and Hoyau, circa *1551*

low. And she pushed François out of the room, bolting on his heels the door that she instantly shut behind him.

"Upon my word!" thought François, "it needs a sharp fellow to understand women!"

. . . . . .

An intense darkness reigned outside, barely letting one distinguish the silhouette of the roofs and signs against the sky. No light anywhere. The greasy pavement stuck to one's feet. François had to take his direction blindly, for he was not accustomed to such blackness. Round him nothing stirred, and nothing gave the impression that, on both sides of the street, in the houses, people were sleeping, deep in heavy sleep, snoring, or turning on their beds. The silence was such that it formed, as it were, a wall through the thickness of which François was making his way, and the silence impressed him.

"God in heaven!" he swore, stopping in his progress.

He fingered the coins in his purse, and, as he was not yet very far from the house, where Marion perhaps was reproaching herself with having turned him out into such a night, he was tempted to turn back, when a rough voice hailed him.

"Hi, there, whoever you are!" called out the voice.

François took care not to answer.

"I'll come over to you, and twist your neck for you!" went on the voice in anger. "Where are you?"

A paving-stone hurled in the air crashed to the ground with a great din, and François could guess that, behind him, some individual, and an alarming one, to judge by the strength of his wrist, was running in his direction. He took to his heels, and cleared off without heed for anything else, and, still in flight and taking the shortest cuts, speedily arrived at the meeting of the rue de la Harpe and the rue Poupée. And there, judging himself to be clear of the rascal who had chased him, he took a deep breath before going back to his bed.

The cry of a hawker: "Old clo'! Old clo'!" roused him next morning. It was raining. Other hawkers eyed the windows as they went by, calling out in shrill tones the commodities they had to offer their customers. There was an old man whom François recognized, and who moaned out: "Salted — herrings!" There was an enormous old woman who trundled a little cart and bellowed every few yards: "See my fine little angels! Fine little angels!" and pointed to her Brie cheeses on their straw mats, ready to cut them in slices as her customers might desire.

François felt hungry. He went down to the kitchen, slashed into the lard, took a hunk of bread, and came upstairs again without paying any heed to Huguette, who told him what she thought of him for the mess he left, then shut himself into his room and began to eat. He was in excellent humour. All the cries coming up from the street cheered his heart. In spite of the rain splashing on the window-panes, and the dullness which had been the price of his visit to Marion, his mind was clear and he felt a keen relish in living and spending himself.

"Ha ha!" he said gleefully.

And just then he caught hold of a stout book on the dresser, opened it, and read several long paragraphs, the sense of which struck him. Usually they just made him restive. He could not understand how there could be any point in stuffing one's head with these formulas which he could only barely remember and idly mixed up in his mind. But this morning the more he read, the more pleasure he found in reading and in setting the whole in order. Forbidding though it might be, the text of the *Doctrinale* struck him as clear, and, closing his eyes for a moment, he recited it word for word, and congratulated himself thereon.

"Who has changed me?" he said to himself in stupefaction. "Here I am studying! Master Guillaume will be pleased!"

He was highly pleased himself, and almost more surprised even, so much zeal and facility did he discover in himself. Syntax, indeed, for a youth who has been a-roving all night, offers few attractions. Yet did François not weary over it. He went on from one chapter to the next, stopping over the examples to master the rules, pursued them further, began again when he had read carelessly, tested his memory, and then rising and pacing up and down his room, he rubbed his hands.

Warmed by his study and finding charms therein which he would never have suspected, François was still feeding on the *Doctrinale* when his uncle, astonished at not seeing him downstairs for dinner, went to rouse him in his chamber.

"Hullo, there!" exclaimed the chaplain. "Are you forgetting the time?"

François remained dumbfounded.

"It's midday and after," said Master Guillaume, coming over to the open book. Unable to believe his eyes, he turned over several pages, dreading lest they should be hiding some culpable diversion. "What! You were in your syntax?"

"Yes," answered François.

His flushed cheeks and shining eyes, and the healthy exaltation that seemed to spread over all his features, touched Master Guillaume's feelings. He fixed his gaze on the scholar, and then, feeling him so ingenuously proud, he shook his head and said: "There is a time for everything, my child. Now come to table. Huguette will be crying aloud if you keep her waiting. Hark to her!"

"I hear her," said the scholar gaily.

And indeed — a deaf man would have had his eardrum split by it — a shrill voice was filling the staircase, squealing: "Will you come down, Master Guillaume! It'll be cold! Come down! As for the other, he's already eaten, the good-for-nothing!"

"When was that?" asked the chaplain.

"This morning," answered François with a burst of laughter. "But it was from desire of learning — and I'd a mighty appetite!"

I

Throughout the day he had such energy in all he did that his worthy uncle, knowing him to be inclined to excess in all he undertook, was careful not to put checks upon his zeal by any observations of his. What a boy this François was, one day as abstracted as a dormouse, and the next all agog, active, impetuous! In vain did Master Guillaume try to know the lad: every time he escaped him, disconcertingly. How was one to be his director? The good man had nothing for his pains, for as soon as he ventured on something, the boy, who the evening before had been so confiding and so eager to learn, fell back into apathy and seemed no longer to have understanding of anything. And yet he was very intelligent. Ah, if only he had the will! But no. The effort of which he was capable was renewed only at intervals too rare to be of any use; and in his heart of hearts the chaplain, far from rejoicing to see François clambering up to his room four steps at a time, as soon as the meal was hurried through, reflected sadly that with such a temperament one must, alas! be prepared for everything.

What did the future hold in store? Master Guillaume, as a wise and prudent man, had fears for his nephew. His small property — it had taken him a long time to acquire — would no doubt pass to François on his death. That was quite natural. But between now and then how many misadventures and deceptions the child was preparing for himself! How many wasted years would be flung away! And health goes too if it is not looked after. Health? — The taste one has for doing well —— Poor François!

'Oh, but God will be at his side," said the chaplain to himself suddenly, checking himself as his thoughts had run on at leisure. "I don't want to doubt that. God knows he is honest and good ——"

And standing up, Master Guillaume called to Huguette for his cloak, left the room and its dying fire, and returned to his occupations, while François, plunged in his reading, did not even lift his nose at the creaking of the door.

It was November, and one of those gloomy days which, about three o'clock, have no more strength left to them, and just glow dully rather than give any light. From the neighbouring roofs, with their flat tiles, long reflections were thrown. They gleamed under a sky that was big with rain, very low, and of a heavy grey that seemed to overwhelm everything. The beams of the house fronts seemed to form visible veins in the plaster, and round them the dampness was gathering. Down below, on the soaking slabs, the noise of footsteps resounded dully, and the creaking of wheels, when a covered cart passed down the rue Saint-Jacques, found no echo.

"Well, evening's overtaking me," thought François.

He went over to the window, still holding his book, and looked out. Evening was indeed closing in. Here and there, amongst the stalls, lights were trembling. The sky became clearer, in contrast with the houses, the street, the dripping walls, and then grew gradually darker while, in an instant, the panes glowed on a level with the shops, and all the way along flung a yellow, narrow light, oblique and flattened.

François did not insist. He stretched himself like those animals which lie attentive in the day-time to some inward dream, then scent the night as their master and give a sudden snort.

"Right!" he said. "I'll go and find Colin to show him what he's managed to teach me. It's the least I can do. He'll laugh. Ha, ha, ha! But the money's mine. I earned it."

Whereupon, putting down the *Doctrinale,* he took his hat and set off at a good pace, with Marion's two crowns in his right-hand pocket, underneath his gown, and in the other the key forged by his friend.

He felt no scruples, but, on the contrary, a sort of placidity which made him find it entirely natural that a woman of evil life should have given him these two crowns.

"It's the usual thing," he said, weighing it up as he walked, full of the idea of meeting Colin and telling him of his exploit. "Marion has got them from some citizen, and I get them from her in turn. So it goes on, from one to another, from hand to hand, until they return to the said citizen and Marion takes them once more. — A pretty trick! And most marvellous!"

Before long he arrived in front of the threshold of a humble, broken-down dwelling, the passage-way of which led into a little courtyard in which Colin's father had his workshop.

"Is Colin there?" he inquired.

A man with bent shoulders and a hard, sad face, gave answer: "Colin? The devil shield him!"

"And why?"

"Because."

"Ah!" said François, "I thought I should find him here."

The man, who had raised his head to reply, resumed his work in silence. He leaned over his vice and tightened it still further. This was the father of Colin de Cayeux.

François addressed him: "Colin will be back to-night, won't he? He's out on some errand?"

But his questions did not seem to interest the other at all. So he shrugged his shoulders, passed along the Seine, and came into the rue de la Juiverie, where as usual Montigny awaited him.

"Hey, François!"

François turned round.

"Good-evening," said Montigny.

"Good-evening."

"And Colin?" asked François, still burning to relate his glorious exploit.

The other made a vague gesture.

"But I want specially to see him," said the scholar.

And looking him straight in the eyes, François observed that, for the first time perhaps, Montigny was worried.

"What!" he said, but without raising his tone too much. "What's wrong then? You mistrust me?"

"Not a bit," muttered Montigny, and as the scholar insisted, he went on, with a disagreeable air: "Don't talk any more about it. Come along. We're going to drink."

"At the 'Pomme'?"

"Choose for yourself," said Montigny.

And then François drew a crown from his pocket and displayed it with pride.

"Look!" he proclaimed. "It's my turn to pay."

"One crown?"

"No, not one alone, but two," François informed him, his animation growing.

"How's that?"

"I'll explain."

And leading Régnier de Montigny to the "Pomme," he called out, as soon as they were seated in the back room of the tavern: "Hi, there! Mugs!" — with a voice so self-assured that the landlord himself came running to the table and asked what they fancied.

"Ambrosia," said François.

Montigny was silent. He had a preoccupied air, and gazing sadly in front of him, he lent only a casual attention to the young scholar's story.

François shook him.

"You're worried about Colin, aren't you?" he inquired.

At that moment the young Turgis, who was about

the same age as François and claimed to assist his father and the servants, came up to them. He was fat and blown out, with pale colour to his face.

Montigny gave him a chilly welcome.

"Have they sent for those mugs yet?" he flung at him.

"They're coming," declared the other, placidly.

And he clapped his hands to hasten the service, while François and Régnier, irritated by the proximity of this self-important personage who had the air of watching over everything and not taking any trouble himself, sat there without opening their mouths and watched the people around them.

At this time of day there was a goodly number round the tables, drinking and throwing dice. There were regular customers; and there were casual ones, talking loud and full of zest. Under the ceiling of painted rafters they did business, as is often the custom in such places, where the sly ones don't mind the expense, but call out: "Here!" as soon as glasses are empty, or make a discreet sign to the serving-maid. Merchants bluffing each other on purchases of corn or wool, disputing, banging on the table with the bottoms of their tankards. Lawyers from the Palais in grimy gowns, jumbling up their papers and growing excited and gesticulating. Gamblers rattling the dice, and around them, standing or seated, calculating the throws, stood the connoisseurs of the play, vague rogues, drunkards. — François recognized Jehan le Loup, dead drunk. He was singing, leaning up against the wall. Near him, Jehan Rosay, who had only one eye, and vomited when he had drunk too much, in order to be able to drink more, was entertaining Taillelamine with a project which, judging from the explanation, must have been very elaborate. The said Taillelamine, with legs crossed, ostentatiously displayed his fouled stockings; he was a proved cheat, and while the other man was using up his saliva and his time, kept one eye on the dice and the other on the ground, whenever a coin might fall. Casin Cholet, who loved arguments, alone in a corner, drank a great measure of wine, sucking his moustaches, and frequently scratching himself. And lastly, little Guy Tabary, his cheeks round and shiny like apples, went from one table to another in search of invitations.

"Alas, François!" he sighed pleasantly at the sight of the nectar filling his glass. "I'm thirsty!"

He snatched a cup from a servant-girl and held it out at arm's length.

"Pour out!" he asked.

François did so, and Tabary, tossing off the bumper that had been given him, moved away satisfied. The young Turgis likewise had disappeared.

"Régnier," said François softly. "I swear to keep the secret, but don't keep me pining. I want to know where Colin is. Has he left Paris?"

"Yes," answered Montigny. "Last night. I took him by the Seine road."

"And when ought he to be back?"

"That depends."

"Depends on what?"

"He alone can say," answered Montigny. And breaking into a forced laugh, he nudged François with his knee under the table, for two individuals who had been their neighbours had come rather too close—in order to overhear.

5

This first absence of Colin was not a long one, but it had the result of withdrawing François for several weeks from the influence of this doubtful young character. That of Régnier de Montigny was barely preferable. Nevertheless, it was exercised only nonchalantly, for at bottom it mattered little to Montigny whether one ruined oneself or no. He who was a ruined character asked nothing further. He settled down to his dissolute existence, found pleasure in it, and when sometimes he had time to think about it, he felt no regrets at having sunk so low.

"Ah!" he exclaimed jestingly, "provided that if you do fall, you don't hurt yourself, that's something!"

And François admired him. Régnier de Montigny compelled sympathy more than did Colin, who lacked delicacy in his ways and always shocked one by his grossness. His birth gave him a great air, and assurance and impertinence and, even amongst the wenches, a quality that held them all in sway. And so Régnier profited by that and extracted abundant prosperity from them. It was known that his father, Jean de Montigny, squire of the royal bakeries, elected by the city of Paris, had been pillaged by the Burgundians, and so had left nothing at his death, or so little that it was not worth mentioning. This enhanced the prestige of Régnier, who did not hide the fact from anyone that his sisters had shared the "nobleman's" modest heritage without any thought for him.

"I had to be glad for their sakes," he would expound in a detached tone, "and then take myself out of their sight so as not to cost anything."

"And you've never regretted it?"

"Never," answered Montigny.

It was not in his nature. Neither regret, nor envy. What did it matter to him! At twenty-two he wasn't going to vex himself, was he? In lieu of his sisters, the girls of the town helped him out of his difficulties, and, first one and then another, they provided with a good grace for his numerous needs. Since his adventure with Guillemette, to whom he had administered a good thrashing, Régnier de Montigny, to speak the truth, had found a better place for himself. His new friend was a girl named Jeanneton. He lived with her. And when people were astonished that he could sponge upon this girl, he whistled, and made no reply.

"And who knows," said François on these occasions to the importunate ones, "whether you are right, or he?"

But Régnier stopped him.

"Be quiet, youngster," he threw at him calmly.

He led him down the narrow rue de la Juiverie to the "Pomme de Pin," or sometimes, it might be, when his slate there was scored up too heavily, to another cabaret styled "Le Trou Perette." This den was a kind of cellar, with bare walls and a floor of trodden earth.

Seated on casks, you drank hot cider there, and brandy, and a very famous wine of Arbois. But the company was often so mixed that brawling would be the outcome of it and the watch, summoned in haste, would come running up. And everyone took to his heels as best he could, between the dark blacksmiths' booths along the street, and striding through the cross-ways, he would reach some fresh hostelry where credit was not yet extinct.

"Have no fear," said Régnier firmly, when he saw François at such moments trembling in every limb. "And try this stuff. It smells of the vine, boy, good and strong, and of the rock."

"Yes," answered François. "The real thing!"

And emptying his glass to hide the fear he felt within him, he thought of Master Guillaume, and was concerned at the thought that, if he were caught, his uncle would then know how his nights were being spent. At the same time, the memory of Marion, of whom he awaited news, filled the scholar with a dull apprehension. He did not know whether he loved Marion, and did not dare unbosom himself to anyone. But the image of this creature kept his whole body on the gridiron, and he frequently regretted that, instead of making the draining of tankards and then bolting helter-skelter his sole pastime, Montigny did not prefer to take him to the rue de Mâcon to frolic at Marion's at their ease.

Montigny, as a matter of fact, had a woman in a

house where they were kept busy late with stout merchants, and he felt no desire to be noticed in the company of another, for Jeanneton would have heard of it. He was faithful to Jeanneton, in appearance at least, and, as he had very early passed the age when one reckons less on the profit than on the appetite of the senses, he did not understand why François so often eyed him with a sulky look.

"So he's sleepy, is he?" he said joking. And shaking his companion, he shouted in a loud and merry voice: "Hi, there, François! You're asleep!"

"Not a bit of it!" retorted the other.

"Yes, you are! Wake up!"

And standing up, he proposed to him: "Come along! I'll go with you. It's time now."

François followed Régnier, his head down, trying to drag out the journey's length in the hope that perhaps they would meet Marion on the way. But not once did she appear, and François no longer knew what to conclude.

Every day, having risen early so as not to betray himself in the eyes of the chaplain, the scholar thought of nothing but this woman, and when he went to the rue du Fouarre to the class taught by Jean de Conflans, his master, as of many others too, in the study of logic, Aristotle, grammar, and syntax, he stared like a zany and took nothing in. And yet it was now the end of November, and barely four months were left, no more, before he would have to face the first examinations.

François paid no heed to that. He gave idle answers from his bench to the questions of his master, sometimes well, often badly and with much confusion of the little that his good uncle had taught him; and he remained unheeding either of blame or of praise. The stuffy, airless room of the rue du Fouarre was hateful to him. The constant smell of dirt, of the straw that was spread on the floor, of dampness and leather, caught his throat, and he contrasted it, in his disgust, with another odour, an insinuating one, this, which he had never forgotten: that of the girl whom he loved. For he did love her. Her and her only. He desired her ardently, and nothing mattered to him in the world but Marion.

It was then that Colin, who had returned to Paris, saw François, and judged him to be looking ill.

"What's wrong?" he asked. "Are you sick?"

François told him his tale.

"Well, then," said Colin at once, as he went into the little room in the rue de Mâcon while François waited for him. "You stay here, and if I call, run up!"

But Colin came back alone, after less than a quarter of an hour, and, irritated with François, he said to him: "You've let someone else get your place, you nincompoop! Someone else has it."

"What's that?"

"Yes — another. Another, I say," grumbled Colin. "That's how things are."

And he swore by the name of Christ and spat in front of him with an air of such contempt that the poor vexed scholar accompanied him without so much as opening his tight-clenched jaws until they had found Régnier.

"Would you believe it?" began Colin, pointing him out to Montigny with outstretched finger for his humiliation ——

But the scholar turned and put up fight. He had had enough of hearing Colin snap at him and treat him like a baby. And why? For Marion. — A fine business indeed! A girl like that! What was she, after all? Nothing at all — less than nothing at all! It mattered precious little to *him!* If Marion had slipped through his fingers, he would replace her — and quickly enough. And whenever he chose. Nothing difficult in that!

"Bah!" mocked Colin. "If you go on with another the way you did with her, I have my doubts!"

"Oh, well — we'll see that in good time," said François drily.

Régnier made the peace between them. Quarrelling at a first meeting! Did they think of that? Colin had certainly better things to do than to ill-use François for some business about a woman! What madness was inflaming his spirit?

"First of all," said the scholar, "I got two crowns out of Marion. — Ask ——"

"Precisely," Colin reproached him.

And stretching out a black and horny hand to him, Colin exclaimed: "Right you are! Agreed!" — and he fixed the scholar in the eyes with his hard glare, forcing him to respond to his gesture.

I

Peace being concluded, Régnier and Colin spoke to each other about other matters, in that language they used between themselves when they wanted not to be understood. Listening to them, François picked up here and there scraps of their conversation, but the sense of it remained foreign to him, and in the end he said: "What *is* that jargon?"

But his friends left him shortly afterwards, and he went home with a heavy heart, and not at all sure whether he was suffering more from the faithlessness of Marion or the scene he had had with Colin. This scene stuck in his mind, intolerable, vexing him, taking the heart out of him, for he had promised himself to win, not insults, but flatteries from this man who never minced his words.

"But there!" exclaimed François. "Is it my fault? He flew into a temper."

Really, it was too unfair, too stupid. And then, having left him there in the lurch, he had gone off with Régnier with not so much as a good-evening! Did people behave like that? François felt himself taken down a peg. He did not sleep all night, and in the following days he could find no savour in anything. What a life! A week drifted slowly past, hour by hour, in repining and dejection. François did not leave his room except to attend the University lectures in the rue du Fouarre, and so tired and pitiable was he that Master Guillaume took fright. He was unwilling, however, to let his uncle know the pain from which he was suffering. He refused to answer him, avoided him, and felt no appetite until one morning, having told himself that perhaps it was not for Colin's sake he had this vile humour, he suddenly burst into tears on Marion's account, and forthwith recovered his right mind.

"Sure enough," he said, through the flowing tears that made him feel ashamed. "I was mad . . ."

And that evening he went up to Colin in the tavern and said to him, in all sincerity: "Colin, I know I'm not worth much, but I've profited from hearing it."

And Colin answered him: "You're worth more than you thought, youngster."

"Yes, if you help me."

Colin smiled; and then, making room for the scholar, who was filled with contentment at this response, he called out in his rough voice: "I will help you; I promise. Ho, there! Wine for my friend, François de Montcorbier! He's thirsty."

And people turned round in the room to look.

Such a welcome brought back the pleasure of living to François, and the result was that he spent his nights outside, in the company of the locksmith's son. And he learned to know him to perfection, for, along with him and Régnier, he explored taverns of every sort, where they drank without spending a halfpenny. To meet the reckoning, Colin played at dice, and whether at the "Trumelières" or at the "Truie Qui File," whoever took him on, lost, and had to pay the score. François was dumbfounded. But once, when the stakes of the game on the table made up fourteen crowns, no less, he could not contain an exclamation. Colin gave him a mighty kick on the shin, and he held his tongue. The dice were loaded.

"God help us!" he said a little later, to show that he had understood. "You have a twin set of dice on you and you change them!"

"And I rake in the brass!" was all Colin's reply.

During these expeditions it would often happen that sundry persons of surly expression would join in with Colin and converse with him secretly of activities in which François had no part. They were vagabonds, thieves, sorry creatures, with faces as long as an ell, and broken-down shoes. Colin spoke to them in the language he used with Régnier, and these individuals answered him in this same rude and obscure tongue in which François could find no meaning.

"Twig the cant?" he heard Colin say one night to a man who had come forward and greeted Colin as Colin de l'Escailler.

"De l'Escailler?" said François to Régnier. "Why that name?"

"It's the name for the Coquille," Régnier told him.

"In what language?"

"In the cant language."

"Ah!" said François. "And what was it that Colin asked him?"

"He asked him if he understood the cant, if he

twigged —— Cant, a jargon, what you will. Do you understand?"

"I'm beginning," said François.

He bent an ear to the remarks that Colin was exchanging with the stranger.

"But they go so fast," he confessed, "and the words escape me."

Régnier nodded his head.

"You've time enough to shape yourself," he said, stretching himself. "Colin wishes you well. He'll teach you. You'll see, it's a language that's easy to get the hang of when one's given a lesson or two; and it allows a man not to make any mistakes."

"For what reason?"

"For the sake of the matchmaker," said Régnier in a low voice.

And he sketched a gesture that signified the rope and a grimace which was that of a man round whose neck it is being slipped before he is turned off; and François guessed that the "matchmaker," in this queer language, must be the hangman, and he felt a shudder go down his spine.

From that day on, no matter what François did to control himself, and though he was determined to listen to Colin and Montigny talking in their secret language, he could not prevent a shudder whenever the word "matchmaker" turned up in the conversation. He had a profound disgust for the executioner, and was amazed at the frequency wherewith his name was brought into question. What on earth could his friends have to discuss that they should be perpetually concerned with the hangman? It wasn't just card-sharping or fooling with the wenches that meant such a frequent use of this word! Indeed no. Dicers and vagabonds did not come within the rope's ordinary reach, and François could not explain why the rope should always, more or less, be drawn into their arrangements. He felt an unreasoning fear about it. Here was a mystery into which, no doubt, his two friends did not wish to initiate him, for he was too young and might betray them. But what was the mystery? That journey which Colin had never spoken of, those doubtful encounters at night with personages of outrageous appearance whose whole bearing was more than suspicious, gave François something to ponder over. He told himself that it could not be gambling alone that had brought Colin to become the friend of such sinister and degraded creatures. Nor women either. These people were scalawags; worse perhaps, they were from among these vagrants who had been arrested in the spring and put to the torture to make them confess their evil deeds. And as everyone was then told that they had kidnapped children, slit the eyes of some, chopped the legs of others, the scholar, who knew that such a charge would involve a disgraceful death by hanging, had little mind to be met in company with their kind.

"Listen, Colin," he said one night. "Have you never thought of the risks you're running?"

"Yes," said Colin, quite dispassionately. "And then?"

"It's madness!" exclaimed François. "Madness!"

Colin winked his small eye, and then good-humouredly explained: "There's nothing to be got in this world without risk, my boy. Everything has to be paid for. Everything's a game, and that one is sometimes worth the candle."

"Oh, but don't talk so loud!"

"My skin!" insisted Colin boldly. "Do you think I cling to that?"

And he left François torn between the fear of displeasing him and the apprehension that, if he did not keep away from him, he would perhaps have a terrible price to pay.

Amongst them all, there was one tall fellow, ill-clad, always dirty, and smelling like a goat, who filled François with such repulsion that, on meeting him with Colin and Montigny, the scholar was left gaping. This person made use of a frightful jargon which was often quite untranslatable from its borrowing of terms from the country *patois* and the dialects of the north. But he accompanied his words with gestures which lent meaning to them; and it was with stupefaction that François interpreted their meaning. He disentangled that this dreadful creature answered to the surname of "Piez Blans,"* in allusion to his foreign origins or to his repulsive filthiness, and he was a bandit of some note. He carried on operations round about Orléans, in the

* "White-feet," a cant term for a stranger or foreigner. [*Trans.*]

plains and woods, and was the chief of a band of malefactors. In speaking, he had an accent which deformed words with a singular rudeness of effect. He said *men* and *nen* for *mon* and *non;* he blasphemed in English dialects and German; and, though he never exactly laughed, he produced in moments of jollity a kind of grating noise which recalled that of the enormous iron grilles of prisons as they swing round on their hinges. Sunburnt, with sparse red hair under his furred cap, with neither beard nor eyebrows, Piez Blans was not a loquacious man. He would often look at his hands as if their great size must have satisfied him. He had been a soldier. And this was obvious at once, for all his gestures and ways of moving to and fro, of marching and of eyeing people up and down, were stamped with his old calling.

"Heigh! Forward march!" he would shout in a stentorian voice when he had drunk too deeply, or else he thundered out this song, marking the measure in the manner of the old soldiers on the roads:

> "*Trou du cul Pierrete,*
> *Choques des talons,*
> *Chuces la pignete,*
> *Vyde les gallons!*"

or again, showing off on his left hand a massive gold ring, bearing the name and arms of the man he had taken it from, Piez Blans would offer it for admiration and derive much pride from this!

That recalled to him things which he confided to

nobody, for the instinct of self-protection in this brute was such that it always made him hold his tongue just in time. It was no good questioning him: he fell back upon his tongue-tied trick, listened to you, but gave no answer.

"You're right," declared Colin to him on these occasions. From the moment of knowing him Colin had taken him as a model. "Often enough it's the one who talks too much who is lost."

And he drank to the health of this curious personage, who sometimes would allow a glimpse, under his leather coat, of a German coin struck on one side only, which he had sewn in there himself as a charm against bad luck.

François detested Piez Blans. He had not the same reasons as Colin for respecting him profoundly, and he was uncomfortable at his always being present at their meetings. He could well have done without such a man. His grossness, his astuteness, the cruelty which one could read in his eyes, not to mention his smell, were not such as to make him an alluring personality. But François did not know how to persuade Colin that he was spoiling himself by yielding to the old soldier, and every time he drew back from undertaking the task. As for Montigny, he had little more marked sympathy for Piez Blans, and, without going to the point of frankly disapproving of his comrade, he awaited an opportunity of giving his opinion.

However, the days were flying past, and to the winter's rain there succeeded a snow which, as it fell, laid and maintained a frozen layer of mud upon the streets. In the very hearts of the taverns, close to the fire, the cold was so keen that even the hardiest roasted their soles beside the flames, and, as they steamed, spat on the floor, coughing and listless. Only Piez Blans seemed to remain insensible to the cold. He pushed Colin into the corners, explained to him nobody quite knew what, and then, watching him while he spoke in his turn, would take him again with authority. Neither François nor Régnier were in the secret. They contented themselves, from their place, with interpreting the sense of the words from the attitudes of the pair. In the end Colin allowed himself to be convinced, and the glances that he stealthily cast were fixed and gleaming. Between Piez Blans and himself, without the slightest doubt, a project was being formed which they were agreed not to divulge. And then Piez Blans disappeared.

"*Bon voyage!*" cried François.

Colin pricked up an ear.

"Yes," rallied Montigny. "God preserve him!"

"He's a man," said Colin. "He has got the better of the proofs against him."

"As he just goes on robbing people outside Paris," said Montigny, "that's an easy task."

"Perhaps!"

Montigny shrugged his shoulders.

"I know," he answered at once, with humour. "I know that anyone who gives you bad advice pleases you."

"And if I am pleased to take bad advice?"

François tried to intervene.

"No," said Colin, in his rough voice. "It's Régnier's affair."

But as Régnier had no mind for the quarrel which Colin was stupidly seeking, a scornful silence met him.

"You are a witness," he proclaimed, turning to the scholar with a short laugh, "that instead of answering, he shuts his mouth. You see. He's wrong. And later, when some time has passed, he'll regret it."

"What time?" asked François.

"The time till I return."

"Ah!"

"Go on!" burst out Régnier, who was listening in spite of his air of aloofness. "I was sure of it. Go on! Go on! You'll have more need than I shall for repenting it! Piez Blans commands: you obey. Well, it's your own choice."

"You're annoyed?"

"Not a bit," said Régnier. "Only take care you aren't behind the bars."

And he rose up quickly, caught the scholar by the arm, and went out without any greeting to Colin or anybody, while François, utterly taken aback, asked him: "Behind the bars! Tell me, what do you mean by that, Régnier? Explain. Behind the bars? What sort of misfortune is that?"

"Ay, a misfortune. A great misfortune!" answered Régnier dully.

6

From December until the spring returned, Colin remained away from the city on the high roads, taking instruction in his contact with Piez Blans on the way in which he led his gang to go out and meet travellers. He shared his wandering life, and like him, a sword under his arm, he was soon only one beggar the more. The life suited him. Frequently, after tramping cross-country through part of the night, he would find himself, at day-break, spying from behind a hedge for the moment when the women and children and old people would be left alone beside the hearth, and then he would make his appearance. His companions, old soldiers for the most part, peasants, pedlars, and vagabonds, hardened him in his job. Sometimes an order came from Piez Blans to stop all work and take advantage of the rest to sleep and take some enjoyment for themselves; sometimes, on the other hand, a lieutenant would come upon the scene and urge them on to reach as quickly as possible a certain village that had been marked down, and there to attack in conjunction with some other band.

There were rough days in the course of which Colin managed things to perfection, and paid less heed to the blows he dealt to defenceless people than to the manner in which the manœuvre was carried out. He was seized with an idea and breathed not a word of it, for the moment did not seem to him favourable for its execution. Piez Blans, who suspected nothing, but congratulated himself on the zeal Colin brought to his task, explained to him sometimes how he kept his hold of the country. From Orléans to Chartres and from Vendôme right to the Loire, he was in sole command. Beyond these frontiers, other adventurers of his sort had their own bands who pillaged and held for ransom throughout their country-side and led a jovial, generous existence. Between these chieftains there did not yet exist any liaison, except that when following up fugitives on to the preserves of their neighbours, they had to lend a helping hand to each other, and then go shares in the booty. They were independent. They had flung off the control of the great Coësre, to whom in the past they had paid annual dues varying in amount from threepence to a couple of crowns. This great Coësre, the supreme chieftain of the vagabonds, lived in Paris, and they laughed at him as at some outworn scarecrow that no longer scares anybody or anything. By what right did he claim to raise this money tax on each of them? Piez Blans, who was tight-fisted with his gains, vowed he would be drawn and quartered before he would pay out a single farthing to the great Coësre, and his friends, the captains of the marked-out territories, likewise gave their oath to ruin him.

"Let him come here and fetch it," proposed one of them. "I'll hand it over all right ——"

"With some pricks of a pike as well!" guffawed the other.

And a certain Olim Cernay, who had a lordly way with him and wore a long-tailed cap in mockery of the rich bourgeois whom he attacked, declared: "If he comes, I'd like to have him to myself, my worthy friends!"

Then Colin felt his idea taking shape, for he understood, without saying anything, that if, instead of remaining in Paris, the great Coësre visited his vassals and led them towards some enterprise on a big scale, no one would deny him longer.

"What's going on inside you?" asked Piez Blans when he noticed how his friend Colin was absorbed in gloomy reverie. "Regretting the old days?"

"You're cheating yourself," answered Colin. "Let it be; you'll see."

"What shall I see?"

"Nothing has happened yet, but a day will dawn when everything may."

And Colin, sweeping the horizon with his gaze, far across the tillage and the woods that stretched into the distance, winked his small eyes and added: "I'm sure of it."

He did not use his time badly in getting information of the habits and frame of mind of these troop-leaders. An abler man than Piez Blans, he made friends very quickly with the boldest among them, flattering them; and, frequenting their company, he plied them with questions. And when he managed to speak with them in confidence, he explained that by dint of not giving each other more support than they were doing, they would risk being beaten and dispersed in the end.

"Ho! Ho!" was all their answer. "And by whom, eh?"

And they laughed, so farcical did the notion seem to them, and paid for drinks for Colin in order to divert the flow of his remarks.

Then Colin went further, and told how, coming from Paris, he knew that an ordinance had been signed, or was going to be, for the organization of a standing army, and that they would come to think differently.

"But who'll lead it?" they asked, without believing a word of it. "They'll need someone who has knowledge of the business and can fight us one after the other! Eh? Have they found him?"

"Patience!" said Colin.

Olim Cernay was always thrown into a crazy rage by these conversations.

"You're mad!" he flung back at Colin. "It might be possible to find him, but he'd have to be mighty clever to dig us out from where we are, by God he would! We'll soon send him flying out of here, my friend!"

Then, passing abruptly from anger to a singular mistrust, he fixed Colin in the eyes and did not interrupt him further.

It was after having in this way made understandings with everyone, and having secretly disturbed each of them in his manly assurance, that Colin decided to return to Paris. He handed up his sword to Piez Blans and came back by the roads, by easy stages, talking now with the mercers carrying their bales on their backs, and now with the rogues, whose language he spoke when they called on him to stop. The kindly weather gave him confidence in his project, and was agreeable for tramping. The twisted apple-trees had blossoms on their boughs; the bushes had their little green shoots; and in the spongy fields, soaked by the winter's floods, the primroses were forming patterns of brilliant and diapered colours. Everything was fresh to the eye, clear, frank, and limpid. The smell of the fields where the corn was beginning to shoot, the smell of the woods and the wells, mingled in the air; and the birds were flying past with scraps of straw in their beaks, or sat singing themselves hoarse on the branches.

Until he caught sight of Paris from afar, between the gentle slopes of the valleys, Colin went at the pace of a man preoccupied with an idea. But as soon as he saw the high surrounding walls silhouetted against the sky, he quickened his step, and felt his heart jump with joy. On the left, between the poplars, the Seine folded its curves, struck kindly by the sunshine. Along the banks women were washing linen and then putting it out to dry on the grass. Colin took pleasure in it all. He could recognize, beyond the water where it flowed between the islands, the Louvre, and the Petit Bourbon, with its heavy towers and pointed roofs and bell-turrets, and there, to the right, the crenellated walls of the quarter of the schools, amongst which only the spires of churches stood up.

"After five months!" he said to himself as he passed the Saint-Germain gate, the arch of which oozed damply and kept a rare coolness. "I'll have news to hear!"

And thinking of Régnier, he felt a desire that it should be from him, for friendship's sake, that he should first be told how things stood.

François was bachelor when Colin resumed his usual habits, and Colin was glad, for he liked François and wished him well, in his fashion. But bachelor! When the blood burned him with the hottest desires!

"Enough of that!" he said. "This is not time for rubbish! I've better things to undertake here to convince them and attach them to me. They are not fools, neither the one nor the other of them. Lord, they'll follow me!"

Chance smiled on him. That Saturday, the eighteenth day of April, when Colin swore to bring reason to François and Montigny, there "were judged and condemned, by the court of the Parlement, two rogues or beggarmen and one woman of the kind, to be hanged and strangled, and for that purpose there were set up gallows-trees without the gate of Saint-Jacques and the gate of Saint-Denis." Everywhere it was the sole topic of conversation, this approaching execution, and the women made ready for it, for they had never yet seen one of their own sex perish after this fashion. There was great discussion of the point of right, and whether a woman, instead of being hanged, ought not rather to be buried alive as the usage demanded. The men, for the most part, pronounced against the judgment, and especially the younger amongst them; but it was answered that, this woman being a gipsy wench, ought to be dealt with according to the law of her race. She herself had chosen the rope. So nothing could be urged against that. As for feeling too much pity because a rogue should be put to death, that was pure waste of time.

"Good," judged Colin. "That depends."

And he feigned indignation because François, who more than anyone was lamenting this sentence, yielded to his nature on the morning of its execution.

The morning came. In the open space near the Windmill, or the chemin Saint-Denis, an immense concourse surrounded the gibbet from day-break. Over their heads it raised its gloomy structure of beams, everyone gazing at it as if for the first time. Colin, Montigny, and François, amongst the throng, argued in low voices. Colin incited them. He told them that this woman had not asked to be strangled, as the story was told, that she was not guilty, and that, in any case, he would greatly have preferred not to attend this horrible spectacle. If he was there, it was simply in the secret hope that perhaps it would not take place.

"Yes," responded François, "please God it may be so."

"God has nothing to do with this," scolded Colin.

François was pale. He went on: "I hate them."

"They're afraid," said Colin, always in a low tone, for fear of anyone's taking offence at his words. "Afraid of a woman. It's laughable!"

François shuddered. He felt so great a pity for the wretched creature who, in a few minutes, was to be seized by the hangman, that the blood throbbed in his veins with sudden beats, and then flowed back violently to his heart. He felt his throat compressed. He was choking.

"Lean on my arm, François," said Régnier.

But François did not hear him. The sight before his eyes, the people, the dull sky, and, to the right, the heights of Montmartre, brought him back to reality, and so painful was this reality that he felt a horror at being there, like all these others, greedy for he knew not what.

A blurred, rayless light showed up the landscape, with its small round trees: an unreal light, such as one sees in dreams, motionless, falling upon the accoutrements of the soldiery over yonder, by the scaffold, but not making them glitter. It produced a fantastic sensation, the effects of which François could feel, and the more he was astonished by it within himself, the more did this dreamlike sensation become intensified and penetrate him with its baleful quality.

"Ah!" exclaimed someone. "The chimes!"

François shook himself.

"The chimes!" he repeated.

I

There was a kind of pause, and at the same time a spasm of anxiety so acute that the whole crowd shuddered. Turning towards the walls of Paris, and gazing between the towers at the arch of the Porte Saint-Denis, men and women stood expectant.

"Here they are!" said Colin, tapping François on the shoulder.

Filing out from the walls, a procession of horsemen advanced, flanked and preceded by so vast a concourse of people that, in the open space, the curious pressed closer together, and were seized with a singular uneasiness. Whilst the archers maintained the escort in the path they had to follow, and thrust the people back, one could see the slow approach, with the balancing movements of the animals, of the horsemen in their lively colours. They were recognized. They were, a great number of them, ushers of the Parlement and sergeants, who, stiff and stern in the saddle, formed five ranks deep behind the provost, that figure clad in scarlet, whose steed likewise was covered with red stuff falling to his hoofs.

Before this well-aligned mass, which now halted, now moved forward again in compact movement, appeared the woman who was to be hanged and one of the condemned men, conveyed in a cart surrounded by soldiers. The said woman, "all dishevelled, clad in a long robe girdled by a cord binding both of her legs above the knees," held herself up with one hand on the side of the cart. Gazing over towards the gibbet, she was pale and attentive.

I

François saw her as she passed, twenty-five paces or so from where he stood, carried forward in a swarm of armed men cased in iron, swaying as the cart pitched in the ruts. Her black hair made her seem livid, and her staring eyes, with neither fear nor intimidation in them, had such power in them as they fixed the gallows with their gaze that the women crossed themselves.

"Dear God!" they groaned. "Alas and alas!"

François was on the point of thrusting himself forward. But Colin, who was keeping an eye on him, held him back by the sleeve.

"What!" he breathed. "You won't prevent anything. Be careful. This is no place for that sort of thing. Listen! What do you want to do?"

"Let go of me!"

"No," said Colin.

François began to shout: "Let me go, I say! Let go!"

"Stop that!" scolded Régnier.

He helped Colin to control François, and the lad, despite his efforts, found himself forced to stay where he was between his two friends. How could he have escaped? Gripped by them, and tightly pressed between thousands of on-lookers who were hoisting themselves on tiptoe, François was now panting for breath. With the stupor of a drunken man or a newly roused sleeper, he stared at the platform of the scaffold, whereon, in a moment, the hangman and his assistant would take their place to carry out their task, and he felt an abominable pain. Soon, too, a shivering fit seized him and grew

The Bastille, the Temple, and Montfaucon, at the time of François Villon. From the Grandes Chroniques de France, *illuminated by Jean Fouquet*

stronger, shaking his limbs so sorely that Colin and Régnier, exchanging a glance, tightened their grasp. François did not even notice it. He moaned as he shuddered, and sometimes too let forth lamentations in an unintelligible voice.

"What's he saying?" asked Colin.

Régnier shook his head, and François, agonized by the long wait, became cold as ice. His teeth were chattering.

At last the executioner was seen, helping the condemned pair to mount the steps: they were pushed from behind and in full view of everyone. A dull roar greeted them, and then a deathly silence, and in the midst of it one of the ushers began to read the warrant of accusation. There was only one rogue by the condemned woman's side, for the other was appointed to be strangled at the Porte Saint-Jacques while the other was hanged here, but he did not appear to be in any way moved. He was led over to the gallows themselves, and with a sort of refinement, which François appreciated so that he felt himself turn green with horror, he was executed first. There remained the woman, trussed in her bonds. The hangman moved across to her, took her in his arms, and set her down under the gibbet. At that moment she appeared to everyone so slender and agreeably formed that men turned away, or else craned their necks still further in order to gaze on her. François closed his eyes, opened them again, and felt himself overwhelmed with dread; and watching, with a horrible fixed gaze, the gipsy woman stretching her neck while the rope was passed round it, he repeated under his breath, very quickly: "Woman's body — woman's body!"

"What's that?" grumbled Colin in a surly tone. "Shut up!"

But he himself, hardened though he was, remained petrified at the instant when the hangman, up there on the scaffold, pushing his victim into the void, bent down and then straightened himself.

"Come on," said Montigny, getting the words out with an effort. "Let's be off. François!"

"François!" said Colin in his turn.

"Must get back," went on Régnier.

The crowd bore them along in silence.

. . . . . .

The mounted sergeants who had escorted these functionaries of the Parlement were driving a way for themselves by force through the crowds. Sometimes one of the horses whinnied and began to snort, but, held in by its rider, wrenching at the bit, fell into step again and tossed its head with quick breaths.

"Look!" said Colin. "What a crowd of men at arms! They've earned their pay all right."

"Yes," insisted Régnier. "Earned it by dishonour."

"But very respectably," went on Colin.

As François was going along beside them without opening his mouth, they said no more, and came down the hill into Paris by the rue Saint-Denis, where the people who had remained behind their benches and stalls watched the others approaching. Reaching the Halles, Colin struck across to the left, and reached the rue Saint-Martin, which all three followed, with dejected looks, as far as the water. — There Colin, who had a plan in his head, proposed a drink to set them up and something to eat as well. François and Régnier accepted. François might have been anywhere, at the world's end perhaps. He was stricken by an emotion so strong that, far from having a notion of the place where he was being led, he imagined that he was still there beneath the gibbet, amongst the mob, still staring open-mouthed at a body swinging at the end of a rope. Only one body could he distinguish, so frail and tender that his flesh was chilled at the sight of it. One body only. It was that of this woman, and there it would remain exposed for several days, stiffening and hardening before it began to turn soft and ooze into decay. It was hideous, this woman's body turning endlessly, imperceptibly, on itself, and hanging there a dead weight. It was hideous and revolting, and yet François did not feel nothing but disgust. He had as it were a feeling of love and pity for this tortured body; for, as the rope twisted and untwisted with the creaking it has when one bends an ear to it, he seemed to hear the body living, and preparing itself for a secret work which, from within, was to fill it with an imperceptible gurgling. Ah! he knew it well, perhaps? He was sure of it as of the stench which the wind drove down in summer from Montfaucon, and mixed with others coming from the earth and the trees to make all as one. And in his inmost heart, that overwhelmed him, for the image of the gipsy woman took the place of the smell, and he was stricken at the thought that she was no longer amongst the living.

From these reflections he was rescued, without his understanding where he was, by bursts of laughter, and several women were laughing at him.

"A fine gallant!" cried one. "He's dreaming."

"Whose? That's what I want to know," asked another.

"No," said François in reply.

But discovering Colin and Montigny in their midst, he softened and looked all round him.

"Here's your glass," said Colin.

"Ah, that's right!"

"Aren't you thirsty?"

"Yes, yes," stammered François. And as he drank, he leaned over to Montigny and asked him whereabouts they were.

"At Grosse Margot's place," said Régnier.

"Really?"

"And this is Jeanneton," he went on, pulling by her tall, pointed head-dress a girl seated beside him.

François smiled, and murmured: "Régnier has often and often spoken of you to me."

"And of me?" asked a buxom creature whose breasts, rounded like a pair of globes, were more than half out of her velvet gown. "Régnier has never told you about *me?*"

"Oh," said François, "he couldn't have said anything pleasant and delectable enough!"

"Hark to him!" she simpered, taking the flattery. "He looks dry and timid, doesn't he? But his speech is honey!"

"He's the devil, I think," said Colin.

"Yes, yes: that's right! The devil! Ha ha!" exclaimed the company. "But he's pretty! Dark too! And knows his way about! And sharp enough!"

"Peace!" cried the woman to whom François had so ably replied. And in her own house she made herself obeyed. "Devil or no devil, I don't care."

And she came over, adding, as she stroked the young man's hair: "I'm Margot."

"François!" said Colin then. "If you go straight on, it's a good place."

"Straight away?"

"Find out for yourself," chaffed Colin. He had not foreseen that the hostess would take a fancy for the scholar like this.

François did not waste time. He had turned towards Margot and let himself be flattered without daring to speak to her, for she laughed while she caressed him, and, highly skilled in handling people, she took heed of nothing.

"Make yourself comfortable," she said to him. "I'm going to sit close beside you."

François moved back.

Now, Colin had brought the scholar and Régnier to

this place only to acquaint them with the plan which he had in his mind, and he began to tell how the man and woman who had just been executed bore themselves at the moment of death. The girls checked their laughter.

François asked him: "Why torment us, Colin?"

"Because, if you have any honour in you, it befits you to take action."

"How so?"

Colin lowered his voice, and, as Margot's husband came forward politely to inform the girls that they were wanted elsewhere, and made them leave the room, preceded by Margot, he traced so lively a picture of the morning's scene that François felt himself suddenly shudder.

"Amongst men," said Colin, "there must be courage to join hands against such atrocities. I've come back" — and he named Piez Blans — "bringing the word of several captains whose minds are made up not to tolerate any longer the way things are going on here."

"But how should I be of service to you?" asked François in reply.

"That will mean a great deal of money," said Régnier.

"Exactly," said Colin.

"And where is that to be got?" asked François timidly, feeling this conversation to be insensate. "Have you got any?"

"I shall have some," declared Colin, "if you support me, and let me explain to you how you can manage it.

Each of the captains, for a march on Paris, can count on more than two hundred soldiers. And moreover, we shall raise others as we fall in with them."

"At Dijon?" asked Régnier.

"Yes," said Colin, "and in Paris too, for we shall need to have comrades in our town to supply their effort. As for money, those who style themselves the Coquille men will get the money all right, so long as they do not spare themselves at it."

François thought he was dreaming.

"You go and get me some of those fine gold goblets or a pyx," said Colin then; "they're easy to get in the churches at night; or in the coffers you'll find fine ringing crown pieces, or groats or florins, or doubloons, or nobles. They'll go towards the expenses; the first melted and beaten down, the rest ranged with great care against the day when they will be useful for the better recruiting of the *gueux* in the country. Meanwhile, I'll go and find my men and exhort them to make ready jointly for striking the great blow. Am I talking sense?"

"Ha!" answered François. "Yes and no."

"And you, Régnier?" asked Colin, rapping on the table.

Régnier looked at him, and said: "It's a good scheme. I'll follow you."

II

7

"Colin must be going out of his mind," thought François, after weighing what was to be said on all sides of the problem, and having realized that engaging himself in such a venture meant the risk of his skin. "It is attempting the impossible! What is he judging by? I'll not mix myself up in it. As for Régnier, he'll sniff the rope in it and back out!"

But he had thoughts also for Margot, the hostess of the cloister of Notre-Dame, and he had a great desire to see her again without his two friends' knowing anything about it. She had made an impression on him. She was tall and strong, still young, and with charms so appetizing that they made his mouth water. Had she only wanted to make mock of him the other day? François was perplexed. Frequently he examined himself in his mirror, and, sighing to find himself so unworthy of this handsome and robust woman, he reproached himself for thinking such things. Never yet had he felt so disgusted by his dull complexion, his hollow cheeks, and that mouth of his, too large and very unpleasing. He was small, ugly, ill clad, and timid and penniless to boot. As for prizing open these great coffers! Ah, Colin was talking there! Did he think that one had only to wish, and one would be rich? Where were these famous coffers? And how were they to be opened? Come along! Why did Colin go cheating at dice when he could take the money in handfuls where he was, and then show you the place? François would scarcely have hesitated. For without money, no wine, and no women either, he concluded. And certainly not Margot. The temptation then became so strong that it decided François. In broad daylight, he went into the hostelry, and Margot, full of smiles, came at once to meet him.

"You, at last!" she exclaimed.

"Yes," replied François, highly satisfied at his welcome. "You haven't seen Montigny, have you?"

"It's too early."

"Oh, well ——"

"But where are you off to?" asked Margot, as he made as if to go out by the door. "Just arrived to go off again?"

"Well, you see —" stammered François, pointing to the end of the room towards the hostess's husband, who was watching them sulkily.

"What!" said Margot. "Not at all."

And as the scholar hesitated to take her at her word, she called out commandingly: "Antoine! Go and fetch us some wine!"

Immediately Antoine picked up a jug and a candle, took the key of the cellar, and went quickly downstairs. He was used to the caprices of his wife and, so as not to appear ridiculous, he showed himself delighted that she had always the same tastes as his own. That allowed him to be looked on with a friendly eye by Margot's gallants, even if it meant giving them a cold shoulder when she flung them over, and throwing them out if they tried to come back. Fat as dripping, a coward and a wheedler, the man cared for nothing but a quiet life for himself. Wine and women were only a secondary consideration to him.

"As for dicing and cards," he used to say, "I leave those to them who are up in the game."

He, indeed, was as expert as anyone, but applying himself always to self-effacement for the prosperity of his commerce, he brought the wine and the bread and cheese, sat down apart, counted the day's takings, and went to bed. Jeanneton, waiting for Régnier, remained in a corner, alone at her table. Régnier arrived late, and Colin with him. Colin had a mistress in the house, Colette by name, and very harshly he treated her. In front of François, being annoyed at not having won him over, Colin behaved in an exaggerated style. He stormed at Colette, passed several nights without joining her, deceived her, bullied her, and then, when he had in the end to say good-evening to the scholar, he did it in such a way that his temper was put down to the count of the trouble he had had with the girl.

But François was not deceived by that. He knew that Colin bore him a grudge for being so well looked on in the house. It was stupid: Colin—jealous, envious? François was amused at the idea, and in bed, while he took his pleasure in the caresses of Margot, he shamelessly made merry at being thus in the best room, and had a sense of satiety.

In this way he took his revenge upon Colin, and quite unwittingly submitted him to a harsh ordeal, for Régnier was a witness of the scene, and the girls also, admirers of François. —

"Yes and no," he had answered to the locksmith's son when the latter had unfolded his absurd project. Events seemed to justify the scholar. Now yes. Now no. Life was like that. Just chance. Who could tell? And yet François felt gratitude towards Colin for having introduced him into these circles and supplied him, for going out at night, with a false key, which doubtless he had not forged with this intention.

And highly prized this key was by the scholar, now that he had become acquainted with Margot; it allowed him to escape from his room, about eleven o'clock, without waking Master Guillaume. But François used it in his own way. If he spent his nights abroad and did not come home till dawn, he remained in his room fully clothed and studied the lessons which he should have done the night before, and very quickly mastered them. His love-affair transformed him. It gave him energy, high spirits, wit, and self-assurance. It whipped his blood. It made a new lad of him, and when Master Guillaume, amazed to notice how much François had managed to alter in so short a time, admitted as much, François replied with a laugh which told a good deal.

He still went to see his mother, every Thursday, at

the Célestins. But it made no difference to him when she thought that he was not looking well; François was no longer vexed by that.

"It's this Latin," he would declare cynically. "Studying by candlelight makes you pale, you know."

"Ay, ay," answered the old woman. "And how thin you are!"

"Bound to be," said François. "Come, come, don't worry yourself about that. When I've taken my second stage at the University, I'll get fatter to please you. I promise."

"But goodness me! Shall I be here to see it?"

"Certainly. Two years soon go by."

"Two years!" said the good woman. "And during these two years you're still going to go on learning and stuffing your head?"

"No doubt of it!"

And then, thinking of her years, the old woman softened and sketched a poor little sign of the cross on her troublesome boy's brow to shield him from harm, and she kissed him, and made him promise to look after himself better.

"I'll go and say a prayer for you in Notre-Dame," she sighed simply. "For you. To help you in your work."

And as François could make no answer, his mother, who knew perhaps how much he stood in need of her prayers, recited a *Hail Mary* to herself, and drew him closer to her and, fumbling, made him join his hands as she used to teach him long ago when he was a little boy and followed her to church to wonder at the stained-glass windows.

Of these visits François retained the kindest of memories, but they did not prevent him from making for Grosse Margot's establishment that same night, and behaving there in the merriest style. The ramblings of his poor old mother had no real effect on him. He called them to mind when chance reminded him of them, but he gave them no heed. Did he not see all around him an alliance of the pure with the impure? Here was Notre-Dame, beside which he was pacing, and there, behind the cloister, an easy stone's throw away, he could see the house of ill repute, frequented by all manner of people. Was he doing wrong in going there? The front of the cathedral, with its doors embellished with images, and its gallery of kings, did not make him halt on his way. On the contrary, he hurried on the faster, and if he chanced to address a humble greeting to Her he had so often prayed to as a child, or put himself under Her protection, he thought no more of it the moment after.

Neither his mother, nor his uncle the chaplain, when they preached their sermons to him, could thwart in François that instinct for pleasure which was his; nor could they even instruct him against himself, for immediately François would begin sulking and grumbling. Master Guillaume had his suspicions that his nephew was tricking him. He saw as much from his fatigue and his tired eyes. But not yet realizing wherein the deception consisted, he would sometimes take the scholar out to dine with some of his friends, and introduced the young bachelor to them, not as a mere boy now, but as his newly won scholastic status entitled him.

François made the most of it. He had at least the chance — tedious and long drawn out as these evenings seemed to him — of enjoying good cheer, and of planting seeds of sympathy of which he might one day have need. The table of Jacques Seguin, prior of the Abbey of Saint-Martin-des Champs, was a meeting-place, apart from the Présidente de Scepeaulx and two women styled La Davie and La Regnaulde, who enlivened the meal with their piquant repartees, of such men of mark as Master Jacques Charmolue, Germain Rapine, Guillaume de Bosco, Jean Tillart, the examiner in the criminal chamber, Raoul Crochetel, Pierre Malaisée, the King's surgeon, Jenilhac, the treasurer of the Sainte-Chapelle, and often enough Jean Turquan, the lieutenant of the provost of Paris. Ladies and gentlemen conversed freely in front of Master Guillaume's nephew, and never a suspicion crossed their minds that his attention to their remarks was induced by any other wish but to make a good impression. Ah! if they could have guessed how François laughed in his sleeve, and mimicked them all when he was telling Margot of how he spent his evenings, they would have kept closer watch on themselves. There was Jean Tillart, for instance, a man full of solemnity who suddenly yielded at the dessert to a spirit of buffoonery; François could reproduce exactly his bearing and the tone of his voice. He talked through his nose like the examiner himself, squinting at the corsage of the old Présidente, whose tricks he had mastered and whom he represented as a pert, stuck-up old maid; or else, retailing in cold tones the elaborately polished conceits with which Pierre Malaisée embellished his conversation, he looked you up and down so alarmingly that a wild laughter mastered him in spite of himself, and drew shrill little cries from his mistress.

"Stop! That's enough!" she cried, half swooning with hearing him. "François, you're too silly!"

"And Jean Turquan?" asked Antoine, who delighted in these imitations. "Does he still sing *Marionette* as if he were burying a corpse?"

"Of course he does. Like this —" said the scholar, suddenly rising and beginning, with a great rolling of the eyes:

"Elle est gente et godinette,
Marionette!

Sufficit! Even when he's singing, I get frightened!"

"Ah! Ha ha!"

"You're frightened?" said Antoine in astonishment.

"He smells of flames and ropes and torture. I'm not lying. What a man! Enormous!" (He puffed out his chest.) "And rich!" (He drew a farthing from his pocket and felt its weight as if it were a crown.) "Lewd!" (He embraced Antoine.) "And so polite!" (He belched.) "A model of a man! Oh, the bastard!"

But while he was thus describing with a wealth of gesticulation and grimaces the criminal lieutenant of the provost of Paris, François checked himself. For he was afraid, as he piled it on, lest evil fortune should some day transpose the roles, and make him play a less harmless farce in front of Jean Turquan in person.

"I'm wrong," he said to himself.

And he passed on to another guest with some new foolery.

It was with these extravagances of his that he enchanted Margot.

"Here you wouldn't recognize them. They're hot as embers, and restless, and make-believe. And as for paying, they count their ha'pence."

"You fleece them, I'll be bound?"

"Lord help us!" answered Antoine in his oily way. "Don't fear for that! I've got my head screwed on the right way!"

"So much the better!" said the scholar.

But he was not malevolent. Neither good nor bad. A true boy of the people, quick to note a trait and sharpen it immediately, and then direct it against the fool who had given it into his hands. Margot herself did not go free when the mood was on him, and her anger was all in vain; François depicted her with such dexterity that she ended by laughing and saying: "Go on, François! Don't you see any other faults in me?"

"Of course I do!" answered François.

And one evening when Colin and Régnier were seated

with their doxies, he recited this ballade which he had composed, miming it as he spoke it:

> " *Se j'ayme et sers la belle de bon hait,*
> *M'en devez-vous tenir ne vil ne sot?*
> *Elle a en soy des biens à fin souhait.*
> *Pour son amour sains bouclier et passot;*
> *Quand viennent gens, je cours et happe un pot,*
> *Au vin m'en fuiz, sans demener grant bruit;*
> *Je leur tens eau, fromage, pain et fruit.*
> *S'ils paient bien, je leur dis:* 'Bene stat!
> *Retournez cy, quand vous serez en ruit.*
> *En ce bordeau où tenons nostre estat.*' "

"Ho there!" cried Antoine, quite dumbfounded. "What's all that? I take your meaning!"

"Proceed!" said Montigny, gravely.

> " *Mais adoncques il y a grant deshait,*
> *Quant sans argent s'en vient couchier Margot;*
> *Veoir ne la puis, mon cœur à mort la hait.*
> *Sa robe prens, demy saint et surcot,*
> *Si luy jure qu'il tiendra pour l'escot.*
> *Par les costés se prent; c'est Antechrist.*
> *Crie et jure par la mort Jhesucrist,*
> *Que non fera. Lors j'empongne ung esclat;*
> *Dessus son nez luy en fais ung escript,*
> *En ce bordeau où tenons nostre estat."*

"But that's *me!*" broke in Antoine again, jubilant at the picture. "Margot, what do you say to it? You've been telling him tales?"

"Be quiet!" she answered. "You or someone else, let's hear it to the end. And then we'll discuss."

"What?"

"Go on," she cried. "What comes next?"

"Yes, the next!" cried Antoine, abruptly changed by the answer he had drawn.

"Listen," said François.

And with a tone of irony, addressing himself to Margot and imitating her, he went on right to the envoy of his ballade, and while Antoine was laughing on the wrong side of his mouth, he recited, carried along by the rhythm:

> " *Vente, gresle, gelle, j'ay mon pain cuit.*
> *Je suis paillart, la paillarde me suit.*
> *Lequel vaut mieulx? Chascun bien s'entresuit.*
> *L'ung vault l'autre; c'est à mau rat mau chat.*
> *Ordure amons, ordure nous assuit.*
> *Nous deffuyons onneur, il nous deffuit,*
> *En ce bordeau où tenons nostre estat.*"

There was a moment of stupefaction. Antoine was observing Margot. Colin watched Colette, and Régnier, Jeanneton. They all refrained from saying what was in their thoughts, for they all recognized themselves in these verses of François's, and did not know how to express their astonishment.

"You're a poet?" said Régnier to him at last.

"Oh," retorted François, "I've done my best to depict this place."

"And you've succeeded," said Antoine. "True, you might have portrayed me more nobly. Running for wine, that depends on the people. There are ways and ways."

"Bah!" answered François. "I've kept the good way. And you, Margot?"

But Margot turned her back on him, and Colin, who had not yet expressed his feelings, rose gaily, and, talking as if to himself, declared: "There! You house him, and you coddle him, and that's how he shows you his thanks."

"Hark to Colin!" said Margot then to François, offended. "He's right. Treating me like a bad lot!"

François seized her in his arms.

"No!" She defended herself. "No and no and no!"

"Margot!"

"Oh, I'm angry! Angry!"

And she went off to bed, on her dignity, whilst Antoine and Colin, in one corner, talked mysteriously of what had happened.

François was in distress. He did not dare to join Margot, nor yet to go away, from fear lest by yielding place he should lose all his standing. Approaching Régnier with a sorrowful air, he said to him: "Where is the harm, Régnier? Do you blame me?"

"You are young," said Régnier.

"Maybe!"

"And Margot is a woman: she would have preferred you to paint her in the fairest colours."

"How so?"

"Well, say, by comparing her with some great lady, as is proper."

"Oh, indeed?"

"Yes," answered Régnier. "It's true. Women hardly ever like to be treated as they really are. They need eulogies."

"I don't understand," answered François, in all seriousness. "What eulogies? The sort that are so dusty with age and ludicrous that just using them is so much nonsense?"

"That's what it is."

But François's disappointment touched him, and he said in a low voice: "Your verses are excellent. They are consistent; they stand in high relief; and what they describe has the accent of life. Go on without thinking of Margot. You'll get other satisfactions out of them. You are a poet, I tell you that straight out. Have confidence in yourself, and some day you'll be feasted instead of being disowned."

"You think so?"

"I do. Your name will be known. Your poems will be learnt by heart, and the ladies and young men will greet each other with the words: 'Do you know François de Montcorbier?' "

"You're joking?"

"François de Montcorbier!" repeated Régnier loftily.

And then François, drawing him by the sleeve, and shameful at having to confess that he had had this in his mind, explained to him: "De Montcorbier is my name no longer."

"Why that?"

"I've changed it," said he. "François de Montcorbier sounds poorly to the ear. And it is difficult to remember. But if you take the first letter of each line of my envoy there —

Vente, gresle, gelle. . .

— you will get the name I've chosen."

"And what is that?"

François recited the envoy of his ballade, and Montigny was deeply impressed.

"What do you think of it?" asked the scholar.

"Ah!" said Régnier. "Villon! You're right, boy. That is better. That sticks in the mind at once. But what will your uncle, Master Guillaume, have to say to it? You've taken his name from him?"

"Bah!" retorted François. "He will never know!"

8

And so it came about that François, keeping it dark from his uncle, wrote other poems, which he recited to Régnier and Antoine, for Margot, since the episode of the ballade, remained hostile towards him. They were very smutty verses, fanciful and crammed with humour, in which the scholar hit out at sundry characters of the streets and taverns who, by their ridiculous ways, aroused his maliciousness. Montigny was delighted with them. As for Antoine, he was much too sharp not to have realized that Margot's annoyance would last only for a time, and that he had everything to gain by not rebuffing François.

"Have patience!" he said to him in a crafty tone. "You must let her come back."

"And she'll come back to me?"

"She's dying with desire to," declared the stout fellow. "I know her all right. It's still spite that keeps her from making a move in your direction, but don't you go and spoil things by hurrying."

"No," said François. "You're a good counsellor."

And a short while afterwards, true enough, Margot took her seat at François's table, and, without any reference to their rift, called for Antoine to serve them with something to drink.

"A drop of the best, eh?" said the latter, knowing

from which cask to draw the wine of reconciliations. "I'm hurrying!"

"Quicker!" commanded Margot.

François eyed her.

"You've got something against me?" she said, with a great air of submission.

"No," answered François.

"Well, come nearer then! Come along! Nearer!" she murmured, enticing the scholar. "Ho! The sulky fellow! Give me a kiss!"

François paid up without much enthusiasm, and then, as Margot clasped him full in her arms, and gave him back ten kisses for each of his, he put her gently away from him, and said with an affected smile: "How can anyone believe you, Margot? You throw me over — you take me back. — What's your game?"

"The game of love."

"Indeed?"

"Yes, indeed," said the hostess, thrown into a lively desire for the reconquest of her friend by his trick. "Don't push me away! That's wrong of you."

"Ha ha!" he sneered. "It was you who taught me."

"François!"

"How do you mean?"

Margot seized hold of him tenderly, and leaned her head on his shoulder. Ecstatically she sighed: "What do you want me to give so that we can be just as good friends as we used to be?"

"We'll talk of that later," said François suddenly.

And he showed Margot any number of little tendernesses, for Antoine was coming up from the cellar, with a large pot, and cheese and bread.

The same night that François and Margot made up their quarrel, someone came to bring news to Colette that Colin had been arrested at the "Pomme" and locked up in the Châtelet. Colette broke into shrill cries, and burst into tears. Jeanneton, anxious for Régnier's safety, demanded explanations.

"He's been up to some of his games," was the evasive answer from the man charged by Colin to tell the news. "Some sergeants, disguised as merchants, were trying the luck at dice with him for who would not pay the reckoning, and Colin did not mistrust them. He's a good sort."

"No, no!" struggled Colette, as they attempted to calm her. "What did he say about the sergeants?"

"They caught him cheating," declared the man. "And immediately they jumped on him, and a job they had to hold him and bind him."

And, in order that Colette should gather the object of his mission, he added: "This will mean some expense."

"Yes," said Colette.

And she asked how much.

"He must have a bed, and some food, while he's waiting to be taken from the Châtelet to some other prison, for he's appealing to the bishop, being a clerk —

and quite right too. — Well, twenty pistoles — is that too much?"

"I'll go and take them," said Colette.

"To-morrow, then."

"And what are you drinking yourself?" she asked, wiping her eyes.

François felt overwhelmed by astonishment.

"Twenty pistoles!" he reckoned.

"That's the price," answered Jeanneton. "Before Régnier I had another lover, and he cost me the same sum for having to help him when he was in quod."

But the man ate with good appetite, and Colette talked to him and filled his glass up as he emptied it. It was late. Antoine was yawning. Margot was just going to go off to bed when Régnier turned up.

"François," said Margot gently, "are you coming?"

"Yes," he said with regret, for he would have liked Régnier's confirmation of the tidings. "Wait."

But Régnier was not informed, and François rejoined Margot saying: "If I were to tumble as Colin has done, would you help me?"

"Oh!" said Margot, "can you ask it?"

"Then just act as if I were in trouble. That's the best way. I'll at least have the advantage of it."

"How so?"

"By your handing me over the twenty pistoles," answered François chillingly.

And never did he have more pleasure than next day in pocketing that money.

It was almost a fortune for him. He laid it out under his window, behind a panel of the room, and then, satisfied with taking enough money to drink and amuse himself every day, he neglected Grosse Margot's place, in favour of the "Trou Perette," where he spent as freely as he liked. A pleasing spot! As soon as François showed his face there, everyone celebrated his arrival.

"Ah! here he is!" they said.

Régnier like the rest. But it was a Régnier dumbfounded by François's generosities and suspecting — with a certain admiration — where the money came from.

"You do well," he said approvingly, when the scholar, half drunk, called with loud cries for more tankards.

"Quick, wench, quick! Make haste! It's François Villon who pays. He's got the money all right."

And François added: "Lord help us! It'll all go to the good of the house!"

"Ha ha! A great lad is Villon!" shouted the men whom he was treating. "Look at him. He's got the money, and he knows how to use it!"

Sometimes, egged on by Régnier, who had revealed the news that his friend was a poet, François would recite some of his verses. He was applauded. He recited them with unmatched spirit, a sense of comedy and an intensity which left everyone astounded, and soon his ballade of Grosse Margot was famous to such an extent that wherever he went he was asked to recite it for the general entertainment. A fine entertainment, indeed, it was. This dark, dry-looking lad, in his tattered gown, had such a trick of miming, and putting life into his poem, that he quickened the blood in your veins, dominated you, subjugated you. One was held by him. One laughed. One yielded utterly, and when he reached that cynical avowal, so splendidly expressive, of the envoy —

> *Vente, gresle, gelle, j'ai mon pain cuit.*
> *Je suis paillart. . .*

it was as if one had really heard the falling hail rattling outside to make you appreciate all the better the generous life of the comrades seated beside the fire.

At the same time there was admiring wonder that François, although so youthful, should show himself freed from all the prejudices. And indeed he was! It was himself whom one could see in those verses of his; and that money he brought out in handfuls from his pocket — one heard how he had got hold of that! A certain old monk, Brother Baude by name, a rake with the women, swore it on his cross, and, out of the running though he was at the "Trou Perette," he was listened to. He rose when François had finished his ballade, and, questioning him with force, cried out that it must needs turn out so, for such instruction was not in the books.

"You are my master!" he said to François. "And you make me alive again to the motto that I love. Ho there! More wine! May poetry reign, amen! I salute you!"

And in a hoarse voice that whined out of habit, he

struck up a song, so as not to be left lagging behind Villon. It was that song of which he had written both the words and the queer tune, beginning with these words:

Tire-moi par mon cordon —

and everyone roared with delight.

This Brother Baude never left François now, and took him for his diversion to many a place which the scholar knew nothing of. With the advancing summer, the nights became milder and lighter, and the dawn broke very early in the sky. But Brother Baude did not give a rap for that. He got himself as tipsy as if these nights would last an eternity, and then, turning up with a great hullabaloo under the balconies of ladies where musicians were tuning up their instruments, he gave them a drubbing and sang himself, alone, in his dreary style, till the ladies lost their temper. And then François had just time to make himself scarce, for chamber-pots were emptied on your head for your persistence, and the watch came running on the scene.

"Look alive!" cried François. "Use your legs!"

And giving his companion the slip there, he took to his heels through the narrow lanes and, in an instant almost, had reached the hostelry of Grosse Margot, where his mistress came down to open the door for him. The more faithless the scholar showed himself, the more attachment Margot showed him. She never asked questions as to where he had come from, nor whether he had deceived her, but, eager to serve him, she helped him to clamber up the stairs and get his clothes off, and then pushed him into bed. François was delighted. He had in this woman a companion of whom he could never have foretold that she would yield so easily to all his whims. It was vain to keep her dangling in suspense every night before going to join her, for she did not grow weary, and when François hailed her from the street in company with the monk, it was a question of sleeping all three of them, even if Margot had to stay on alone with Brother Baude in the morning at the hour of François's leaving them.

Brother Baude made no complaint, it can be imagined, nor Margot either, but it ended with things not going as they used to at the tavern, for no sooner did the monk appear than he was called "the crabbed monk," and the guests took their leave. Antoine refused to serve him. It was the very deuce with this monk, who sat at his table there in the room in the morning, quite shamelessly, and drained tankard after tankard. In spite of his long striped cloak of the Carmelites' order, he had scarcely the manner of persons of standing, nor had he even the false and hypocritical ways which at least preserve appearances. He blasphemed in your face, and went down himself to the cellar, and, toying with Margot when the fancy took him, he would have gone further with her if Antoine had not come near.

"Ho, my friend!" said the monk. "Off with you! You're spoiling my pleasure."

But Margot burst out laughing, and, after a moment,

she sent back Brother Baude, begging him not to push François to drink too much when he rejoined him.

"He's easy to lead away," she said to him. "And then what would I have left for me?"

"Nay," said he, "I'm here, you know."

"You—you aren't the same. Ah! Ah!" Margot scolded him. "Go on! Off with you!"

"Till to-night?"

"Till the devil!" grunted Antoine, and coughed and spat and then added: "Lord! He's a fat brute!"

The misfortune for François was that Brother Baude, who styled him his master, had really such power over him that he guided him towards the taverns where the girls of loose life and the clerks of every rank made free with each other. A dense atmosphere seized you as soon as the door was opened, and cries and snatches of song taken up in chorus were your simultaneous welcome. These songs worked upon Francois's imagination, exciting him. He gave tongue, and Brother Baude, who was never a laggard in such company, bellowed like any ruffian of them:

"Beuvons du vin,
Et chantons, de cœur cler et fin:
Alleluia!"

It was the favourite refrain of the topers and rolled interminably on, on a rhythm in double time, heavy and long-drawn-out, until, standing up and uplifting every man of them his glass, the frequenters of the place roared till they were hoarse:

II

> *" Benoist soit qui bon vin bera*
> *Et qui bonne chère fera!"*

"*Alleluia!*" intoned Brother Baude.

None the less, out of the sum that Margot had handed him François now had only five or six crowns left over, and they too vanished as if by magic. In vain did the poet rummage in his hiding-place. Not one ha'penny could he lay his hands on, and very disappointed he was.

"What! Already!" he said to himself.

"Yes," said Régnier, "the money you get from women is quick-come, quick-go stuff."

"And where does it go?"

"Where youth and pleasure go," answered Brother Baude. "Into nothingness."

"Right," said François then. "I shall consider the matter."

That same night he forced himself to excite Margot's compassionate feelings. She felt some satisfaction in finding him penniless, and had thoughts of having a better hold of him by the fact. He told her of his plight, but Margot did not seem to take it in.

"But I need money," insisted François harshly. "Well? What have you got to say?"

"I haven't any more," answered Margot.

"You lie!"

But Margot stuck to it.

"Give you my money?" she said. "Just for you to take it to others? No, thank you!"

"You see you *have* got some!"

Margot shook her head.

"I have some — some —" she repeated. "In a manner of speaking . . ."

Or, when François was pushed to extremities by these stupid answers, he struck her, and she whimpered: "It's true. No — no — I've no more. — You've taken all I have. — Enough, François — stop. . . ."

Brother Baude, who was present at the scenes and took care not to intervene, then had an idea.

"As Margot refuses," he expounded with buffoonish dignity, "leave her alone. To examine what one needs helps one to obtain it. Come. I want to take you."

"Where are you going?" Margot asked them.

They went along the streets, stopping a long while in front of the stalls where the sellers of tripe and fish, fruit and cheese, were crying up their wares, taking them for honest folk.

"How much?" inquired Brother Baude.

They gave him a price, and he pushed on further, dragging François with him, although he could make nothing of it and stared at all this merchandise with an undeceived air.

"Here's some fine fish!" said Brother Baude gravely, to the herring-women of the Petit Pont. "Are they fresh?"

"Fresh as a flower!" they answered. "Just look at that fish now; isn't he like living?"

"And my chickens!" cried a shrill voice.

"Yes, yes," answered Brother Baude. And, slipping

through the crowd that thronged the narrow space reserved for persons on foot, he nudged François with his elbow to make him move forward.

They had both formed the project of providing themselves with a meal, to which all François's friends would be invited in honour of the poet. A huge and sumptuous feast, such as none had yet known, to last from dusk till dawn, when the first fine nights arrived. Régnier was in the secret, and judged the idea excellent. But alas! for such a crowd of guests — and they had to be counted as double the number on account of the girls who would have to come — Margot would have had to loosen her purse-strings very far indeed, unless, by some subtle arrangement, they could succeed in providing themselves with all they wanted.

There lay the difficulty. And insurmountable it appeared, when Brother Baude, having taken his friend strolling at his leisure among the wares exposed for sale, said to him: "Now the time for action has come. You know where the tripe is, and the big fish too. You're going to go and take 'em."

"But how?"

"Wait!"

Quickly he led François to an old-clothes-dealer of his acquaintance, who togged him up in fine clothes against a promise that they would not be kept for more than an hour. Then, running to the "Pomme," where Guy Tabary, Vallée, Guillaume Charruau, Philippe Brunel, and others were used to forgather, he told them that this very night, without the Porte Saint-Denis, a merry gathering would be held, provided they lent themselves to giving him useful support now.

François understood what was expected of him, and broke into a loud laugh.

"Wait a bit!" decided Brother Baude, who was assigning a clear duty to each one of them. "Tabary, you shall go and post yourself near Notre-Dame, and François, to begin with, will join you there. You, Vallée, keep on the Place de Grève. Guillaume, rue Poupée for you; and Philippe, rue de la Verrerie. Shift for yourselves. Whatever François brings you, run with it to outside the Porte Saint-Denis. I'll be there with two or three lads who will have the wherewithal for cooking. Promise?"

"Agreed!"

"And on your way," the monk recommended, "just tell any of the girls you may meet that there's room for them at the picnic, for eating and drinking, as well as for other things. But only the most pleasing ones, mind! You understand? And good-humoured too, because for old fellows such as there are — no, no ——"

And to François, who was eager to be off, Brother Baude said: "Success depends on you. Off with you, quick, and come back furnished in plenty with the best that you can find. You know how to manage?"

"You'll see by the weight!" answered the scholar.

"Be on the generous side, won't you?" the monk added further. "Better too much than too little."

François was off like a flash, and, adapting his gait and bearing to the noble appearance he now displayed, made his way to the herring-woman pointed out by Brother Baude, and caught hold of a fish.

"Seven sous," said the good woman.

"Why not twenty? Ho, ho! I have a taste for them, and I'll need a basketful. Seven sous! Won't you take something off on each?"

"He's taking the biggest!"

"By our Lady!" exclaimed François. "As far as choosing goes ——!"

He could not refrain from laughing, but in a seemly fashion, as a well-bred man who doesn't take offence at the pretensions of market-women, and at the same time went on piling up the mullet and the carp. He counted them: seventeen, eighteen . . .

"You're going to clear me out!" exclaimed the fish-wife, in high delight.

"Well, a good part at least, if not quite altogether," said François. "Would you be angry if I did?"

"Oh, but of course not!"

"And where am I to put them?" asked François, pointing to the choice that he wished to take away.

"Don't you worry about that," said the good woman cheerfully, "I have someone for running errands. Jacquot!" she called out. "Come here! Take a basket!"

"That's right. A large basket," added François. "As for the money, Jacquot will bring it back."

"Is it far?" asked Jacquot.

"Over by Notre-Dame."

"Right," said Jacquot. "You shall go in front, sir, and I'll follow up."

When François set off, flanked by his porter, he was much embarrassed at the prospect of sending back this man without paying him, for he was a fellow it would be safer to have no awkward dealings with. All the way along the rue Neuve he kept a steady pace, in spite of his heavy load, and kept saying briskly: "On we go! On we go!"

Guy Tabary, who was waiting on the look-out, saw them approaching, and François as he passed gave no sign of recognition. He was looking for the means of reaching his ends when suddenly, catching sight of a penitencer receiving a woman's confession, he bade Jacquot stop.

Going over to the priest, he whispered in his ear: "I beg you, sir, to make haste, if you please. To-day is my opportunity of taking you to a nephew of mine who is conducting himself in a manner offensive to God. He is not really bad at heart, but he is mad, and will talk of nothing but money."

"Yes," the confessor agreed. "I shall hear him."

François came back to the porter.

"This priest will pay you, my friend," said he. "Put the basket down from your shoulders and have a rest from it. Look, he'll soon be finished. There! This way, nearer! Keep just there."

And while François was giving directions to the fellow, he made a signal to Tabary, and Tabary snatched up the basket and was off.

"He'll give me a few coppers for the job?" asked Jacquot meantime, highly pleased with the fine manners that François was passing off on him. "It was a heavy load I had."

"You'll have four," said François, and off he went in the opposite direction from the one chosen by Guy Tabary, touched the Seine at the Hôtel-Dieu, where Régnier, who was strolling abroad, was amazed to see him in this fine get-up.

"Quick! Quick!" the scholar said to him. "Come with me and I'll tell you the story. . . ."

Régnier guessed that something was in the wind, and ran behind François to the "Mule," into which they both disappeared and offered explanations in a flash.

"Ah!" said Régnier. "I'm in it!"

"The devil!"

"And what have you still to get hold of?"

"Tripe."

"By God, I thought as much!"

"Well, listen," said François abruptly. "This is how we must try. While I am arguing about the price, you must come up and forthwith butt me with your backside, in mockery."

"I get it exactly. François, you've a good head!" said Régnier. "Let's make haste ——"

"And I'll lose my temper and fling the tripe at you. You'll pick it up and then we'll get away ——"

"Ah! Ha ha!" roared Régnier.

And in this way François, holding in his hands the liver and the famous tripe he was so fond of, contested with the woman the price she was asking, when Régnier joined in the discussion in the agreed way.

"What are you up to?" stormed the scholar. "You lout!"

And he did as he had said, to the despair of the tripe-vender, who rejected the sullied wares, and refused to put them back in her buckets. Whereupon François put on a mighty vexed air. He shouted out and stormed away, while Régnier took to his heels, bearing off enough food for twenty, and while the good woman, who saw him making off, set up a great outcry.

Régnier was already well away, and Villon made haste to escape at full speed, as far as the rue Poupée, where he found Guillaume.

"Here," he gave the word, "we shall provide ourselves with bread. Come nearer, Guillaume, and when I come out of the bakery there with a little boy carrying the loaves, be diligent in following us close."

"How far?"

"As near as possible."

François, escorted by a lad laden with gilded rolls, which he carried on his head in a basket, arrived over near Guillaume, who dogged their footsteps. In the rue Hautefeuille, Villon helped the lad to empty his basket, and then said to him: "Make haste. Run now and fetch what has still to be delivered. I shall be there

— that's my house — and I'll pay you for the whole lot. Do you understand?"

"Yes, sir, I do."

Guillaume also had understood. He tied up all these rolls in his vest, and vanished.

"Remains the wine," said François to himself. "Without wine everyone would choke, and Baude would send me back to fetch it. Wine! Wine! Lord help us, how is one to get that? People take care of it, and I need it in a can."

Plunged in meditation, he proceeded to the rue de la Verrerie to take the advice of Philippe. But on the way he had an idea. It was not one can that he needed: it was two. And he would fill the first with clear water for the execution of his scheme. He discovered the necessary cans at the "Trou Perette," and poured the water into one of them as he had promised himself. Then, holding this one under his coat, and handing out the other empty, he asked friend Turgis at the "Pomme" to serve him with some white wine. It was done, but Villon looked and exclaimed: "What! Bagneux wine? You must have misheard. It's Beaune I wanted, and fine and red too."

"You asked for white!"

"Not a bit of it!" contradicted François.

And in a flash he exchanged the can of white for that of the clear water, passed it to Philippe, and advised him to be off. He himself, a little later, set off in search of a second tavern, where he acted likewise, and then a third, until, provided now with wine enough for all, he turned his thoughts to the roast.

Quick as an arrow, François arrived at the Place de Grève, where Vallée was cooling his heels. Satisfied at having taken everyone in so deftly, he led his friend over towards a cook-shop, and engaged in conversation with its owner as if he wanted to buy from him. Whereupon Vallée, addressing himself to the merchant, cried out loudly, pointing to François: "What does that scoundrel want?"

"It is a matter between this gentleman and myself," answered Villon.

"In that event," said Vallée firmly, "show your money first."

"Money?"

"Let us be," said the merchant, overwhelmed by the fine clothes and solid air of François. "Pay no heed to this rascal, sir. I'll deal with him in my own way."

But Vallée suddenly dealt Villon a blow in the face with his fist, the merchant of the cook-shop tried to catch hold of Vallée, and François grabbed several fat capons, well cooked and with tender flesh, and escaped into the street. There Vallée joined him, and in an instant both were running and out of sight and dividing their plunder, hastening in the direction of the Porte Saint-Denis.

II

9

Five or six months later, Villon, who had become notorious by these thievings, was on his way to Margot's, when he found himself surrounded by a band of students who forced him to remain in their company.

"But don't tug me about so!" cried François.

"On you go! Forward!" cried Tabary to him.

He seemed to be highly excited, and the others, who had been drinking, were dancing, clasping each other round the waist and setting up a great din.

"We're going to cross the water," cried Tabary, "and then on the other side ——"

"No," answered Villon. "We shall be arrested on the way if you don't stop this shindy. Do you hear me? Guy Tabary, I command you to make them be quiet. If not, don't count on me."

"He's right! He's quite right! Silence!" ordered the most sober amongst them. "François Villon is speaking to us. Silence there! Listen!"

"Do you want me to take you to the Halles?" said François. "I know taverns there where we'll be welcomed."

"Yes! Yes! To the Halles! That's the thing! On you go, François. Show us the way!"

But François restrained them with a gesture.

"If you make such a row," he declared, "nothing will come of it. The watch will get mixed up in our party, and thrash the lot of you, and so, good-bye to an evening of pleasure! Keep your mouths shut from here to the bridge, and don't be more than three or four together. Otherwise you'll be very soon sent your ways, as you well know. It's always best to go past the arch of the Châtelet without a noise. Gently. — Hi, Tabary, don't get excited. I said three or four. Are you deaf? Take it or leave it."

"Well, come with me," said Tabary. "I'll keep as quiet as you want."

"All right," François accepted. "We two first, and then the rest of them. Bear in the direction of the 'Truie Qui File.' On we go! Step out, Tabary! Are you primed up?"

"Right to the top!" answered Tabary.

And heavily he leaned upon Villon, who got him across the river without his noticing it. The rest of the company followed as had been arranged, and soon along the streets there could be heard laughter, and strange groanings, for on the way to the "Truie" certain of these cheerful young persons thought it necessary to warn people of their approach. Some gave imitations of the cries of a stuck pig. Others, with great blitheness, bellowed out at the top of their voices:

"Venite *tous nos bons voisins,*
Si chantons à ce bon vin
Salutari nostros.
Si nous beuvons vin de hault prix
Nous n'en pouvons être repris."

Startled by the shouts, some citizens were showing themselves at the windows and making protests against the scholars. But the latter booed at them, or else, slamming back the shutters which had not been pushed to, set up a devilish din, shouting: "No mercy! No quarter! Kill and plunder! Cut them all in pieces, comrades! Death to them!"

François incited them.

"That sign there!" he said. "Smash it!"

And the sign, torn from its hinges by the most resolute of the band, who hoisted themselves on each other's shoulders, came crashing down with a tremendous din of clattering ironwork.

"This way!" came François's word, not leaving them time to recover. "Come on! Break everything! Smash everything! And then you'll get something to drink."

"Some Beaune wine!" cried Guy Tabary, increasing the reward and the tittering.

"Ay, ay! Beaune wine!"

"Enough till you burst!"

"For everyone!"

"Ay, ay; for everyone!"

"Whoooeee! Whoooeeee! Grrrooo! Ho-eee! Ho-eee!"

They whistled shrilly at the same time, and banged on the doors and stalls, smashing them, and some, who had laid hands on sticks, laid about them with violent blows which brought down the window-panes in the houses and set the signs all a-clatter.

II

"Good!" said Villon. "Now bear left. We're nearly there."

The songs and shouts redoubled in the narrow lane where the cabaret of the "Truie" was situated, but, whether because all this din had alarmed the innkeeper, or because the hour was in reality unduly late, François and his friends found the doors tight shut in their faces, and nobody to answer.

"Mine host!" called the scholars. "Ho, there! Host! Open! We're thirsty!"

They gathered round, ceasing their laughter, and called out once more.

"Hi, landlord! Wake up! We'll pay for your wine!"

François knocked with great politeness at the door, and asked: "Are you by any chance in bed?"

"Oh, we've waited long enough," grumbled Guy Tabary. "We'll open for ourselves ——"

And he picked up a large stone, and hurled it against the panels.

"Do you hear?" he cried. "Do you mean well or ill?"

"Bah! May the fellow choke himself!" cried one of those with the sticks. "We want drink!"

Villon wanted to intervene. But it was too late. His companions hurled themselves forward, and cobbles torn from the gutter were flung with vigour while shouts and oaths and threats burst forth. But the shutters were strongly secured and folded in, and the efforts of the scholars had no result.

II

"I'm going to fetch the watch," said someone abruptly in a neighbouring house.

They poured their scorn on him. Then they resumed their siege of the tavern, but without managing to displace the stout iron bar, which, held within by bolts, did not budge an inch.

"All together! All together, all of you! Shove on it!" proposed Tabary.

And they shoved, cursing like devils, striving, sweating, swearing, starting again twenty times, quarrelling. The bar held firm. So unyieldingly that some grew tired, and stood watching the vain efforts of the rest.

"Leave it alone," they said.

"No!"

"Yes!"

"By God!" swore François, "time toiled is time spoiled. You won't move that shutter, never! But go on, get a fist on the sign up there. Come on. Who's got the kick left for that?"

"It's very high up," they answered.

And there the sign was, a huge disc of iron cut in the shape of a swine, the noble animal whose name the tavern bore, swinging away above their heads, hanging from an enormous arm, and seeming to defy them.

"Here!" called Tabary suddenly.

"What is it?"

"Give me a hand."

"All right. Look out, there! Stand back and let's get near."

"But what is it?"

"A ladder!" announced Tabary proudly. He was too drunk to carry it. But there it was, above the porch.

There was an eddy in the crowd. Everyone wanted to climb the ladder at the same time, and François had to intervene. He ordered the sturdiest to hold it firm, for it was too short, and then he selected the one who was to unhook the sign, and encouraging him to hoist himself up without fear, asked: "Have you got it?"

"Look out! I have it! But look out! It's heavy! Mind your heads, stand back!"

At that moment the guard hove into view, coming in their direction as fast as their legs could carry them, armed with pikes and maces, and preceded by torches.

"Come down!" called François. "We're caught!"

"I should think we are!"

"Get out of it!"

"And the ladder! Oh, curse! The ladder ——"

The ladder fell to the ground, and the scholar, who had not had the presence of mind to jump, crashed to earth with a dull thud.

"Off with you! All of you!" shouted François.

Such a panic was there in the quarter that, fleeing in every direction, these stout comrades did not trouble to ask whether the other had broken his neck, but learned it next day from people who had not been present at the affair, but recounted it with a wealth of detail. Villon feigned ignorance of it all. For several days he kept lying low in his room, and when Master Guillaume spoke to him of these riotous lads and enjoined him to have no dealings with them, he listened to his uncle with an ingenuous air, and agreed with his injunctions.

About that time there was already endless talk of the misdeeds of scholars who, fearless of a beating, made off with the signboards in Paris, or flung them on the street. Anyone might have thought that they had some inexplicable grudge against those signs, for, in one place or another, they lay there in the mornings, wrenched from their hooks, in front of the doors, or else, worse still, had totally disappeared. The watch was helpless. The "Three Kings of Cologne" had been captured at the Innocents, or the "Nun Shoeing the Goose" at the Saint-Denys archway, or the "Two-headed Man" in the rue Saint-Martin, or the "Goblet" on the Place de Grève, or the "Bull" in front of Saint-Bon. Why were they stolen? To what end? It was very queer, and the good people, outraged by such scandalous behaviour, made no concealment of their way of thinking. What! Were such acts to go unpunished? However, when night came round, these same people, who gave themselves such truculent airs in the daylight, hid themselves close in their houses as soon as a clash broke out betwixt the students and the watch. Sometimes the watch got the worst of it, sometimes the clerks, who were taken to the Châtelet and later released on the demand of the rector; and the rows began all over again.

Apart from the signs, the merchants complained to the Prévôté on other counts: one had been robbed of

The Page of the Registre de la Nation de France *recording François Villon's scholastic degree*

thirty chickens at one swoop, another of casks of wine, or of arms — to wit, a small cannon — or of costly clothes, or shoes, or fat, or jugs, or dishes. The complaints accumulated. Every morning they poured in from the various quarters of Paris on to the table of Master Robert d'Estouteville. But, although he strengthened the supervision of the streets, he could not succeed in preventing these thefts. In vain were patrols increased in number; winter passed and then the spring, without bringing any noteworthy improvement. And soon a rumour ran round that a young woman had been seized at Vanves and carried off by scholars, who claimed to be keeping her in their possession.

Incredible as this abduction was, it had indeed been carried out, and François knew something of it. Along with Guy Tabary, Brother Baude, and Régnier, he had determined to stupefy the whole of Paris by a series of extravagant exploits. In a certain house on the slope of Sainte-Geneviève the prizes were amassed, and there too the young woman of Vanves was held prisoner. Brother Baude was her sentinel, brought her food and drink, and dubbed her "the queen of the university." She was a peasant woman, and had been told that this house where she was lodged would belong to her, provided that she agreed to live in the cellars, where, by night, François and his friends came in great mystery to visit her.

Well, in order to create general astonishment, François Villon took it into his head, at the beginning of the winter, to make a bold stroke. To that end he gathered the scholars together and told them how, in a very secret place, he had a great store of clothing, daggers, hoods, and brimming casks, and how they must needs lay their hands on some fantastic object or other in Paris, round which, dressed like rich seigneurs, they would engage in a fine frolic. He claimed that on this occasion they would drain every cask, and that a woman of wondrous beauty would preside over the festivity to the sound of flutes and bagpipes, which some knew how to play.

"But what is to be taken?" asked a certain Farcy. He was a little fellow, and was always on the jump so as to attract notice. "You've only to say — I'll help you."

"We too," joined the rest.

"On one condition," said Farcy: "that there is something to drink!"

"You'll get that all right!" answered François.

He led them down to the right bank of the Seine in scattered groups, as far as the rue de Martelet Saint-Jean, and there, in front of a large house, he showed them a stone of a curious shape, resembling a bladder.

"Ha! that's the boundary stone of the 'Pet au Diable'!" exclaimed Farcy with a ringing laugh.

"Are you crazy?" François said to him. "If anyone hears us, he'll give the alarm, and a useful thing that'll be. — Ha! Do you understand?"

And in a lower tone he asked: "Where are the stakes?"

"Here," said Tabary.

"Right. Well, come forward. What? Forward with 'em — take them, the rest of you! Easy, there. — Under this side slip the bars. Have you got them? All right. Raise away. And meantime Régnier and Tabary will go and find a cart."

The stone was tightly fastened to the wall, and it took nearly an hour to remove it from its chains, then slowly to get it moving and rocking. Only then did Régnier and Tabary come back with the cart that François had sent them to find. They held it lowered against the stone, the vast bulk of which was painfully loaded on, and then, each helping as best he could, they set out in silence by the Place de Grève, the Pont Notre-Dame, the Pont de l'Hôtel-Dieu, the Place Maubert, and the rue Saint-Jean-de-Beauvais. As this street ran uphill, a halt was made before going further, and François gave vocal encouragement to the scholars, tugging and panting and cursing.

"Stick to it!" he said to them. "Once more now!"

"Oh, no!"

"Here!" cried François. "All together — heave!"

They bore leftward by the rue du Clos-Bruneau, then by the rue Saint-Hilaire. But there they stopped, finally, and François was satisfied; he did not ask that the stone should be taken any further, for this was a good place for it.

II

Next day the feast took place. The scholars, instead of going to their lectures, collected round the stone, and crowned it with foliage and flowers. François Villon had given his orders. Long strings of students, in the traditional single file, wound their way over Sainte-Geneviève, preceded by musicians, and brought in their wake such throngs of people that everyone was at a standstill. In both directions the street was blocked. At the windows and on the roofs crowds of inquisitive folk stood open-mouthed with astonishment at all this din, and heightened it with their own remarks. The whole day long there was no word save of laughter and gambolling, dancing, and singing. At night Tabary and Régnier brought the casks of wine on the same cart which they had stolen the night before, and deposited them in front of the boundary stone. There everyone partook. And then came "the queen of the university," so called, whom Brother Baude, disguised as a herald and drunk as a lord, escorted through the company of scholars. She too was drunk. Crowned with small flowers, she tore them off, kissed them, and distributed them to her loyal subjects, what time François, standing upon the stone, at the sound of a trumpet saluted their presence.

"Ha!" exclaimed all the throng of clerks and loungers. "Hurrah for God and the queen!"

"Come!" cried François. "Gather around me! Range yourselves about, and then listen!"

Boom!

An explosion rang out abruptly, terrifying the women

and raising the tumult to a climax. For the small cannon, concealed behind a heap of branches, had spat out its charge without anyone's expecting it. Immediately the festivity collapsed into a mad Bacchanalian rout. Seizing hold of the girls, and the gossips, and the stall-keepers, who had come to see the boundary stone, the scholars forced them to dance with them, and to kiss them; and the women for their part did not stint themselves. Masters of the University, mixed up in the crowd, had perforce to join in the party, and drink, and make merry. They were not allowed to escape. What madness! Flutes and bagpipes played without a break. After one dance, the next. After one bumper of wine, drawn from the cask, a second, and then a third.

Dead drunk, Farcy had succumbed in a corner, and as he got rid of what he had drunk, the bystanders could hear him saying appreciatively: "This Saint-Aulnys is capital! Ha! It's a sad blow to me not to keep it. Ha! ho! ho! ho! Even when it comes up again, it tastes good!"

Everywhere, in the glare of the torches, there was nothing to be seen but frantic couples, whole-heartedly abandoned, leaping and linked together. François harangued them from the post he occupied. He too was drunk, it may be, but less with the wine than with satisfaction, for this festivity was his handiwork, and he derived boundless joy from the fact. Although not a word of his speeches could be caught, he went on endlessly improvising them in prose and in verse, addressing himself to Brother Baude, who crossed himself and threw him kisses in return, to Régnier, who was cutting the purse-strings of those who had been overcome by the wine, to Guy Tabary, to Farcy, to the queen of their election, who, smeared with dregs from the wine, was howling out filthy refrains. What better could he have desired? He received acclamations. The cry went up: "Long live François Villon!" And the women, looking at him, asked: "Who is it?"

And he, guessing their questions, broke off his fine speeches to answer them: "A fine drinker, girls, a fine drinker! Free and gladsome! Ask anyone!"

Till dawn broke, things went on thus at Saint-Hilaire, to the great scandal of the inhabitants, who could not get a wink of sleep, and to the pleasure of the scholars, who, heedless of everything, scattered, singing, through the streets. François led them, escorting the queen, and then, as the cold grew sharp, he returned to the Porte Rouge by the quickest route, reproaching himself, as he went, for having overstayed by more than an hour the time at which the chaplain was wont to rise.

It was the first time, thought Villon, that he was going to be caught out, and sure enough, he had no sooner turned the corner of the rue Saint-Jacques, to turn up the rue des Mathurins, than Master Guillaume appeared at the window.

"Where have you come from?" he asked in a severe tone. "Answer me — where have you come from?"

He came down and faced François, catching him by one arm and shaking him so roughly that François said: "If you treat me like that, I'll run away, I will!"

"Where, indeed?"

"Where I know of," said François. "Come, I'm hardly at fault."

He drew back, pointing to the street.

"Yes," exclaimed Master Guillaume. "It is just as I thought. I've heard all about your tricks!"

"My tricks?"

"This boundary stone you've stolen from in front of the noble demoiselle de Bruyères's house. Ha! You've much need to feign astonishment. You are known to be one of these young ruffians who break down the signs at night, and commit all kinds of excesses. You have been denounced to the provost. Yes. You. You — François Villon by name. — Wretched boy! — You see that I've been well informed. Yesterday, while your rioting was afoot, they came to tell me that Mademoiselle de Bruyères had lodged a complaint."

"She's mad!"

"Hold your tongue!"

"An old madwoman!" went on François. "And as things are so, I'll go and tell her who I am, and then we'll see. For accusations like that you need proofs!"

"François!"

"No, no. I've the right to defend myself."

"And the provost?" asked Master Guillaume. "How did he get wind of your being one of the crowd who smashed the shutters of the 'Truie'? Can you explain that?"

"That," said François, "I don't discuss."

He shrugged his shoulders and said, very quickly and with a disagreeable air: "I'm tired just now. Let me be, Master Guillaume. You can cross-examine me some other day. I want to sleep."

Master Guillaume raised his eyes to heaven, and was silent.

"To sleep!" repeated Villon dumbly. "Think of it! Day and night, none of us has had a moment's repose."

"And you drank like brutes?"

"What!" countered François. "Like brutes? What brutes?"

"It is enough to look at you," groaned Master Guillaume. "You, whom I thought to be honest and well brought up! You are the same as the poor boy I see here in front of me, defeated, broken, and so wretched! Ah, I am ashamed, I despair! It cannot be possible!"

"It is."

"What? You dare? You confess! God in heaven! No, no. You did not understand me. — I was questioning you to get you to deny, to protest! Eh? Do you hear? François!"

"Why should I deny it?" said the scholar in hard tones. "I am the man you have drawn. No reason to excite yourself, uncle. When anyone's chosen his side, the only thing to do is to let things take their course. — There's always a chance turns up to pull oneself up. —

Between ourselves — that does turn up — sometimes well — and sometimes ill ——"

"What are you saying?"

François stopped short, and had the strength to pull himself together. But suddenly pushing aside his uncle, who was looking at him stupefied, he climbed the staircase with a heavy tread, and, once in his own room, he slammed the door so violently behind him that a pane of glass in the window fell and smashed.

"He is a monster!" said the worthy old man in his consternation. "He has been ruined; they've made a scoundrel of him! How is he to be saved?"

Trembling and discomfited, he went next morning to pay a visit to the provost, in his rich house in the rue de Jouy, and confided in him his apprehensions. Robert d'Estouteville, who knew his chaplain, let him speak on at his ease, listening to the story and taking notes. Then he said that, in order to do him a personal favour, he would see that the matter was settled conveniently, provided François pledged himself to keep the peace.

"You must bring him to me," he said severely. "I shall admonish him myself, and that will be better."

François, as it turned out, refused to go and see the provost, on the pretext that he had only to summon him directly if he wanted to speak with him. To give himself up at this invitation, of his own accord — without any guarantee that he would be set free afterwards —— Oh, no! he wasn't so stupid as that! No, François would listen to nothing. He could do quite well without the remonstrances of this high-placed personage. It was nothing to him. As for trifles, what did that matter?

"But he does not wish you any ill, believe me," said the chaplain. "He's a good man, and peaceful in intention ——"

"Yes, yes," said François.

"He is well disposed towards you."

"In that case, all the more reason for my not troubling his temper," replied the scholar. "Suppose I were to annoy him by some reflection of mine; why, from being good and peaceable, I should make him peevish."

"Oh! how hardened you are!"

"No, uncle, I'm just as I ought to be. There is nothing to be gained by putting too high a value on oneself. As for politeness, you will make my excuses to this noble gentleman. You will tell him that I have been ill, and shall go to his house later."

"And when will that be?"

"Never!"

Nevertheless, the story of the boundary stone took on the proportions of a real scandal, and François Villon no longer knew what to make of it. Mademoiselle de Bruyères made a great fuss about the damage done to her, and lodged a volley of complaints with the provost, claiming that the matter should be brought before the Parlement. Régnier, Guy Tabary, and Brother Baude saw that the joke was going too far, and sought out François. They told him plainly that it was time to do something. From the reports of the old lady, all of their names were brought up, and, what was more serious, there were a good many other papers joined with these of this case, which had been drawn up by the sergeants, who had picked up information here and there and knew the case thoroughly.

"Through your uncle," said Régnier, "we must join Robert d'Estouteville, or otherwise we are done for."

"And without delay," said Brother Baude.

"Right," answered Villon. "Leave me to see to that."

"What about it?"

"I have an idea."

That same evening, shut up in his room, Villon rhymed a certain ballade in honour of Robert d'Estouteville's lady, and, in poetic play, he wrote its first lines in such a way that they formed an acrostic, making her own name; and very pleased with it he was. Ambroise de Loré, or "*la prévote,*" as she was called in Paris, doted on poetry. She gave great receptions in her house at which all the society of the time was received and welcomed with signs of the most gracious courtesy.

With his poem in his hand, elegant but modest in his dress, François Villon presented himself at the provost's lordly house. He said he was expected, and was accordingly led through several large rooms, luxuriously painted and adorned, to where Robert d'Estouteville stood with some ladies at his side. At first he did not understand.

"But it was in the morning that I wanted to see you," he said to Villon in a crabbed way.

"Oh!" said François, feigning extreme confusion. "I can't have understood aright."

"I dare say," said the provost. "From what I hear of you, you know how to set about avoiding a reprimand. But just you wait, you won't miss anything. — Come along, boy. You'll have your allowance just the same ——"

He presented François to the ladies.

"Know who this scholar is," he said to them smiling. "He is the most troublesome and the most mischievous in Paris. He has stolen the boundary stone of the 'Pet au Diable.' Ha! You see, he makes no denial."

François was taken aback.

"If I had known," he answered, "that I should have to show shame before so brilliant an assemblage, I should have taken good care to have nothing to do with it."

"Ay, ay," went on the provost. "If I had known! He's clever. And what's that you're holding there rolled up in yon piece of paper? Is it a petition?"

"Oh, sir," stammered Villon, "I don't dare to ——"

"Give it me," said the other, casting a glance over the wretched paper. "What! Verses? Are you a poet, then?"

He read Villon's ballade, frowning the while, and then, astonished at its being so well turned and so agreeable, he looked the scholar in the eyes and said: "Your uncle did not breathe a word of it to me."

"He does not know it," said François gently.

"Like the other matters!"

François nodded, and then, seeing that Robert d'Estouteville was handing the ballade to his wife for her to read, he bowed, and said to her: "Madame, I have tried, on your noble name, to make inspiration come to me."

"But these verses are delightful!" exclaimed Ambroise de Loré in her surprise. "And they do me honour."

"And myself too!" exclaimed the provost. "An amusing affair, devil take me! By day this young fellow writes poetry instead of studying, and by night he haunts the taverns, plays with the wenches, and goes a-thieving. — A sad business for his uncle. Poet and rascal all at once, eh? What have you to say about it?"

"I shall learn wisdom," promised François, who could detect in these words that Robert d'Estouteville was not granting him pardon. "I give you my word for that. I have had enough of folly with all this. I'm punished for it now."

"You really bind yourself to it?"

"Yes," said François.

The provost softened a little, but without giving too many signs of it.

"Well," he said, "come back to-morrow morning. I'll have a word with you then."

10

The provost's lecture was terrible. But out of it François profited, in that he was then admitted by Ambroise de Loré to her receptions and managed to make friendly connexions with wealthy young men who influenced him in the direction of a better way of life. Association with the subtle Jean Raguier was highly profitable to him. Villon also came to know, at Ambroise de Loré's, that brilliant entertainer Jean Chappelain, head of the sergeants of the Châtelet, and some of those gentlemen from the prison of the Châtelet who, like Master Garnier, Jean Mauteint, and Nicolas Rosnel, enjoyed and profitably exploited the provost's favour. They were stiff and very important personages, who could talk to ladies in a tone so light and free that François was fired with the ambition to express himself thus, for hours on end, to charm the female friends of Ambroise de Loré. For amongst them there was one called Marthe, who had conquered François almost instantly.

She was overwhelming in her freshness and sparkle, and her successes had made her neither proud nor too bold.

François did not pay court to her, but devoured her with his gaze, and Marthe noticed his presence and was pleased by his not acting towards her in the way to which she was accustomed. None the less, he irritated her with his fanciful airs. He made her laugh. That lad a rascal! Marthe knew others, more gay and more alluring, such as Pernet de la Barre, for instance, who, being assigned at the Châtelet to the duty of supervising the women of the town, had no hesitation in recording his adventures and making you believe them. A droll fellow, Pernet. He had spirit, though, while Villon, in his short gown, was really too much lacking in the conventions and had a very cowardly air to him.

"He was caught the moment he set eyes on you," said Pernet to Marthe, pointing to the poet. "He has lost his tongue, and has no more assurance ——"

"But it is incredible. So bad as that?"

"I assure you."

"Well, bring him to me. I don't want him to be discomfited by any fault of mine!"

François thought he was dreaming. Marthe welcomed him with so good a grace that he spent a full minute at first in admiring her. Then he thawed and answered in his fashion, which was picturesque and lively for such a setting. Pernet excited his natural spirit. Marthe smiled at him, and soon, between the three of them, a kind of comradeship was securely established, and they took delight in it.

"He's no fool," the girl weighed him up. "Nor vulgar either."

And when she spoke of him with Pernet, who was perfectly familiar with the poet's existence, he answered her: "Oh, he will astonish you!"

II

On two or three occasions, when Marthe and François happened to pass each other in Paris, they found pleasure in exchanging greetings. François blushed, and was embarrassed, but the girl did not appear to notice it. Sometimes Pernet de la Barre accompanied Marthe on her walk, and Villon joined them. They went as far as the cemetery of the Innocents, chatting, or listening to the sermon, or looking under the vaulted arches at the striking paintings. The place was not altogether grisly. On the tombs, book-venders and small mercers spread their wares. Women selling cakes, cracknels, and wafers hailed you. Between these long charnel-houses, where the dead lay rotting, the rich and grassy soil reminded all who passed of their human lot, but nevertheless there were fewer mourners to be seen there than gallants with their ladies, or than girls who, under the guise of selling linen to the passers-by, inveigled them to their dwellings for a very different trade.

"Look!" exclaimed François. He had stopped in front of the dance of death, where it unrolled its long fresco of men and women, half putrescent and devoured by worms. "It is excellent to know what will happen to us all some day, so that we can disport ourselves and find our diversion beforehand."

He described the hideous accumulation which, above their heads, in the garrets of the cloister, the grave-diggers made of the remains when they extracted them from the pit in order to leave room for others. There was something frightful in these descriptions, and Villon, growing more and more feverish, traced a picture so sombre and horrible of the garrets filled to overflowing with bones, that Pernet de la Barre said to him: "Have you some sorrow that you are hiding?"

"I?"

"Oh, no," said Marthe immediately. "What sorrow?"

She cast a slow glance at François, and in it he could read a somehow sad and mocking tenderness, restless and disconcerted. What ecstasy he derived from it! She understood. She had clearly discerned that in all he was saying he had addressed himself to her, and how sincere was his feeling. But what could he hope from Marthe? François supposed that she favoured La Barre, and for too long for him to be able to change anything. He was quite certain that there existed between Marthe and Pernet a liaison which neither the one nor the other avowed. This certainty discouraged François, and inspired him with absurd considerations in front of the frescoes of the Innocents; and it animated him with so sulky a humour that afterwards he reproached himself for it. But after all ——! Could he prevent himself from loving Marthe? In his little room, where he worked now by candlelight at night, he felt himself filled with her gentle presence. He lived with her, sought her, and called on her name. He wrote poems, tore them up, and then, by dint of always postponing till later a decision which gripped at his heart, he withered and pined away.

He then made the acquaintance, under the roof of

Marthe, of a most curious woman, Catherine de Vausselles by name. She was not so much beautiful as provocative, though well formed; she was decked out with the utmost care, and, suspicious in the friendship which she lavished on Marthe, she caused François a profound irritation. At first sight she struck him as insufferable, and he said not a word to her. But he soon came to feel that, as Catherine made advances towards him, he had to defend himself, for although she was hateful to him, he himself, it appeared, had kindled interest in her.

Marthe had realized this little comedy. She questioned François.

"Why rebuff her?" she asked. "She's a very sure friend."

"The truth is," answered Villon, "that she will make a fool of me, with my appearance such as it is."

"Not at all!"

"And if it were not towards her that my only thoughts are turned," went on the poet, looking Marthe straight in the eyes, "what would you answer?"

"I would answer that you were making a big mistake."

It may be that Marthe, in questioning François in this way, was binding herself as the accomplice of Catherine de Vausselles. For the latter, turning up at a very opportune moment, engaged the poet in conversation and sometimes, in the evening, asked him to accompany her.

"I don't live very far away," she said, "but I cannot

wander about Paris all alone at night without the risk of compromising my reputation."

François escorted her in silence.

"Tell me," asked the young woman, "do you love Marthe?"

"I?"

"Yes. You. Why avoid it?"

And she laughed as she added: "Alas! Marthe is not free."

"Free to love?"

"No. To go out as you and I do."

"That is true," observed the poet. "You depend on nobody."

"Nobody indeed. Confess that I might be envied."

"Indeed, yes."

"And yet," went on Catherine, "what advantage is it to be free? None at all. I go to bed early, I rise early. I have no pleasure."

This confidence threw François into a ludicrous state of confusion, and the young woman then remarked: "At least you're no chatterbox!"

Then, abruptly wishing him good-night, she dismissed him. But one evening, when he had been sent off somewhat quickly, François turned in his track, gazed up at the window of the room which he thought was Catherine's, and stood there motionless in the street. There was a light up there. But it went out, and a moment later the door was opened a little way and a woman's figure, which Villon recognized, appeared.

"Aha!" he exclaimed, going up to Catherine and catching hold of her, "where are you going?"

"Where I think fit," was the answer he got.

"Where's that?"

"Follow me, and you'll see for yourself."

"No," said François; "follow you? I've no wish to do that."

"Well, then," said Catherine. "Let me go."

François was holding her, and she sought to free herself, not supposing that he would be insistent. But he clasped her more firmly and declared in a low tone, the words coming from between his teeth: "You shall not go. So much the worse for you. I swear you shan't. Don't try to escape. I'm keeping you."

"If you like," said Catherine. "Do as you please — although —— Keeping me? To what end will you do that?"

François took her still nearer to him, drew her close, and said in a whisper: "So as to have you for myself."

"What?" exclaimed Catherine, astonished and impertinent. "You've actually made up your mind!"

He replied, with shame in his voice: "It is you that I love, not Marthe. Listen, Catherine, I loathed you for your ways, and now I can't any more. Whom were you going to meet, going out like this?"

"My lover, of course."

"And who is he?"

Catherine shook her head.

II

"Every night you tricked me like that?" asked François.

"Tricked you!" protested the girl. "Don't be stupid. — And let me go," she added after a short silence. "Look, you're hurting me."

François hesitated, and then, slowly unclasping his two hands, he muttered grudgingly: "There! I obey. Now you can go or stay. You are free."

"Yes," said Catherine, drawing back at once. "I knew that you'd listen to me. It's a pity —— But perhaps it is better that it should be like that."

"Why?"

"Because, remaining in your company, something disagreeable would certainly have befallen us."

Starting to run at these words, Catherine vanished before François had recovered from his surprise and had time to bar her passage.

"Ha!" said the scholar to himself, "with this one more than with others I'm learning what women are worth. When you hold them, it's madness to listen to what they're saying."

He was furious at having been made a fool of, and he swore to see Catherine again in order to prove to her that he had been able to profit by the lesson. But Catherine took care not to show herself. In vain did François wait several nights for her at the door of her house, pacing up and down the street and dragging along like a soul in pain. To right and to left he looked, pricking up his ears at the slightest sound, and raising his eyes to the front of the house. And then at dawn he went off, chilled to the bone, having found out nothing that could enlighten him. The keen cold of November pierced the scholar through and through, freezing him, and the dreary rain that poured down during the long hours of his watch soaked him to the skin. In this narrow street, up which the north wind of winter came rushing and blowing sharply, François kept on spending long hours like this, when one night he was startled from his reflections by a headlong rush of running feet. It was a band of students. They ran together, bearing sticks and weapons with which they smote the shutters of the shops, and then, hurrying on the faster, made off at top speed, shouting and bellowing.

"Where are you going?" asked François of them.

"The boundary stone's been taken from us," they answered, "and we're going to get it back."

"Who did that?"

"Master Bezon of the Châtelet."

"Oho!" said François. "If you try your strength with that fellow, you run the risk of his keeping you."

"We are armed," answered one very young lad.

"And the stone is set down at the Palais de Justice," said another. "Nothing's easier than to take it off."

"You think so?"

"Of course!"

"Good luck, then," said François.

And, far from accompanying them, he turned down the street on his endless pacing to and fro.

II

He let Marthe know of his passion for Catherine, and she was much amused. She made a show of being sorry for him, and then, as she was a woman, she told him that Catherine only wanted to test him before belonging to him.

In Paris now, whether at the Innocents, or at the butts of Notre-Dame, whither it was customary to repair in the afternoon to watch the archers at practice and the players of *soule* striking the ball with their sticks, Villon wandered to and fro in search of Catherine. He gazed at the people about him with melancholy, wondering why the young woman did not come any more for her walks. None the less it was good to walk abroad on these spring days, still cool, yet just warmed by the sun. On the roofs of the houses the sunlight made the slates gleam, and the sky was blue, with that faintly mauve blue of the periwinkle, and veiled with light clouds, which gathered closer as the evening came on. Sometimes Marthe and Pernet would come upon François, seated all alone on a stone pillar behind the cloister, and, approaching him, would chat with him for a little. Sometimes there were girls who recognized him, smiled as they passed, and called him by name, rallying him for his brooding air; but he made no answer, remaining distant and preoccupied.

Antoine himself had not his former influence over François. Sometimes, when at his business, he was drawn by the sunshine towards these places filled with leisured folk, where one could see the lively, sparkling water of the Seine, its green banks, and the houses, with their variously coloured façades, flanking the Place de Grève. If he halted and asked kindly after Villon's health, the scholar was silent, and shook his head and made a pretence of following the comings and goings of the archers on the meadow, shooting their arrows at a tall mast crowned with a bunch of flowers.

"You are out of humour," said Antoine, who could not understand anyone's wasting his time like this. "Come along with me. I've had some Anjou wine sent to me."

"And Margot?" asked François. "She'd send me packing."

"Not a bit of it! She still has kind thoughts for you. She often thinks of you. Lately you were passing along in front of the house with the most noble Pernet de la Barre and the lady he was accompanying, all three of you, and Margot wanted to make a sign to you. It's quite true. I had to hold her back from doing it."

"But why should she make signs to me?"

"She is jealous," said Antoine, assuming a peculiar air, and rolling the edge of his stout apron between his fingers. "I know it. All that day she did nothing but scold and grumble. Ha! Do you see? I'm telling you facts as they are. Come along now. Instead of hanging about here, stuck in front of these clumsy and lazy fellows of archers, who cost us good money in taxes, come with me. You'll be received as no one ever was. Well, are you making up your mind?"

"Not yet," said François in reply.

But nevertheless he stood up abruptly. For there, in the crowd, a woman whom he named to Antoine was coming forward.

"What!" said Antoine. "Was it for that you were here?"

"Yes," said François in an acid tone. "Now go away."

"She is not beautiful."

"She is better than that," said François.

"Perhaps!"

"What do you know about it?"

"I know," said Antoine slowly, "I know that a woman who is rigged out like that deceives you with appearances. Have you lost your wits? Or have you no eyes any longer to see with? She has a crooked nose and big feet. She is dried up. Think it over, François. And come along ——"

François repulsed him.

"Come on," repeated Antoine.

"No."

"You won't?"

"Take yourself off from here!" said the poet, rushing forward before Catherine de Vausselles.

But Catherine was not alone. And the greeting she extended to Villon struck him as cold and reserved, to such a point that she herself noticed it, and she smilingly asked him: "Do you still feel a grudge against me?"

"None at all," answered François.

"Ah! I thought you might!" she said negligently.

"For as I saw nothing more of you, I argued that you must be angry ——"

François looked at her. She was dressed in a long robe with very tight-fitting sleeves, trimmed with a narrow strip of fur, which also encircled the opening of her corsage and set off the delicate gleam of her bosom.

"Angry! I might well have been angry!" went on François, who was becoming troubled.

Catherine took his hand and pressed it.

"I forbid you to judge me so harshly!" she exclaimed.

And then, in order to explain her gesture, she drew Villon towards her friends and presented him to them.

"Oh, we know each other," said one of them, who frequented the house of Ambroise de Loré and belonged, like most of the elegant young men of good family who were to be found there, to the provost's guard. "Monsieur Villon writes verses."

"Very fine verses," said another courteously.

François had to bow.

"Yes," said a third personage, who was unshaven. "There is a certain *Ballade of Grosse Margot* which has spread the fame of the author far and wide."

He was a priest. And addressing Catherine, he added: "But it is a cynical and foul ballade."

At the same time he looked at the scholar's hand, which the young woman was still holding in one of hers; and the expression of his face changed suddenly, becoming almost hard and full of hatred.

"Ah, you think so?"

"Without doubt," he said. "To celebrate this Grosse Margot, who keeps open house quite close to here, Monsieur" — he indicated Villon — "has neglected nothing."

François smiled.

"Stop smiling, sir," said Sermoise to him angrily, "or I shall go off."

"Sermoise!" appealed Catherine.

"No!" he answered. "It is your fault. You flatter him so that he may jeer at me. And you find this amusing! Very well, very well. I know what is left for me to do. Adieu!"

"But —" said François. "For good, you're going?"

"Oh, we shall meet again," grumbled Sermoise, turning on his heels and going off in dudgeon.

His departure rejoiced Catherine's friends greatly, and François, who was the cause of it, triumphed.

"He has a poor sort of character," said he, alluding to the priest. "Can you imagine anyone's getting so angry? He's a nincompoop!"

And proud of the success he had achieved, François already thought that he had rights over Catherine. But she took the arm of one of the youths escorting her, murmuring: "Take me to the *soule* players, if you please, Robert. I want to see them from close to, and then we'll go along the riverside."

François followed. He had eyes for nothing but the free and easy way in which Catherine leaned on the arm of his rival. Was it to annoy him? Villon hated her. He reproached himself for loving her, and especially for his tolerating her flaunting him with this impudence. He felt a desire to flee, he in his turn, without saluting anyone, to go far away from this woman who found a mischievous delight in showing him that he meant nothing to her, and laughed at the ceaseless trifles poured out by Robert, simpering and making shrill little exclamations and feigning to be overcome with pleasure.

How hateful this walk became to François! Suddenly he stood still, waited, and turned back with lowered head.

Yet all around him the couples were idling and frolicking on the grass. Girls were smiling to the gallants, watching for them, trying their fortune. In the clear air one could hear the shock of the balls being struck by the players, and sometimes too, very distinctly, the singing whizz of the arrows as the archers shot them. On the meadow the pigeons settled in pairs, or flew off with the mechanical beating of their wings. The water of the river was spread out before him. The sellers of cracknels and wafers hailed their customers, and the sinking sun cast over the throng, over the lofty square taverns of Notre-Dame, and on the fronts and roofs of the houses, a copper-coloured light, which made the evening glow with rosiness.

"Antoine was right," said François to himself, with a sorrowful smile. "I am being punished for not believing him. But after all, could I really have expected such perfidy as this?"

II

When he came near the cloister, the scholar turned round in spite of himself and looked for Catherine in the crowd. He caught sight of her seated in the distance, on the fold of her gown, between the two young men. At once François felt his eyesight grow cloudy. He turned aside to the left, walked on a few paces, and found himself in front of Grosse Margot's.

"Well, back again so soon?" said Antoine, who was taking the air on the door-step.

"Yes," answered François.

"Come in, then," said the landlord.

He called out to Margot, and she came. Going up to the poet, she took him by the arm.

"What do you want?" asked François.

"Nothing," said Margot. "Sit down: there. Sit down. Do you recognize me?"

He nodded affirmatively. "It's my fault," he murmured. "I ought not to have left you."

And then, discovering Colette and Jeanneton drinking at a table, he greeted them with a discreet "Good-day!" and in a low voice he questioned Margot about Colin.

"Oh, he's far away from Paris," said Margot.

"And Régnier?"

"Régnier? He still comes in."

"Good," observed François. "He at least knows what he wants, but as for me ——"

The aroma of the wine coming up from the cellar, to which Antoine had gone down, put fresh life into François. He looked at Margot, yawned, passed a hand heavily across his brow, and sighed.

"I feel better," he stammered abruptly, as if he had at last woken from a long dream. "Everything is in its proper place, and you're there, Margot, by my side, as it used to be. . . ."

He felt a strange sensation pass through him, and, little by little, the scene of the room, and the presence in the room of the girls, of Antoine, of his old mistress, brought back to him a thousand memories which he had thought were lost. A sudden emotion brought tears to his eyes. But he pulled himself together, and as the landlord set a tankard of his famous Anjou on the table, François made a proposal: "Will you drink with us, Antoine?"

Antoine did not need to be asked again, and politely thanking the scholar, who poured out for him, he pushed his glass towards Villon's, touched it, and smacked his lips.

"Yes," declared François after he had tasted it. "What a wine! That consoles you for women!"

Margot tossed her head and said: "It depends on what women."

"True," observed the scholar, "true. There are women and women."

And in pleasantry he hailed a wretched creature, with tarnished features that seemed almost to be eaten away, who had been standing near the door, not daring to come forward.

"*She* will answer us!" he exclaimed.

"Bah!" said Margot. "She knows more about it than we do."

"Who is she?"

"You know her very well. It's Magdeleine, she who was the helm-maker's wife. At least, she claims to be!"

Timidly the old woman approached the table.

François broke into laughter.

"What is the worth of the best of women?" he asked.

"As much as a man."

"And otherwise?"

"She's worth naught," said the old woman, "when age has taken her and made her as I am. Just look! It's pitiful. — And don't laugh, my lad, for even if I'm talking like this and complaining to everyone of being poor and withered and thin and small, I was so beautiful in time gone by, and loved myself for my beauty — but what's left of it all?"

"Yes, very little," laughed François.

"Still less," groaned the old woman. "Less than less — nothing at all, you might say. Ah, there you are, merry, and here am I — I, who would have taken you in the old days as I used to take them, clerks and merchants and churchmen and all the rest of them — what can I do? Yet I had a man, very like you, but he's dead now these thirty years. Do you hear? He mocked me. He beat me. Ha! all men are made the same way!"

"Sometimes!" grumbled Antoine. "Oh, you're in your dotage, old woman!"

II

"Let her be," said François.

The poor old soul twisted a smile on her face, and then, as Antoine rose in disgust and went over to a customer round whom the girls were hurrying, she spoke the word very quickly to him: "Aha! Give me something, boy. — Give me something while that fat fellow's not here. I'll go and get myself something to eat."

But Margot replied with anger in her voice: "Eat indeed! Just imagine it! It's to get drunk she wants — with your pence too!"

And she chased the old woman away; but not before François, secretly and under the table, had passed her the little money that he possessed.

11

During several weeks, in order to forget his love for Catherine, François resumed his old relations with Grosse Margot. And they both appeared to be delighted with the situation, although it no longer had the glamour that it once had. He would arrive at night, and sit down, then lean his chin on his hand, and find neither savour nor pleasure in anything. Marthe herself had no particular attraction in his eyes. He no longer went to her house. And as for the receptions of Ambroise de Loré, he renounced these out of spite, for at the mere thought of showing himself in his poor clerk's clothes in the midst of so many rich young men, he turned moody and no longer dared even to look at himself. All day long, shut up in his uncle's house, the hapless François brooded in his melancholy. Occasionally, weary of this sorry life of his, he sought consolation in study, but books brought him no help. When he had moped the whole day long over it all, there was nothing for it but to join Margot, whom he came to like more and more, and experience the sense of his own degradation. The more he frequented her company, the more he felt the measure of his failure. However, how could he have managed without this wench to prevent himself from thinking of Catherine? He had no choice, and when he watched at Margot's the comings and goings and the tricks of the three girls there, he was bound to reckon himself lucky that he was looked upon with a kindly eye.

Now that the fine spring nights had come, the windows remained open behind the closed shutters, and the noises of the street penetrated into the room and so clearly that you could imagine yourself outside. Now it was the watch making their round, now a drunkard passing and reeling as he went, now a band of gallants belatedly serenading. And one night, not far from midnight, Régnier arrived in haste, hammering at the shutter and demanding to be let in. He must have had companions with him, for the laughter of several voices could be heard, and their louder knocks and their calls for Antoine.

Jeanneton had risen from bed. From behind the door she answered him: "Coming, coming!"

But Antoine, just as he slipped the key into the lock, changed his mind, and asked: "How many are you?"

"Good God!" grumbled Régnier. "Make haste! You can see for yourself then."

"No," said Antoine. "I want to know."

"Ha! Vixen!" said a voice. "Will you open?"

At that moment a violent argument broke out in the street between Régnier and the sergeants of the watch. Blows were exchanged, mingled with the clatter of weapons and stifled cries. Then oaths, the fall of a body on the cobbles, other blows, in more rapid succession, while Jeanneton, as if mad, kept repeating: "Monsieur

Antoine! Monsieur Antoine! For God's sake, take pity on me! Have pity on me! Let Régnier come in! It's him! Hark to him! He's begging you!"

François strained his ears and listened.

"Why don't you help me, Monsieur François?" said Jeanneton.

"Best wait till they've finished first," he answered pitifully.

"But they will kill him!"

"Not at all!"

"Oh!" exclaimed the girl. "What cowardice! You're afraid for your own skin! All right! I'll tell Régnier what sort of man *you* are! Yes, I'll tell him all right. Fine thanks you'll get!"

But the uproar had suddenly ended, and only Jeanneton's lover could have been left outside, for he was rattling the shutters again and calling for Antoine, and warning him that he would give him a good thrashing if he didn't give him refuge without delay. His fury seemed to be choking him. He raged and stormed.

"What!" he said, half mad with rage when he saw the poet opening the door for him. "What! You were there and you didn't so much as come out?"

"He was afraid," explained Jeanneton.

"You wait," said Régnier, thrusting her back.

And shaking his blood-stained hand before he wiped it on his clothes, he went on: "Afraid? Ha! I see how much we can count on you!"

II

"Régnier!"

"Go on!" he added brutally. "Enough of that! I'll give you a lesson. I'll ——"

But Régnier had a deep wound in his shoulder from which the blood was pouring, and Jeanneton made him sit down so as not to move about any further and to let himself be bandaged.

"It's nothing," said Régnier.

"And your friends?" asked Antoine softly. "Where are they?"

Margot was outside in the street inspecting the damage.

"Here!" she called out in a piercing voice. "Come on, quick!"

"What's wrong?" asked François.

She called for Antoine.

"Fetch some water! We must wash the steps."

"Look here, Margot," said François. "I can do something to help."

"No, you can't," said Margot.

"Why not?"

"Because of the blood," she said. "It would turn your stomach."

And she pushed in front of François, who, put out of countenance, stooped and picked up from the ground a dagger. He did not know what to do with it, and drew the remark from Régnier: "Look out, everybody, please! Here's Master Villon wanting to cleave us all asunder!"

"So long as he doesn't wound himself," remarked Jeanneton.

François blinked, threw down the dagger, and looked angrily at Régnier. But everyone laughed, and he went off without uttering one word.

Next day it was known that Régnier had been found at Grosse Margot's and taken to the Châtelet, and that, by order of the provost, the establishment had been closed down. A certain Jehan Rosay, who had used violence against the watch along with Montigny, was likewise arrested, and active search was made for a third person whose name was kept dark. François was afraid that he was involved, and kept indoors. He was afraid that he had been incriminated in the business, and although he congratulated himself on having had no hand in it, he reckoned that it was high time he changed his way of life. Fear tortured him. It almost cured him of his feelings for Catherine, and turned his mind into healthier channels.

"Once and for all," he said to himself, "let's get clear of all this, and then we can think matters out."

Working in his chamber right up to the dinner-horn, and hardly venturing even to take the fresh air under the dial of the church of Saint-Benoît, in the rue Saint-Jacques, he kept watch on himself and kept himself calm. The days grew slowly longer, and then summer came, then autumn, and the time for the examinations. And François, who had been studying devotedly — such was his constant dread of a denunciation — presented himself for his master's degree, and was duly received. In his honour Master Guillaume gave a great dinner. He addressed François by his new title, and the youth, full of happiness, felt himself a different man, for in the mean time Margot had reopened her place, and there was no more talk of that vexing story, which, so far as Régnier de Montigny was concerned, had been brought to a conclusion by a decree of banishment.

"You have done well," said Antoine to his friend François one evening. "Meddling in shindies always gets one into trouble, invariably."

Laden with large baskets and string-bags full of provisions, Antoine was bargaining for fish with the herring-woman at the Petit Pont, for Friday was a day of abstinence in his household.

"What good have we ever had from having Régnier in the house?" he went on. "We've had to buy back our licence. Ah! Often enough one never stops to think, one drifts along with the chance current, and one clinks glasses."

"But how is the house getting on?"

"Well. At least, there is nothing to complain of," Antoine gravely expounded. "Margot has made a fresh start. If you come, you'll see for yourself. There are changes. We have five girls now, all very nice and well-behaved. When will you come?"

"Quite soon," said François.

"You'll be given a royal welcome," promised Antoine. "That is the least we can do. Master François

Villon! Master, eh? Ah, but it isn't everyone who can become a Master of Arts, even if he wishes to! You have to have a strong head for that, young man!"

"And legs."

"Legs? How do you mean?"

"Yes," said François. "To get yourself out of evil ways!"

And laughing, he left Antoine astounded that he had become barely more serious.

Nevertheless, it was quite true that they had already rendered very real services to François. He did not forget it, and he still counted on them, although for the moment he used them only for little strolls here and there about Paris. They bore him over to the Cordeliers to his old mother's, to the Innocents, or round about the neighbourhood of Saint-Benoît, when, having nothing to do, the poet wandered gently through this street and that, taking pleasure in living. Venturing sometimes with a prudent step on to the slopes of Sainte-Geneviève, he went down the rue Saint-Hilaire, where the boundary stone of the "Pet au Diable" had resumed its old position. The sight of this stone amused him, and as the scholars, who claimed to be its guardians, ordered that caps should be removed on passing near it, François doffed his hat and bowed. One day someone recognized him. It was Farcy, the drunkard. He took his part very seriously and stopped people who did not salute it, threatening them with violence.

"We guard it night and day, you know," he said. "And there are several of us here who've decided never to let it be taken back."

"But you're mad!"

"Mad! Hark to him! You just ask in the Quartier if anybody is ever allowed to dispute our orders!"

A stout bourgeois was just then coming up the street, and Farcy called to him to take off his hat. The man obeyed.

"Oh!" said François, "you've taken to it wonderfully well!"

"It has to be done," answered Farcy; "otherwise we should never get anything at all. Some sergeants have turned up before now. They took the stone from us, but we went to fetch it back, and since then they've scarcely ever ventured this way again."

"Really?"

"Haven't I said so?" affirmed Farcy coldly.

And taking Master François round into a neighbouring street, he showed him a second stone of more or less the same dimensions as that which he kept under his supervision.

"Look!" he said with pride. "The old woman we took the 'Pet au Diable' stone from had it replaced with this one, but it didn't stay there very long."

"Capital!"

"That's the 'Vesse,'" explained Farcy, derisively caressing the enormous block of sandstone which, fixed against a wall with an iron belt and very heavy chains, was crowned with foliage. "The 'Vesse' and the 'Pet.' Rather good, don't you think?"

Master François smiled.

"As for tavern signs," his companion went on, "we have a few everywhere, in cellars where we accumulate them against the day when we marry them off. That day, François, you must come and amuse yourself with us. It'll be a fine row, I can tell you! Heavens above, I swear it will! There'll be great doings!"

"When is that to be?"

"When we've got the 'Popinjay,' and the 'Stag,' and the 'Bear,'" said Farcy. "For without them, you see, the best taverns would not be represented at the festivities, and there would be something lacking."

But that moment a youth came up to François, saluted him, and declared that he wished to have a word with him.

"I was going to your house," he said, "to deliver a letter to you."

"A letter? Give it me."

"Here it is."

"And who are you?"

"Noël Jolis," said the youth.

François opened the letter. He read it, and a profound disturbance overtook him.

"Was it Catherine who asked you to bring me this message?" he asked Jolis.

"Yes, she."

"You know her?"

"I live in the hostelry attached to her house, and I see her when she goes out. Yesterday morning I was passing, and she signalled to me."

Master François slowly read Catherine's note a second time, gazed at the young man, and then suddenly resumed the mastery over himself.

"Well," he said, "she can count on me! I shall go ——"

And he shook Farcy by the hand and went off, forgetting to salute the famous stone, in front of which some innocent fellow or other, led by a number of students, was kneeling and singing at the top of his voice.

François went back to Saint-Benoît, brushed his gown, arranged his hair, washed, and then, in a fever of joy, did not know what else to do to pass the time. He had the whole evening before joining Catherine, and the hours seemed so long to him that he went out and ran headlong down the rue Saint-Hilaire to catch Noël Jolis and invite him to drink with him.

"Did she say anything to you about me?" he asked, holding this agreeable companion by the arm. "Tell me! What's become of her? How is she?"

They sat down at a table at the "Pomme," chattering and smiling like two old friends, and told each other so many stories concerning Catherine that François no longer had doubts of anything. Never once had he felt satisfaction or enthusiasm or lightness of heart which could compare with this. Catherine gave him a rendezvous at her house. It was extraordinary. It was more than he had ever hoped for. But Jolis answered him that with women you must expect anything, and that the best thing is to take them as you find them.

"But my mind is made up for that," said François. "To think how I tortured myself in the past, and now here she is, making advances to me of her own accord! Isn't it queer?"

"Quite normal."

"Oh, perhaps!" said François.

He dined that evening with an excellent appetite, and feverishly waited for the bell of the Sorbonne to ring the curfew. And then he slipped out from his room and was at the appointed place in no time. Catherine was looking out for him on the door-step. She half opened the door, signed to him to keep quiet, and then, leading him towards her room, said suddenly: "Do you know who is there?"

"Where?"

"In my room," answered Catherine, stepping back. "Look!"

"Marthe!" said François in his surprise.

Marthe burst out laughing. She exchanged a quick glance of understanding with Catherine, and then, with a reproachful air, she said: "Just so! I had to come here to find you!"

"Certainly," said Catherine in confirmation.

François stopped short.

"I am happy that Catherine has provided us with

the opportunity," he said after a moment to cover his vexation.

"For without her, of course—?" asked Marthe, "I suppose I should not have existed for you, any more than anybody."

"No," said François. "You're my only friend."

"And what of me?" simpered Catherine.

He looked at her without answering. Then lowering his eyes, he sighed and sat down at Marthe's side. But she rose instantly, a trifle annoyed, and said: "Do not put yourself out, Master François. Now that I've set eyes on you again, I shall go away satisfied."

She smiled at him and kissed Catherine. François made as if to accompany her, but she said with a mischievous air: "Oh, taking you from Catherine! She would never forgive me."

And Marthe went off, leaving them alone together in the room, eyeing each other without daring to make further advances.

"I am obliged to you," said the young woman at last, "for having come so quickly without bearing me any grudge."

François did not stir.

"I was sure of you," she went on. "So I wrote you the letter which little Noël Jolis brought you just now. Come nearer—don't be afraid. You seem to be dumb!"

"Stop this playing!" growled François.

"What playing?"

"Playing at harrying me as you're doing. Stop it, I warn you, or else ——"

Catherine moved towards him.

"Else what?" she asked, amused at his anger.

Sadly he thrust her back from him, and then, picking up his cap from a seat, he murmured quickly: "Good-bye, Catherine!"

François was in a hurry to have done with the affair. In spite of Catherine's opposition to his departure, he had already reached the door and was just opening it when, below, the outside knocker sounded.

"Listen!" said Catherine. "You can't go away now."

"Who is it?"

"They're still knocking," said Catherine.

François did not insist any further. He looked round to see if he could find a way of escape. The young woman pushed him into the passage, at the foot of which was a very dark opening. She made him promise to remain hidden there while she went downstairs to receive the irritable person who now was shouting in the street.

"All right," said François. "So be it. Go and open. Go on. Make haste!"

From his hiding-place he heard the door grating and then a man's voice rebuking Catherine, then her excusing herself on the ground that she had fallen asleep. The voice was harsh, and François thought that he recognized it. And he drew back as far as he could when the man, stopping on the landing before going into the room, asked if there weren't by chance anyone hidden in the house.

"Do you want to look?" suggested Catherine.

There was a silence, and then, after a moment, the noise of a fresh discussion rose and made François's blood run cold with terror, for this time he realized unmistakably that the man was none other than Sermoise.

"If he sees me," thought the poet in his cover, "he'll make me pay for the affront he received that time. He hasn't forgotten it, I'll be bound. Oh, he's swearing, he's angry! and Catherine, like a fool, is standing up to him instead of calming him down. Everything's going wrong!"

Ready to leap, he waited. But the door of the room was not closed, and as François had to pass right in front of it in order to get away, he hesitated a long time, gazing at the light on the boards coming from the room where Sermoise was. But the priest was softening. He was talking in a low voice, caressing the girl, and saying tender things in her ear. Embracing her, he pushed her towards the bed, while Catherine gave an intolerable little laugh. For an instant the poet said to himself that she was laughing as if intentionally, so that it would hurt him, and he was on the point of dashing in. But prudence, fortunately, held him back motionless, for almost at the same moment Sermoise slammed the door, and François felt himself delivered. On tiptoe he came forth from his hiding-place, came along the dark corridor, lending an ear to the words of Catherine and Sermoise. Then he reached the steps that led to the street, went down them, and made off like a thief.

What an adventure! It left him next day with a great contempt for himself, and with regrets that he had not known how to profit by the occasion so as to give his rival a thrashing and teach him what sort of a man he, Master Villon, was. Alas, he had shown that only too plainly by his flight! And his contempt for himself grew greater. In the eyes of Catherine he would henceforth count for nothing, whatever he might do; he could not prevent her from passing judgment on him, or especially from rejoicing that she had played a trick on him a second time. For she had played one. François felt sure of it. The presence of Marthe, and then the arrival of the priest, and the way in which Catherine forced François to remain there: all went to prove it. It was a trick of her own sort, and perhaps she was deceived in that it had not turned out as she had desired.

"Very well," said François, weighing it all up. "My turn next."

Nevertheless, disgusted with women, the poet wondered how he would disarm Catherine, for during nearly a month he felt no desire to set eyes on her again, so much had she mortified him by her conduct.

It was now the beginning of December, and the season of festivities was coming near, when one morning, as he was wandering in the quarter of Saint-Jacques, François was astonished at the extraordinary activity he noticed thereabouts. Students were running hither and thither, calling to each other, and forming into groups. Then, armed with staves, they made in the direction of the schools, where there seemed to be fighting in progress. It was the sixth of December, exactly, the feast of Saint Nicholas. Shouts rose up here and there. Villon stopped a scholar and, telling him his name, asked him what was going forward.

"It is the provost," answered the student. "He has given orders to the sergeants, and they've got hold of the stones, the 'Pet' and the 'Vesse.'"

"And where are they?"

"They were in the house of Master Vaudelar just now, and there they were loading up the first of these stones to take it away, when we came on the scene, and now we're guarding the street."

"Come along, quick!" said François.

At a run he scaled the rise leading up to the rue Saint-Hilaire. And there, amid the wild confusion, he saw that carts had been overturned to prevent the sergeants from passing. Paving-stones had been wrenched up, and all along the houses curious spectators were standing grouped together in the doorways, awaiting the next stage.

"This way," cried a clerk suddenly as he ran up. "Come on! Be quick! They're at Saint-Étienne now, at Master Andry Bresquier's!"

There was a furious charge. With loud boos for the provost and his men, the students deserted the post they held, and came down by the rue des Écoles into the rue Saint-Étienne, where they immediately ran into the body of armed men, who charged in amongst them in force.

In the middle of the street François recognized the provost himself, mounted on horseback. He was shouting to the sergeants, urging them forward.

"Break them up!" he was crying, infuriated by this ridiculous riot. "If any resist, kill!"

Fortunately the students had no defence but their staves, and did not persist. Crowded back towards the wide rue Saint-Jacques, they poured ignominy on Robert d'Estouteville, while the archers, forcing a way to the house of Master Andry Bresquier, took into custody a score of young men, and piled on a cart a number of tavern signs, and a couple of blood-stained crow-bars, and butcher's hooks, and knives, and the famous little cannon of which they were so proud. Suddenly some of the archers, who had broached several of the casks in the cellars, began flinging everything that came to their hands out of the windows, and the provost had to restrain their zeal. On his command the pillage ceased. And then Robert d'Estouteville gave with his right arm the signal to advance, and put himself at the head of the little troop, which moved on rapidly to the "Image de Saint Nicolas," where another goodly store of signs was discovered and borne away.

Still abusing the provost, the students followed, and the wild din they made caused great excitement amongst the citizens all round. A second time the sergeants had to intervene, for at the sight of the "Queen of the University," who had been brought out from her lodging, they gave vent to such an outcry that anyone might have thought they were being butchered. This stupid creature, however, offered no resistance to the gentlemen from the Châtelet. Hoisted up on to the cart where the tavern signs were, she laughed uncomprehendingly and gave every sign of being delighted with her position.

"Hi there!" said one lad who had approached the cart and was anxious at any cost to get the Queen down from it. "What right have you to take her off! She is ours ——"

"That's for you!" said a sergeant, giving him a stunning blow.

The youth's name was Boisincourt. He fell to the ground, and for five minutes he lay there, being struck at savagely.

"Boisincourt! Boisincourt!" howled the students. "Give him up! Give him up!"

But the provost put the spurs into his horse, turned sharply round, and in an instant was amongst the boldest of them, who scattered and opened up the street again, so rapid had been the movement.

"There's a man for you!" thought François.

And as he watched the archers falling into step as they led away the cart and dragged the vehicle on which the two enormous stones stood swaying, he bade himself hold his hand, and give no outward sign of his feelings.

II

It was all one to him if the stones were removed from the neighbourhood of the schools and carried in ceremony to the Châtelet. He laughed at it all, when he saw Brother Baude passing, handled roughly by the sergeants, and heard him shout: "Help! François! Help!"

François turned his head, and took himself down another street, without another thought for the monk or anybody else. He reached Saint-Benoît again and told his uncle the news of what he had just witnessed.

Already it was being rumoured everywhere that, in the course of this operation, a sergeant rigged out in the cap and gown of the clerks had insulted them by appearing thus clad, and that, in mockery of the University, others of the soldiery had held him by the arms and struck him repeatedly on both sides, calling out: "Where are your friends, my fine gentleman?"

Master Guillaume was furious at this. Calm and prudent though he always was in normal circumstances, he could no longer contain himself, and to François, who strove to soothe his feelings, he answered: "No, no! Insulting us in our own quarter! Presuming to make mock of us by force! No, no! It is inexcusable. The matter won't rest there, I give my oath for it. The rector must be warned."

"But I'm sure he is," laughed François.

"Well, wait then — you'll see."

And a few days later, as it turned out, Master Guillaume was summoned to the Sorbonne, where a special council was held, and that evening he informed his nephew that the rector had decided to demand in person from the provost the release of the students who had been confined in the Châtelet, and a great commotion would be caused.

"Yes," replied François, "but it is really comical. All this excitement of these exalted personages for the sake of that confounded stone which I myself took away, a long time ago. — Who could have thought it?"

"You're right," said Master Guillaume coldly. And as he saw from his air that François did not take the rector's discomfiture very seriously, he shrugged his shoulders, and breathed not another word.

12

There was endless gossip on every hand in Paris concerning this affair, and everyone heard the tale over and over again, except François, who wandered here and there about the streets, thinking of Catherine and unable to make up his mind. When he met her and answered her smiles with a slight salutation, he returned in a pensive mood and showed an execrable temper. He would have liked to challenge Catherine directly, and humiliate her, but he could not bring himself to it. If a few days went by without his seeing her, he pined for her and fell into deep dejection, or else, walking up and down beneath her window at night, he spied upon the movements of the passers-by until he had distinguished Sermoise.

But all this did not prevent François from realizing that a turbulent spirit was abroad in the schools and that an important stroke was being made ready. It was delivered in the spring, when, after many negotiations which proved fruitless, the rector grew weary of waiting for the provost to free the students whom he had flung into the dungeons of the Châtelet, and took steps to act.

On the morning of the ninth of May 1453, a procession was formed, and went to Robert d'Estouteville's house in the rue de Jouy. In imposing array the professors, masters, and pupils filed past, in ranks eight deep, with neither staves nor knives. They had all sworn that during this solemn manifestation, they would make no answer to any provocations, whatever they might be, and to maintain an absolute restraint. From the start everything passed off very properly. Robert d'Estouteville received the rector, agreed to his request, and gave the order to a certain Nicolas to hand over the guiltless and take caution for the guilty. And then accompanying the head of the University out to the door of his dwelling, he himself announced in a loud voice that agreement had been reached.

More than eight hundred scholars, assembled there in the street, acclaimed him, and the procession, with the rector at its head, set off to reach the left bank, taking the rue Saint-Antoine. And there, unfortunately, as it was noon, a commissary, named Henri Le Fèvre, with some sergeants, crossed the path of the students.

"What is all this?" asked the sergeants, faced by so large a gathering.

Henri Le Fèvre answered, telling them to let the rector pass, and then just as the column was turning the corner of the house where the "Ours" tavern was, he drew his sword and called out: "Help! In the King's name! To arms!"

Immediately the sergeants flung themselves on the demonstrators, striking them with halberd and dagger, and pursuing them with violence until everywhere in the street the disorder reached a climax, and other sergeants, arriving from the opposite direction and understanding what was afoot, spread out the lines and entered into the struggle. The unarmed scholars took to flight. They tried to find refuge in the houses and in the gardens, but wherever they escaped to they were overtaken. The townspeople and merchants hastened to put up their shutters and closed their stalls, chasing them off, and the scholars were forced to run hither and thither, begging to be spared, or grouped themselves round the masters, calling for help.

"Death to them! Death to them! There are too many of them!" was all the answer from the sergeants.

One of them threatened the rector with uplifted dagger, and brutally told him he would take him off to the provost.

"That will be twice in one day," retorted the rector, "for I have only this moment been paying him a visit."

"What! What's he saying? What's he saying?"

"He's an old fool!"

"Well, take me," insisted the rector.

An archer aimed the point of his arrow at him, and declared: "Ha! I'll make him keep quiet!"

And he was just going to fire when, with a shove, the scholars knocked him over, and then, emboldened by this success, disarmed him and rained blows upon him.

They incited each other with cries while their anger rose.

But one of the scholars, struck behind the head by a

sergeant's mace, collapsed, and several of his comrades were so severely set upon that they sank to the ground, to rise covered with blood. Everywhere, more or less, one could see nothing but these fine boys, cruelly assaulted, dragging themselves under the doorways and imploring the occupants to open their doors to them. And everywhere they were repulsed, for townsfolk, fearful of paying the penalty in their turn, were unwilling to take them in. A priest whose face had been horribly slashed groaned and sought for shelter. The archers made game of him. They pricked him when he came in their direction; and the lamentations of the wretched man were frightful.

When they had wearied of this barbarity, the soldiery left the scene, and their victims were picked up. They were carried to the barbers', where their wounds were bound up, and then they were sent to the colleges.

It was the occasion of much heartburning on the other side of the river. The rector in person visited the injured, and asked them to state who it was who had struck them. Some of them knew the names, and these were put down in writing, in order to draw up a report to be laid before the provost. And until late at night the most varied rumours were in circulation, plunging the colleges into consternation.

Meanwhile Master François had gone out to take the air, and was wondering what the meaning of all this business might be, and he managed to find some amusement in it all. If anything could afford him diversion, it was certainly the adventure of the rector, who had envenomed everything without achieving anything.

"There you have it," he said to himself. "When you act so foolishly, you only get what you're looking for."

And he turned by the rue Saint-Jacques towards Catherine's house, and was stepping out faster when somebody tugged suddenly at his gown, and asked: "Is that you, François?"

"Go to the devil!" he exclaimed, and then: "Colin! You gave me a fright!"

"I know," answered Colin calmly. "I saw Régnier, outside Paris. He told me the story. There, keep cool! Where are you off to?"

"Up this way," said Villon, with vexation.

Colin shook him.

"Now, then!" he said in a low voice. "When I speak to you, you must answer me."

"Take your hands off me!"

"No!"

"Colin! What harm have I done you that you should jostle me like that?"

But Colin, still holding him and knocking him against the wall, declared to him: "I've been told all about it, you young monkey, all about your going to Ambroise de Loré's and the fine folk you're familiar with. Do you take me?"

"Explain yourself."

"What I mean," said Colin, "is this: that if ever any

new troubles should turn up for me in that direction, I should hold you responsible."

"Oh!"

"That's how it is," said Colin. "You've had fair warning. Wherever it may be, if it turns out that you can't hold your tongue — look at me — you'll get into the devil's own trouble, and you'll pay the price."

"But what are you saying?" protested François. "Me? Treating me like that! I who ——"

"Come on, now!" said Colin, "come on! You know what talking means!"

And, rolling his shoulders, he joined a few paces away a mysterious figure who had been waiting for him, whom Villon, quite stunned, knew must be Piez Blans.

. . . . . .

What caused François the most distress in this encounter, and succeeded in discouraging him, was that Colin had believed Montigny merely on his word and had not asked for the slightest explanation. François would have given him one instantly, but he had other concerns on his mind, and soon he thought no more about it. However, what was the meaning of Colin's presence in Paris? And why this queer temper, this restlessness, these threats, this need of warning one to be on one's guard?

"Bah!" exclaimed Villon. "Let him look out for himself!"

And he resumed in solitude his nocturnal walks under

Catherine's windows, without doubting that the young woman, seeing him so regularly striding up and down the street, would grow weary at last. Her curiosity regarding François was leaving her. It was yielding to a sense of irritation which, little by little, made her more unjust in his regard and brought her to be less tactful in her dealings with him.

In fact, when she now crossed his path, Catherine turned her head and answered his greeting coldly and distantly. If he followed her, she turned on her path. If he tried to speak to her, she did not listen. And if he humbly beseeched her with his look to have pity on him and his sorrows, she broke into malicious laughter that made him turn suddenly as pale and grave as if he were going to faint.

Villon had only Marthe in whom he could confide, and he complained to her that Catherine had no heart and was driving him to his grave.

"But it was you who wanted to try your fortune at the game," replied Marthe.

"I've had enough of it," said François. "I'm down and out."

"Oh, you astonish me!"

Then, as she felt him to be sincere and cruelly unhappy, she became very kindly towards him and sometimes she embraced him.

The winter passed without bringing anything fresh, and yet a ludicrous rumour was spread abroad to the effect that François had been Catherine's lover. The latter denied it in vain, and in vain called Marthe to witness: victories were ascribed to her which she had never enjoyed. What was not said? François was content to shrug his shoulders, or, if people insisted, to turn away from anyone who congratulated him on his supposed good fortune, and quickly to regain Saint-Benoît.

He took refuge there as a wounded animal might, speaking to nobody, ashamed and disabused. His three young pupils were greatly distressed by it. Then he regretfully went out into the street, and, not knowing where he was going, he invariably found himself once more under Catherine's windows, until one evening when Sermoise caught sight of him.

"Come, come!" answered François to the priest, who had come up to him and grossly insulted him. "Come now! Not so loud with that voice of yours!"

"I'll use it as I think fit!"

"No, you won't," said François. "I'll take care you don't."

"How so, pray?"

"Thus," said the poet.

And forthwith he hurled himself with fury upon Sermoise and threw him to the ground.

"Ha ha! There! Do you see?"

And so saying, he gripped him by the throat, hammered his head on the paving-stones, clasped tighter and struck harder, while the other, mad with rage, struggled to bite him and to catch hold of his dagger underneath his clothes. But he could not draw it, and Villon noticed what he was doing. He gave Sermoise one last blow, more violent still, and, as the priest had turned over, he rose up quickly.

"What have you done?" said Catherine, who had run up beside them at the noise of the fight.

François pointed to Sermoise, and answered: "You see there. He was getting at his dagger!"

"Oh!" said Sermoise with fury.

And struggling headlong towards him, he was about to strike the poet when Catherine put herself between them.

"Out of there!" cried the priest.

"No, no! I forbid you ——"

"Oh! That's too much!" cried Sermoise. "Will you get out of there?"

But François had made off, and, once at home, he slept until the next day with a heavy, dreamless sleep which repaired his weakened forces. It was a long time since he had been so well on waking up. He rose, yawned, and looked out of the window at the sun making the fronts and the roofs of the houses gleam with its light, and then, a good hour before the midday meal, he came downstairs and went to greet his uncle, who was in the garden.

"Ah, good-day, François!" said Master Guillaume. "What's the matter?"

"Nothing. I came to take a walk."

Master Guillaume took him by the arm.

II

"Do you feel better disposed?" he asked, leading him peaceably along. "You certainly look well."

"It's the fine weather," said François slowly, drinking in the smells of the soil and the perfumes of the roses. "I get pleasure from that."

He sighed, raised his eyes to heaven, and smiled, but did not dare to tell his uncle of his adventure of the previous evening. And he thought of Catherine, evoking her at the same time as Sermoise, and a profound satisfaction took hold of him at the thought of his having given this man a beating, this man of whom he was jealous. What had he been thinking about last night, to have insulted him, simply because he was there in the street? He must know what the price of an insult is. The imbecile! Would it be taken for granted that he had to remain in his place if he did not want to be thrashed every time? François only asked to instruct him on this point, but as he remembered the punishment inflicted on the priest, he remembered likewise that he was armed and that perhaps it would be better not to take any risks with him unless he took precautions.

Accordingly, that same day, Villon made the purchase of a dagger, which he carried under his gown, resolved to have recourse to it if he needed to. It was no longer Catherine who filled his thoughts, but Sermoise, and, curious as the fact was, the poet was delighted, for he experienced a relief which he had in no way foreseen.

Refraining from running to station himself beneath

the young woman's windows, François henceforth contented himself with wandering in the neighbourhood, or else he went down as far as the Seine and, before night fell, reached that stone bench under the sun-dial of the cloister whereon he loved to sit and watch the people as they passed about their business. There was a woman who sat beside him, settled every evening on this same bench, and talked to him of one and another. She was young. François caressed her without its being noticed, and little by little, astonished at the leaning he had towards this creature, he found amusement in seeing how troubled she became as soon as he drew near.

After long days without any breeze, a light wind was blowing along the rue Saint-Jacques. May was coming to its term, and then June flamed with all its fierce ardour, and the nights became so overpowering that, stretching out in front of their doors, the shopkeepers decided not to go to bed.

The feast of Corpus Christi was particularly hot. During the procession in which, according to custom, the body of our Lord had been borne through the Saint-Benoît quarter under a canopy crowned with roses and wreathed in gold ribbons, François thought he should suffocate as he followed the line of ecclesiastics, church-wardens, and bearers, crowned likewise with marjoram and white violets. An odour of foliage and flowers, of incense and dust, caught him in the throat, and the cloths decorating the fronts of the houses hung motionless from the windows, without any breath of wind to disarrange their folds. Nothing stirred. Amongst the temporary altars burned the lighted candles, and their flames rose straight up in the air, gleaming with intense brightness.

Right on until the evening, which brought no coolness, but only prolonged the fever of the day and spread far and wide a warm perfume as of churches and bruised flowers, François longed only for the moment when he could repose himself on the bench. His neighbour was to join him there again, and when he was beside her, he took a deep breath, and said: "Will you not stay with me all night, Isabeau?"

"Oh, oh! Master François! Be serious!" she answered.

"I haven't the slightest desire to be that."

"But I'm most virtuous," said Isabeau with a little laugh.

François drew her to himself, and, speaking in a low voice, he explained that all these flowers that had been thrown down and trodden upon in the course of the procession gave off a perfume which disposed one to love.

"Oh, yes," the girl admitted tenderly. "But they'll come to look for me."

"Bah!" said François. "You can go, and then come back."

He was lost in Isabeau and was seizing her round the waist, when Sermoise, whom he had not seen arriving, moved in his direction, and strolled past the bench, exclaiming: "God strike me dead, if it isn't Master François! But here I've found you!"

Murder Scene. From an illuminated manuscript of the XVI century

II

Isabeau leapt to her feet.

"Good-evening," said François drily.

He rose to his feet and, looking Sermoise straight in the eye, asked him: "What do you want? Have I done you any harm?"

Sermoise sniggered, and, as he was visibly moving to feel for a weapon, Villon caught him by the arm and murmured: "Sit down. We shall talk."

"No," answered the priest, drawing back and turning white with anger. "This is no occasion for talking. It's an occasion for your explaining yourself."

"Ah, indeed?"

In answer, Sermoise fell upon the poet with upraised dagger, and, getting in a blow with it, he wounded him so fiercely on the lip that it was all but torn off and the blood gushed out.

Isabeau ran off. François broke free and moved off a short distance, pursued by Sermoise, and in his turn brought out his knife. He crouched. Beside the wall of the cloister he picked up a paving-stone, and then, as the priest advanced with muttered threats, he planted the dagger right in his groin. It remained fixed there while Sermoise staggered.

"Aha!" said François. "You asked for it!"

But Sermoise, covered with blood, flung himself on the poet, who this time, swinging up the paving-stone in his hand, brutally knocked him down.

"Murder!" called out a man's voice suddenly. "Hi there! Murder!"

II

François turned round.

"It's no fault of mine," he said.

"But he must have killed him," said a woman.

"Who? I?"

"Quick!" went on the man, pointing to Sermoise. "Take him along and have him looked after while there's still time. Who'll give me a hand here? Come on, here — gently."

François was dabbing at his lip, and did not know what to do. He gazed at Sermoise, who was being picked up. Several bystanders bore him off to Saint-Benoît. He was left stupefied, watching the people gathering round him, and he kept on repeating: "No, it's not my fault. Look, he wounded me. I only defended myself."

"Get off with you," someone in the crowd advised him. "And quick too!"

"Think so?"

"Of course I do. Be quick!"

"And why?"

"Go on, go on!" said the other.

But François, after a moment's argument with himself, went off at a walking pace by the little lane of the Mathurins. He only began to run a little farther on, and betook himself to a barber's.

His wound smarted. The lip, deeply gashed, exposed the lower teeth and the gum, and was already swelling up and forming a kind of black pad. The barber dressed the wound, and then, for his report, asked François who he was and why he had been struck like this.

"My name is François Mouton," answered the poet.

"All right, all right," said the barber. "You'll sign this."

"I feel so bad, you know."

"Here," pointed the barber, after setting down that the undersigned had had his lower lip torn by a certain Sermoise. "Come, sign here ——"

"What!" said François. "Let me read it."

And as the barber, as a precaution, was going to shut his door, the poet took the pen; but, instead of placing his signature where he had been told, he traced a crooked cross on the paper, and excused himself as being unable to write.

III

III

13

Day followed day, slowly and oppressively, flowing past between that evening of Corpus Christi which had meant for Villon his arrest on a charge of homicide, and that winter morning when he returned to Paris after seven months of a nomadic existence amid country roads and woods, in small towns and in the great solitude of the fields. François was in rags and tatters. More sunbeaten and swarthy than any gipsy, with hollow eyes, and his mouth marked by a hideous scar, he had a disturbing bearing beneath those rags of his, and something fugitive and mysterious in his eye that could not pass unnoticed.

And what hatred he cherished still for the jailers and sergeants and examiners, and for the executioner who had brutally bound him and put him to the torture! He abominated them. He called to mind once more the sufferings he had endured at their hands at the Châtelet, after the murder of Sermoise, and his anguish, his sweats of agony when he had appealed to the Parlement and, more dead than alive, had awaited for Robert d'Estouteville to prevent him from being hanged, and obtained the grace in his favour of a decree of expulsion, François had passed within an inch of the noose. He knew it. He could still feel his flesh chill at the thought, and yet, far from amending his life, he had hardened himself in wrongdoing and refused to renounce it.

III

Colin, whom he had seen at the moment of his leaving Paris, and with whom he had made his peace, had shown himself a generous spirit. At Bourg-la-Reine he had directed Villon to a certain barber, Perrot Girard by name, who, at his recommendation, had looked after him, and given him shelter, and had been content, as regards payment, with answering that, as his patient was a friend of Colin's, he owed him nothing. This worthy man had greatly astonished the poet, but as he received a fair number of suspicious characters, who poured out of Paris in disorder every night, François did not insist, and he found it almost natural that, turning up unexpectedly one evening, Piez Blans came to find him by Colin's orders, to take him out on the Orléans road as far as a certain forking of the way, where they parted company. Piez Blans, who had tramped along without so much as opening his lips, then said to the poet that, by bearing to his right, he would reach an abbey, where food, a roof over his head, and the rest would be assured him. It was the Abbey of Pourras. And not only did François find lodging there, but the abbess entertained him nobly and kept him for nearly a full month to have her pleasure with him. This time being over, François, who was growing weary, returned alone to Bourg-la-Reine, where Colin, he had learned, made sudden appearances at the said barber's. There François saw him, beseeched him to plead with Marthe, in order that the interdict against him should be withdrawn. And after several attempts, Colin, who had a preoccupied air, was able to declare that the girl was acting to that end and had hopes of obtaining papers of remission of the sentence. But he would have to wait, and François, who was destitute of money, was forced to borrow some from Colin and Perrot Girard, who associated him in their united concerns.

"Have I any choice?" said the poet to himself when he returned, worn out, at dawn, and thought of his companion. The latter was dragging him on to the roads, and often, stationing him at some cross-roads, would make him act as watch. At Rueil François realized that every kind of vagabond under Colin's direction was full of discontent. In the quarry pits he was booed and pressed to make some active step. Colin talked matters over with their captains for hours on end, and then, powerless to come to agreement with all his efforts, he cursed like a miscreant.

Now on foot, now mounted on horses furnished by Perrot Girard, the two friends traversed the whole region up and down, and wherever they went, there were violent arguments, until the morning Piez Blans came in person to Bourg-la-Reine and swore he would go on no longer. He was irritated at so much time's having been wasted, and so furious was he that he convinced two hideous creatures who were present at the conversation and were eager at any price to march forward their bands, which were concentrated close to Paris.

"What's the matter?" inquired François timidly.

III

Colin made no reply. Night and day he was at the work, fending off the most eager and deterring them from risking the adventure, for it was a lost cause. News coming from Dijon put him into abominable fits of fury. He smashed everything about him and went off, followed by François, who escorted him as far as Paris, returning the same day and spending himself in all kinds of ways. Sometimes he would harangue groups of individuals in the fields, in their own jargon, adjuring them to turn on their tracks, or else he would lead them into sight of some humble village and let them make an assault on it. This allowed him to push these horrible beings further back in the direction of Orléans or Chartres, where, he said, they had only to show themselves and they could pillage the hamlets and small towns, set fire to the farms, and install themselves as masters. François stood dumbfounded at it all. He now understood the language of Colin, speaking it almost fluently and making great progress in it.

"Oh, well," his companion would sometimes say to him, "you are getting to learn this life!"

"But it lies heavy on me."

"Not at all," retorted the other. "You'll soon get into the way of it."

Shortly afterwards, by the force of events, Villon took part in some attacks in the woods, in several robberies under arms, and in sundry other small matters of business which turned out profitable to him. But he missed Paris. Posted for days on end on some high place where he could contemplate at his ease the towers and the walls of the city, he pined. The pale October sun struck the slates of the roofs and made them gleam, and François called to mind that only just over there, under these roofs which he could see, life had all its savour and joy, all its full splendour, and he fell into a sore melancholy as he thought of Marthe and reflected that she was not hurrying.

It was she, however, whom he went to see first of all, on that January morning, to thank her, and at first Marthe did not recognize him. So altered was he that she stood taken aback, and had to take it on herself to speak to him and beg him to excuse her.

"Bah!" said François with a feigned detachment. "I've had a bad time, but here I am again, thanks to you!"

"Robert d'Estouteville helped me," Marthe informed him. "He is a good fellow at bottom, you know."

"I know it. He has already saved my life once."

"Poor François!"

"That depends."

"Oh, I prefer you to hear it said."

"And Pernet de la Barre?"

"He is very well."

They looked at each other in silence, neither of them daring to make any allusion to the third — Catherine. But at the moment when Villon bowed as he took his leave, Marthe said in a low voice: "She is very unhappy."

"I should like her to be still more so," answered Villon.

"She is no longer received anywhere," went on the girl, "for she commits the very worst follies. Since Sermoise, does she even know the number of her lovers?"

François turned slightly pale. His voice became hoarse as he jested: "So many as that?"

"Oh, yes. And what spoils everything is that she demands money. Now look, if it had not been for this wretched quarrel ——"

"But Sermoise sought it from me."

"Of course he did," said Marthe.

And then François looked at her and declared: "I regret nothing."

And because Marthe, troubled by the tone of voice he had just assumed, kept her eyes steadfast upon him, he recited those verses in which he gave utterance to his grief:

> "*Faulse beauté qui tant me couste chier*
> *Rude en effet, ypocrite doulceur,*
> *Amour dure, plus que fer, à maschier . . .*"

"Oh!" said the girl, in gentle reproach.

But François went on:

> "*Mieux m'eust valu avoir été cherchier*
> *Ailleurs secours . . .*

Better to have sought help elsewhere!"

"But where then?" asked Marthe in amazement.

François made as if to continue.

"No. Tell me where!" she insisted. "Why don't you answer?"

"With you," said François. "And yet that was not possible."

Marthe was silent.

"Forgive me," he said bitterly. "I'm losing my wits."

"And I," murmured Marthe, after a long moment during which she stood motionless before him, "I am sorely pained to listen to you."

She shook her head, and then, moving pensively away, she went and sat down in a corner of the room as he left her.

Out in the street, walking with long strides and reproaching himself for this avowal which he had not been able to keep back, François regarded himself as an imbecile, for his muddy university bands, his worn and tattered gown, accentuated his pitiable physical appearance, and he was bound to admit that he had made a bad choice of a day. He was vexed at his own stupidity, and at the same time he felt a grudge against Marthe. Did she understand that he had yielded to emotion on seeing her once again? It filled him with consternation, obliging him to admit to himself that the girl had no real affection for him, that she was, in fact, like the others, sensitive to appearances and altogether unworthy of being loved by any man. In her place Catherine would not have shown more coldness. At least he believed it, or tried to believe it. Yet Catherine had never displayed any tenderness at all towards François;

but, in proportion as he turned towards her, the poet invested her with feelings which he had not found with Marthe, and he felt a cruel deception in it.

It was then, up near the "Mule," in the rue Saint-Jacques, that he caught sight of Régnier de Montigny. He stopped, puzzled.

"Régnier!" he called in a doleful tone. "Are you still put out?"

Régnier flung wide his arms; Villon flung himself into them, and held him firmly clasped as his best friend.

"I heard from Colin," said Régnier at last, "what you had become."

"Yes," said François, "I had to."

"Of course," grunted Régnier. "There are lots of you in the same plight, and we cannot help it."

"But I don't complain," said François. "If it hadn't been for Colin, I was lost. I owe it to him that I am a man."

"And I, for having been at Dijon to instruct myself," laughed Régnier, his face becoming suddenly overcast.

"You regret it?"

"Things aren't going well," he answered. "There I was lodged with Jaquot de la Mer, amongst the Coquillards, and everything was all right whilst I lived there. Ha! That Jaquot is extraordinary, François! As he keeps a brothel, however, the sergeants don't suspect him of making a living in any other way. And what a living he makes! From all sides, whoever wants to sell horses stolen at Salins, or clothes, or silver, or anything at all, applies to him!"

"Horses?"

"Certainly, horses. That lad is never at a loss. He has purchasers for everything, at market rates, you may be sure, and never a hitch, not the smallest difficulty. — You bring him your merchandise. He lodges you in the brothel while he is getting rid of it, and then he pays you the cash in your hand."

"That is somebody worth knowing," said François.

"Moreover," explained Régnier livelily, leading the poet down towards the bridges, "he has receivers in several towns, even in Paris, to whom you may go and make yourself known. Christophe Turgis, Leclerc, Jacquet Legrant —— Have you ever heard these names?"

"Never once."

"All the better. And yet," continued Régnier, "Jacquet Legrant has given me a good price for a large pyx and two silver cruets which I was anxious to get rid of. He did me a useful turn."

"But why aren't you content?"

"No. Nothing. That's a different matter," said Régnier blankly.

"What?"

Régnier appeared to reflect a moment, but he shook his head, looked sternly at François, and held out his hand to him.

"Farewell," he muttered. "Colin will probably tell you all about it. I can't speak, myself. You know where to find him?"

"He gave me his address."

"Well, come then, one of these nights."

And he left François, for he was going to the other side of the river, and François, deep in his thoughts, walked up towards Saint-Benoît.

This meeting with Régnier had afforded him such comfort that his visit to Marthe seemed no more to him now than a far-off story, and he pushed open the door of his worthy uncle and went into the dining-room, calling out: "Good-day! It is François!"

Huguette was preparing the table.

"Master François!" she cried.

"Yes, none other! And my uncle?"

"He will be back for his midday meal in a moment," said the servant. "But how brown you are, and how ragged your clothes are! Lord help us! Quick — upstairs, and change your clothes!"

"All in good time," answered François.

He went over beside the fire and stood warming his soles at the glow, and watching with a constrained air this room with its shining tiles which he expected never to recognize again.

"Give me something to drink," he said then. "I am thirsty."

Huguette served him, and then she saw him, after emptying his glass, wipe his mouth clumsily with the back of his sleeve, stretch himself, slowly move over to the steps leading to the floor above, and disappear.

"Alas, alas!" she groaned.

A footstep upstairs sounded dully. For an instant Huguette felt startled, for she was so little prepared for the return of François that she did not know what to make of it. In the room, however, the passing to and fro of the poet stopped. Huguette listened. She heard a sound of snoring, and her fear, stupidly, grew greater.

"Well, well," came the voice of Master Guillaume, who had surprised her lost in her reflections beside the chimney-piece. "Huguette!"

By dint of great effort she spoke.

"Master François has arrived," she said.

"François?"

"Yes. He had something to drink, then he went upstairs — and now he is sleeping."

"Poor boy!" exclaimed the chaplain. "Quick! let's see! Set another place. I'll go and wake him up."

"In my opinion," said the servant, "you would do better to leave him in peace. He is so tired out that it would be a pity, Master Guillaume! Believe me. Just with seeing him here, here in front of me, I'm still all of a flutter!"

"And what did he say?"

"Nothing."

"What? Nothing at all?"

"No. He asked after you, drily, without pressing the question, and without much interest in anything at all ——"

III

"And — that was all?"

"That was all," said Huguette, grumbling.

François slept on until nightfall, in a heavy sleep, and when he awoke, Master Guillaume was at his bed-side.

"Ah!" he said, taken aback. "Uncle!"

But Master Guillaume embraced him and answered: "There, there boy! My own boy! Don't talk now. — Huguette will bring your meal to you. — No, no. Stay in bed. Rest yourself. Are you glad to find yourself in your own room again, eh? Wait a moment — I'll light a fire for you, myself. Don't move. Above all, I forbid you to rise."

"Why?"

"You're so thin!" sighed the chaplain, who felt his eyes smarting.

"Yes."

"And that gash on your lip. Does it not give you pain?"

"Not at all," said François.

He sat up in bed, and, more touched than he allowed himself to show, he murmured feebly: "And you too, Master Guillaume, you don't look very well either."

"What did you say?"

"No, not a bit well. I can see it——"

"Come, come!"

"And my mother?"

"I'll go and tell her the news," said the chaplain at once, delighted to be able to talk of something else, "for if she saw you thus, she would get such a shock as might carry her away. — She has aged, but she puts up a good fight; she's got lots of courage."

"Thank you," said Villon.

He closed his eyes, and then, when the wood flamed up and flickered in the hearth, he opened them again, gazed at Master Guillaume, and began to weep.

"Come, François," the chaplain reproached him. "My child!"

François could not hold back his tears, and they flowed over his poor face without his drying them. He wept for all his sufferings and all his shames, and, weaker than a woman, he gave his feelings full play. Did he know whence came this ridiculous welling up of tenderness? He did not seek its source. It relaxed him after so many evils borne without a word of complaint, and gave him a sense of peace, and did him good. And Master Guillaume, so as not to embarrass him, left the room.

"He'll be better after that," thought the good old man.

And, summoning Huguette, he went downstairs. There, after a quarter of an hour, Villon rejoined him fully dressed.

"Don't let Huguette put herself to that trouble," he said. "I shall have dinner downstairs here."

Master Guillaume did not insist. He watched François sitting down, and, when he had eaten, waited without saying a word until François got up.

"Where are you going in this bad weather?" he asked. "Would you not rather stay here with me?"

"I have to go," said François bluntly.

III

Outside an icy north wind was blowing, but the poet paid no heed. He crossed the Seine, reached the top of the rue Saint-Denis, took his direction to the right, and knocked at a door. He called for Colin and Montigny, who were waiting for him. They welcomed him, and then all three went out together.

"Where are we to go?" asked Régnier.

The rue Michel-le-Comte, with its five or six low taverns and houses of ill fame, offered them its pleasures.

"There," said Villon.

He crossed a low and damp threshold, and went on with his two friends into a room where some girls at once ran up to them, took his seat at a table and ordered drinks. There was an exclamation from one of the girls: "Strike me! If he does not know me any more!"

"What's that?"

"Why, it's Marion!" cried Colin.

"Yes, Marion!" François was forced to admit. "Devil take me if I knew you were here!"

"Two years now," she explained, sitting down beside him. "Ha ha! You've got fatter!"

"And you?"

"Try for yourself," said Marion gaily. "You see, fat but firm!"

"And still a good drinker?"

"Still."

"You're right," he said approvingly. And he filled the glasses while Colin and Régnier, caressing their companions, proposed to pass the night.

III

During several weeks Villon lived without stinting himself. He slept at the rue Michel-le-Comte, and in the day-time went out and played dice at the "Pomme." His gaiety came back to him. He was a winner, so he had friends everywhere, and often when he passed down the street, eyeing the women behind the booth counters, they laughed, these matrons, at his poor appearance, but they said behind him: "Master François Villon's got his eye on you, dear! Take care!"

"It isn't me: it's you!"

And hearing their remarks sometimes, he would turn and declare with a roguish air: "It's both of you!"

Never yet had his taste for women manifested itself so strongly. Marion knew something of it. And others. Dark, fair, ruddy, they waited for him in the cellars in the evenings; he contented them shamelessly and was all the better for it. He was faithful to none; he desired them all, and when Marion was astonished at his deceiving her and his still being capable of the most valiant conduct with her, he mocked at her surprise and renewed his exploits once more.

In spite of his successes, however, his thoughts turned to Catherine, and he became obsessed by the idea of her giving herself for money. Was it possible? He felt repugnance at accepting the thought, and wondered whether Marthe had been lying to him. And banishing these thoughts, he said to himself: "For my own part, I've paid already, and too dearly."

But he reverted to this idea of his that Catherine was

venal in her love, and the thought of it stirred a dull annoyance in him. Sometimes it woke him at night, while he lay in Marion's bed. And yet he did not love Catherine. She was odious to him. He detailed those charms of hers which had formerly linked him so closely with her, counting them off one by one, coolly and deliberately; he reckoned them at their worth and inwardly made mock of them. What! He, François Villon, had actually let himself be caught by this dry and pretentious beauty, with a crooked nose too! Well, now for others! That was over and done with! He had gone through his time and he had no mind to start on it again. No, no. Quite the contrary. And if by some chance he met Catherine, she would be made to see it clearly enough. She could see that it was dead, all of it, all of that grotesque love which she had inspired and trifled with and rejected. It was essential that she should see him and realize that at the end of the business the roles had changed.

But François had not foreseen the astuteness of this woman. A few months later he ran across her at the Innocents, and he was astounded to find that she showed no sign of emotion. Noël Jolis was with her. He greeted François, who replied without Catherine's seeming to notice. Then he stopped short, vexed, following the couple with his gaze and feeling his anger getting the mastery of him.

"It's too much!" he murmured.

A few hurrying leaps, and he had overtaken Catherine, getting in front of her, and making a half-turn. Finding himself in her path, he watched her approaching.

"What!" he said mischievously, as he saw her draw back and lean against Noël Jolis. "What are you afraid of?"

She turned pale.

"It shows how little you know of me," François went on.

"Go away!" said Catherine.

François had come too near to her. She laughed with a supreme insolence, and then, eyeing him up and down, she said, separating her words: "Is Sermoise not enough for you, then?"

"Oh!" said François, "there have been others since Sermoise."

"Indeed?"

"So it would appear," he answered, beginning to lose control of himself. "Six workmen do more than one. And as for this charming young person" — he pointed to Noël Jolis — "he is no doubt an extra?"

"What are you meddling with?" said the lad.

"*Primo,*" muttered François, "with what concerns me. *Secundo,* with certain rumours which are current with regard to the most noble Catherine de Vausselles and the conduct of her business ——"

"Enough!" Catherine cut him short. "That is no concern of yours."

"*Tertio* ——"

"Will you be quiet? I'll have you thrashed."

"By whom?"

III

"You know quite well!" exclaimed Catherine, who caught sight of a sergeant in the crowd that was gathering round them, and hailed him. "Go on! how far had you got?"

"To this," François went on imprudently, "that in Sermoise's time you could have warned me. I would have found the money you make them pay, and that worthy priest would still be in the land of the living."

"You hear?" said Catherine to the sergeant, who had come forward. "He insults me without ceasing. Take him. I shall lodge a complaint."

François gave a sneering laugh.

"Come on," said the sergeant.

"Oh, I will follow you," said François. "We shall explain ourselves."

Noël Jolis put in a word: "And you'll be beaten all right," he declared. "Beaten naked. That's the least that can happen to you."

"How do you mean beaten?"

"With rods!"

François turned round in a fury, threatening to lay hands on the young fool who was taunting him in this way. But the sergeant held him back.

"Go on, now," he ordered.

And brutally he pushed François forward, for he was losing patience, and could feel in the crowd a certain dumb hostility.

III

14

In any other circumstance this ridiculous incident would probably have been a cause of scandal amongst François's friends and diminished his prestige. But Colin and Régnier gave small thought to the part of his being given a thrashing outside Catherine's windows. They had darker cares on their shoulders.

"At Dijon," began Colin, "since Régnier came back, Regnault Daubourg, quarryman to the Duke of Burgundy and one of the Coquille notwithstanding, has been put under examination, with torture."

"Did he tell anything?"

"He told everything," said Régnier.

"Then Perronet, the man at whose house there was gaming at night, has revealed the names of the comrades."

Régnier groaned.

"A chain is as strong as its weakest link —" he said.

"No," Colin took him up with his stern voice. "It can be forged anew, and it will hold."

"How long?"

"Be quiet!" he shouted at him. "If you're weakening, you can go."

"Go!"

François seemed much disturbed.

"But Jaquot de la Mer?" he asked.

"Jaquot? No. Not yet."

III

"Then the game is not altogether up?"

"I think not," said Colin. "It's enough for the three of us" — and he laid stress on the *three* — "not to give in. Do you accept?"

"Yes," said Villon.

Then Colin explained to them that for the moment they had nothing to fear, and that in all probability the affair of the Coquillards would not rebound. Jean Rabustel, the procurator syndic of the town of Dijon, had enough on his hands and home, without extending his field of inquiry as far as Paris. It was a year now that he had been struggling with it. One could draw one's conclusions from that.

"That depends," said Régnier. "He has perhaps been waiting his chance to probe the business to its roots."

And sure enough, one after another, by a deplorable coincidence with various arrests carried out at Saumur, Langres, and Orléans, the receivers whose existence Montigny had revealed to François were seized and thrown into prison. Christophe Turgis was the only one to escape. At his house were found the equipment for making forged coins, and certain documents which helped the judicial authorities to lay their hands on individuals who were known to Colin, but who did not betray him. He was not then apprehensive for his own person, although on every hand, on simple accusations, persons whom one would never have suspected of belonging to the Coquille were made prisoners, and put to the torture. There were many girls of the town shut up in the underground dungeons of the Châtelet, and they told what they knew without much heed. Their stories were believed at their face value, their statements were noted, and then they were released, on condition that they informed the police of what they might come to hear. And none of François's friends, nor he himself, felt himself secure any longer.

It was the result of the trial at Dijon, where Rabustel had triumphantly announced that so-and-so had been hanged and strangled, three others boiled alive in a cauldron, the last flung into a pit. Jaquot de la Mer himself had not been able to escape the common fate. He was dragged to the cross-roads of the town and delivered to the executioner, and when the news of his death reached Régnier the latter was seized with panic and changed his lodging the same day, so closely threatened did he feel himself.

"Take care of yourself," he said to François. "If Jaquot de la Mer has paid the penalty, nothing will save us."

To leave Paris was becoming useless. Had not Christophe Turgis, who was thought to be clear of trouble, been seized at Sens? It was abominable. He would be taken, he, François, and the others, and they would all be put to death. They had just to wait for it, and when Colin tried sometimes to gainsay it, he answered with terror in his voice: "What is the good of deceiving ourselves? I know what our end is going to be."

And then, in a whisper, he recited these verses which their friend had written:

"Frères humains qui après nous vivez,
N'ayez les cuers contre nous endurcis,
Car, se pitié de nous povres avez,
Dieu en aura plus tost de vous mercis.
Vous nous voiez cy attachez cinq, six:
Quant de la chair que trop avons nourrie,
Elle est pieça dévorée et pourrie,
Et nous, les os, devenons cendre et pouldre.
De nostre mal personne ne s'en rie,
Mais priez Dieu que tous nous veuille absouldre!"

"It will be time then," Colin answered him. "Come on! You make me ashamed!"

"No. Let me ——"

"Régnier," said François, "these verses concern myself alone. And look you, they haven't brought me to Montfaucon."

"Perhaps!"

"Come, now!"

But François was hardly reassured. The sinister profile of justice at Montfaucon, where, as he had described them, the comrades of the rope swung "this way and that with the shifting wind," filled his mind with the most lugubrious reflections. Although he strove to re-establish Régnier's courage, he still told himself that one cannot escape one's fate twice over. He was afraid. He could sense a hostile presence around him, sly and intangible, and every day he surprised himself thrusting it back from him, rather as in a dream one pushes away those faceless and shapeless apparitions which move along with one. Was it a warning? He dared not wonder. He woke up with a start at all hours of the night, called out, felt anxious to flee, trembled; and his teeth chattered; and when at first gleam of dawn he fell asleep, utterly worn out, the black sleep into which he sank left in him a hideous memory, profound, obscure, and tenacious, and he felt a continual anxiety.

None the less, as winter came on, the affair of the Coquillards seemed to slacken its pace, and while the instruction in the high courts was proceeding, nobody was put to torture. A formidable dossier it was, and complicated beyond reason by the information received from Dijon concerning the language, the functions, and the crimes for which each of the prisoners had to answer before the examiners. Régnier de Montigny owed it only to his vast heap of documents, registers, acts, and scripts, beneath which the judges' desks were positively submerged, that he could count his life safe for a moment, and although his name occurred amongst many others bearing mention, in the hand of the procurator himself, of the form of death by which they had perished, he was left in peace. He did not know that he was so clearly designated, and allowing himself to trust in Providence (he couldn't have said what), he was seen outside again with François and Colin de Cayeux, sitting in the taverns, and playing dice and hopscotch as he used to do, cheating, and laughing, and getting drunk.

III

One evening he arrived very late at the rendezvous, with a strange air, and Colin took him aside.

"What's the matter?" he asked.

"Come out with me," said Régnier.

Colin hailed François, and out in the street they caught sight of a small, timid-looking man, who was waiting there. Régnier introduced him to them. He was named Petit Jehan, a very neat hand at picking locks, in spite of his mean appearance, with his coat too big for him, and his colourless fair hair, which framed his face and hung down stiffly like straws. Régnier had known him before, at Dijon, at the house of Jaquot de la Mer.

"Good," said Colin.

They moved off slowly, all four of them, and went without further delay to a hostelry, where Petit Jehan showed them hooks of all kinds, large and short, long and thin, which Régnier, Colin, and François passed each to the other as they examined them.

"Well, shall we come to an agreement?" asked Régnier.

"That depends!" answered Colin. "We have to know where to apply first."

Petit Jehan gave a laugh which exposed all his rotten teeth, and asked: "Is it true that in the sacristy of the Collège de Navarre there is the community coffer, chock-full?"

"Yes," said François, "at the end of the vestry."

"And is it true likewise," he went on, "that besides

the gateway on the rue de la Montagne, there are other practicable ways out?"

"After ten o'clock, as you choose," certified the poet. "But if you'll believe me, the best thing to do is to jump the walls. Along by the house of Master Robert de Saint-Simon, which adjoins the college, they are not so high."

Petit Jehan clapped him on the shoulder.

"You're something like a man!" he said.

"Of course," said Colin. "You've a good hand for picking a lock, Petit Jehan, but François could show you something in skill."

"I can see that!"

"Let him do it his own way. Before four days all will be ready."

"No doubt about it," said François quietly. "On one condition: that I am given somebody to help in the job."

"Who is it to be?"

"Tabary."

"What! That fat baby!"

Régnier spoke up.

"There are four of us. Consequently we go quarters. What shall we give to a fifth?"

"A kick in the backside!" laughed Colin.

"Why not Tabary, if he accepts?" said Régnier.

And, reverting to his idea, he said: "We'd have to fix a price with him."

"Well," said Colin, "Tabary can help us in making

ready for the affair, I grant you, but after that he is useless."

"So his profit shall be what we decide," said François decisively. "Twenty crowns?"

"Nonsense! Five."

"He won't do it."

"Ten crowns," proposed Régnier. "And further, on condition that he turns out to be useful! What do you think, the rest of you?"

"We can always promise."

"Is ten agreed upon?"

"Between ourselves," said Colin, "where's the risk? If the business turns out well, we leave them for him."

"And if not?"

"If not, we'll see," concluded the locksmith's son.

On the agreed evening they supped at the "Mule," in the rue Saint-Jacques, and waited for ten o'clock without taking too much to drink or drawing too much attention to themselves, and then, as it was Christmas eve, they declared that they were going to bed in anticipation of the morrow's festival. Outside, the keen cold air stung their faces, and the noise of their steps resounded so loudly in the frozen ground that they were annoyed, but soon they thought no more about it. From the top of the wall, which he had climbed, and from where he directed operations, Colin let a rope drop, which he fixed to a stout clamp, and then, at the command, he made his companions go down one after the other, and rejoined them.

III

The rope hung down into the courtyard of the college, and on the other side a wooden rack from a stable, which had helped them to hoist themselves up to the top, was to remain there as they had placed it, under the guard of Tabary.

"The lantern?" asked Colin.

"I've got it," said Régnier in a low voice.

"Forward, then!"

"This way," said François.

He made them bear over by a small covered way as he had fears of their being seen from the buildings occupied by the students while they went across the court, and then they approached the chapel, where Petit Jehan forced the door.

There was a faint light inside under the thick, heavy arches. In front of the high altar Colin seized the lantern, and lit it from the flame of the sanctuary lamp, which burned day and night in its glass cup. Then he rapidly reached the sacristy and inspected the place.

"To your left," François pointed out.

There it was, at the foot of a pillar. A great coffer, bound with several bands of iron, was seen, and Petit Jehan, pulling out his hooks one by one, knelt down to be more at ease and examined the lock.

"Gently, there," Villon advised.

Petit Jehan raised his head, tittered, and said: "Don't be alarmed, my lad!"

Then he began his work, while round him, masking the little flame of the lantern, Colin and François and

Martigny stood attentive, following his every movement.

"There, I've got it!" the skilful fellow told them instantly.

And without any effort he turned his hook, turned a second time, and silently opened the lid. He seemed displeased.

"What's wrong?" said Colin, leaning over him. "Oh, yes — a second coffer ——"

"With three locks, too," grumbled Petit Jehan. "By God, it'll need some time, that will."

"How long?"

"Till midnight at least."

At that moment the clock outside struck the half-hour after ten, and François started, for the sound, released with a great clatter of mechanism, seemed to resound in the very marrow of his bones.

"Go into the chapel," Colin advised him. "You listen there, and then Montigny will come and take your place."

"And if anyone comes?"

"Let him come in," said Colin, "and kill him."

François did not dispute the order. As soon as he received a command, he yielded. Moreover at such an hour there was little probability of his having to intervene thus, for he was set around by a compact silence, and nothing gave the slightest sign of the presence of Colin and his accomplices in the recesses of the sacristy. He himself, behind the door, had no clear impression of

(a) The Portail of the College of Navarre. From Beguillet's History of Paris

(b) The College of Navarre. From a plan by Truschet and Hoyau, circa *1551*

being there at all. He could vaguely distinguish stalls and benches, steps, stained-glass windows, and gilded grilles, and, all along the pillars, a series of resplendent stations of the cross.

"The clock is going to strike," thought François. It struck eleven. He counted the strokes. They fell and re-echoed in the court of the college. At last Régnier appeared.

"How are you getting on?" asked Villon. "Has he opened it yet?"

"Not yet," said Régnier. "The locks are holding."

"And Colin?"

"He is trying his hand."

And sure enough, when François approached the two men, they were both occupied, Colin sustaining the lid while Petit Jehan, cool and collected, was probing the third of the locks with his hook. This was the one which resisted and gave the most trouble.

"Here —— Steady! Come here," said Colin to François. "Come and lean on this."

And he himself took Petit Jehan's place, thrust in a fresh hook, a very thin one, rejected it, felt with another, and suddenly his features grew lighter.

"No?" asked Petit Jehan.

Colin flickered his eyelids and smiled, and François, feeling the catch of the lock yielding, warned Petit Jehan.

"Go on! Go on!" said the latter to Colin, who was running with sweat. — "Go on! Stick to it!"

"This time!" exclaimed Colin hoarsely. "God above!"

He pushed François aside, opened the coffer, and plunged both his hands into it. He first of all drew out various papers, and then a bag of stout canvas.

"This is for us!" he declared joyously. "By God, we've got it!"

François went to fetch Régnier, and then, crouching on the stone flags, they counted the money. Each of them had a hundred and twenty crowns. It was splendid. One hundred and twenty golden crowns which they carried away, and out of which they decided to pay Tabary and to advance enough for the dinner the next day.

"And the box?" asked François.

Petit Jehan put back the papers which had fallen out of it, and all four of them made off. A few minutes and they were back on the other side of the wall, where Tabary was awaiting them.

"Well?" he asked.

"The cloaks?" said Colin. "Where are the cloaks? Come on, quick! And that rack against the wall, when are you going to get that out of the way?"

"All right — just a minute ——"

"God-damned sluggard!" muttered Colin.

Tabary made haste to obey, removed the rack and carried it into the building in which they had found it. Then he came back with the cloaks and asked timorous questions.

"Nothing there?"

"No business of yours," answered Colin.

"Eh? What's that?"

"No, none of your business."

"All the same," Tabary protested, fearful of not receiving his share, "I've a perfect right to be told."

Colin gripped his knife.

"Right? What right?" he growled.

And coming close to Tabary, his blade held low, he advised him brutally to hold his tongue and follow behind if he had any regard for his throat.

"All right, all right," from Tabary.

On the way, however, Colin handed over to Tabary the sum which he had been promised, and, inviting him to dine with them the next day, he went off abruptly, after bidding each of them to separate for the sake of prudence, and to go home.

Next day was fine. François ate his midday meal at the chaplain's table, and rushed to the Cordeliers in the afternoon, where his mother was looking for him. He showed a gay and lively humour, and, without furnishing any explanations, he spoke of a long journey he was going to undertake during two or three months. The old woman exclaimed aloud, but François, absorbed in his project, let her talk, and that same evening he informed Master Guillaume that he was leaving Paris.

"There's good fortune for you!" exclaimed the chaplain. "You've been up to some foolishness then?"

"Who? I?"

"Yes. Otherwise, why should you be going away?"

François looked at him and shrugged his shoulders. "How do you mean?" he said.

"Then you must be mad!"

"Ha, ha, ha!" laughed François, gasping.

He went upstairs to dress warmly, went out, dined with an excellent appetite, and then exposed his resolution to Régnier.

"Colin's doing the same," answered Régnier. "Are you going off together?"

"Colin?"

"What direction?" asked the last-named, whom François led aside into a corner. "I'm going Orléans way."

"Then we'll go side by side!"

"Where are *you* going?"

"As far as Angers," said the poet mysteriously. "I have another uncle down there, who is an abbé and must have some sort of property. Would you help in case of need?"

"Agreed," Colin nodded.

In the streets and taverns, in the houses where the lights blazed in the windows, and in the churches, which threw out their multi-coloured beams into the darkness of the night, people were staying awake, and from time to time the bells pealed out. A little before midnight they began to chime with short, lively measures. It began to snow. It was Christmas. François and his friends betook themselves to the "Pomme," singing as they went, for they had drunk well, and found amusement in surrounding the girls on their way to mass, who ran to escape them. The sounds of chanting, the celestial music, the throbbing of the organs, all gave an air of festivity to the Cité, and the mighty voice of the cathedral's great bell raised its sonorous tones over all these various noises.

"Farewell! Farewell!" François answered it.

Never had he felt himself in a more jaunty humour. He spoke to people and to objects, saluted, tossed off snatches of verse, picked them up again, imprinted a rhythm on them, and when someone was astonished at his retaining this playfulness, he answered: "Well, why not? Is it not natural that on the eve of departure I should write my testament?"

"Ho, ho, ho!" laughed Petit Jehan, "his testament! Don't forget me in it, eh?"

"Listen:

> " *L'an quatre cens cinquante six*
> *Je, Françoys Villon, escollier,*
> *Considérant, de sens rassis,*
> *Le frain aux dents, franc au collier,*
> *Qu'on doit ses œuvres conseiller . . .*"

"And then," asked Colin, as Villon stopped short. "*Qu'on doit ses œuvres conseiller* ——"

"Bah! I've lost it —" said François.

He continued, leaving the stanza unfinished:

> " *En ce temps que j'ay dit devant,*
> *Sur le Noël, morte saison*
> *Que les loups se vivent de vent*

> *Et qu'on se tient en sa maison,*
> *Pour le frimas, près du tison:*
> *Me vint ung vouloir de brisier*
> *La très amoureuse prison*
> *Qui souloit mon cuer debrisier."*

Petit Jehan opened his eyes wide.

"What are you saying?" he said; "keeping in one's house, eh? You're outside — as for your heart ——"

"How?"

"Oh, to hell!" muttered the picklock. "Let's go in here and have some drink: that's better."

He belched prodigiously and pushed open the door of the "Pomme" with his shoulder. He entered the room first, and there, tolerably drunk, he danced a clod-hopping step in front of the serving-wench as he called for wine.

All night long François dreamed and pondered, counting sometimes on his fingers, and thinking of nothing but his testament. But still, he did not neglect to drink, and then, turning towards Régnier, he recited to him five or six verses in succession, laughed, and plunged into his meditations again, counting once more, and gazing at Petit Jehan.

"What are you going to leave me?" asked the latter at last.

"Nothing," said François.

"And *me?*"

"First of all," spoke the poet to his friend Régnier:

> " *Premièrement au nom du Père*
> *Du Filz et du Saint-Esperit*

Et de sa glorieuse Mère
Par qui grâce rien ne périt,
Je laisse, de par Dieu, mon bruit
A maistre Guillaume Villon
Qui en l'onneur de son nom bruit
Mes tentes et mon pavillon.

Item, je laisse à ce noble homme
Régnier de Montigny, troys chiens. . . ."

"Dogs? To run?" asked Régnier.

All around them, drawn together out of curiosity, the customers of the "Pomme" were making merry over the burlesque legacy, and now one and now another asked what François would give them.

Jehan le Loup, the sergeant and his thieving companion, Casin Cholet, who helped him to rob hen-roosts on the evening rounds, called out to him: "We're here, François! Look — François, we want ——"

"Oh, yes! *Item,*" recited the poet in loud tones:

"*Au Loup et à Cholet*
Je laisse à la fois ung canart
Prins sur les murs comme on soulait
Envers les fossez, sur le tart,
Et à chascun un grand tabart
De cordelier jusques aux piez,
Busche, charbon, et poix au lart,
Et mes houseaulx sans avantpiez."

There was a general uproar.

"A duck! Yes, yes! Long live François Villon! Quack! Quack! Quack! Aha! they can't deny it! That's right — a duck!"

III

"No," declared Jehan le Loup, "a duck isn't enough. You're stingy with your property. Now look here, it would be better ——"

And drawing from beneath the top of his breeches a goose, in all its feathers, he flung it down on the table, with a laugh, and told the story:

"She was passing within an arm's length. So I just caught hold of her. Take her, François. She's yours."

The goose had to be properly washed down. Tankards by the dozen, filled by the landlord in person, and joyously offered, were brought up from the cellar. They were drained. Others were duly filled, and while François, surrounded and feasted, was wildly scattering riches seasoned with his wit and energy, the dawn appeared, a livid point, in the window-panes.

"Ho, there!" cried one reveller suddenly as he saw it. "They've sounded the trumpets for the watch up at the Louvre. Here's the new day!"

"And all the gentlemen of the town coming back," said a servant-girl, three-quarters asleep.

Between the black houses with their snow-covered roofs, a blue and icy mist was filling the narrow streets and lanes. The bells ringing for prime flung forth their summons. François stood up.

"Take away the goose with you," said Colin, "and make ready. I shall come for you before noon."

"Right," answered François.

He went off with a lively step, escorted by Petit Jehan, who hammered at the walls, and by Tabary, who

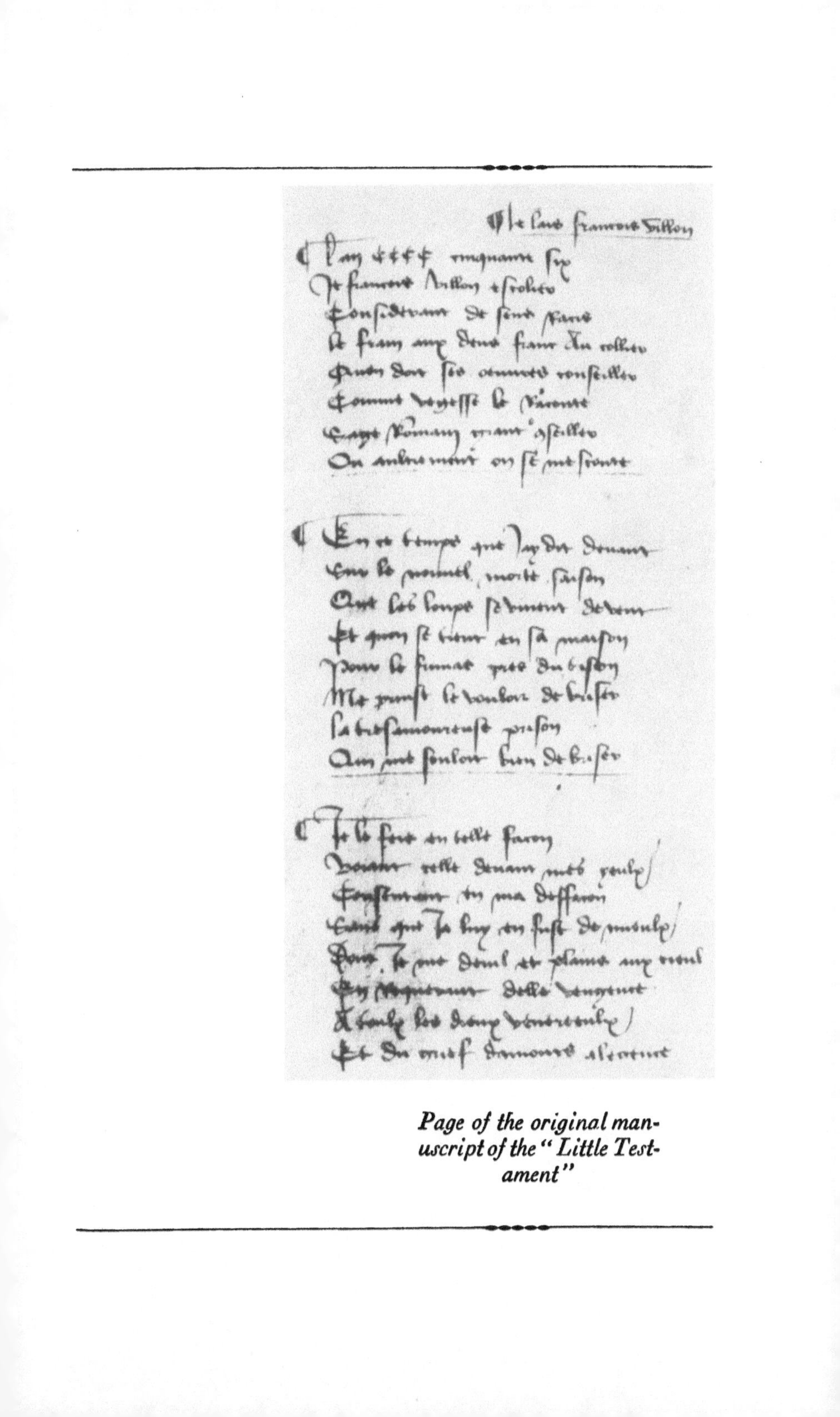

Page of the original manuscript of the "Little Testament"

had not opened his mouth the whole evening through and was watching him, and by five or six others. He bade them farewell and reached his room. And there, recalling his legacies, he straightway took a pen, sat down at the table, and for three long hours he covered sheet after sheet of paper with his small clear handwriting, round and close-set, and then read it through, leaning his brow in his hand. But the conclusion of the poem was missing. He had before him only about thirty stanzas, in which, for pleasantry, the names of the most diverse persons figured in association with the most ridiculous gifts, when suddenly, to round off this clowning catalogue with a comical stroke, he followed it up with:

Finblement, en escripvant,
Ce soir, seulet, estant en bonne,
Dictant ces laiz et descripvant,
J'oïs la cloche de Serbonne,
Qui tousjours à neuf heures sonne. . .

"There!" he said to himself, amused. "They'll be mistaken about that. — That's good."

And catching sight of his great dusty tomes ranged there on the dresser, he continued, gasping with laughter:

Ce faisant, je m'entroublié
Non pas par force de vin boire,
Mon esperit comme lié,
Lors je sentis dame Mémoire
Reprendre et mettre en son aumoire
Ses espèces collatérales,

> *Oppinative, faulce, et voire*
> *Et autres intellectualls . . .*

until, with a very dignified air he concluded the whole, like some foolish scrivener, with:

> *Fait au temps de ladite date*
> *Par le bien renommé Villon.*

He made a fair copy, and then, down there under the window, Colin arrived to fetch him. He called for him as he walked through the snow: "Hi! François! François! François!'

15

Forth from Paris they took the road, accompanied for part of the first mile by Régnier. And then the latter wished them luck, and François entrusted him with the copy of his *Lais* to have a few copies transcribed by Tabary, embraced him, and rejoined Colin. An icy-cold north wind was blowing, whirling up clouds of snow, and when it fell, there was nothing to be seen on every hand but the gleaming white expanse under a low and leaden sky, over which moved the flying squadrons of the crows. Pedlars and humble folk passed along, in bands of eight or ten, with thick fur caps on their heads, some of them leading a donkey laden with the baggage, others stooping their bent backs under burdens and slipping at almost every step they took. Colin went forward without a word. He helped himself as he walked with a cudgel, and François, who also had a staff, smote the ground with it merrily and whistled shrilly between his teeth.

At Bourg-la-Reine they made a loop to the right in their course, to avoid the house of Perrot Girard, which, since the notorious affair of the Coquillards, was like a sort of mousetrap, and they resumed their proper way only after long struggling in the snow. Towards evening, having eaten nothing and having exchanged perhaps not more than a score of words, Colin entered a way-side inn with François, and they bartered the goose for a meal and a cover in the barn.

"Where do you keep your money?" Colin asked him.

François showed him that he was wearing a belt round his body, into which, on the night of the robbery, he had stitched one hundred crowns. The rest he kept in his purse. Colin approved.

"Don't go boasting your wealth at Orléans," he said then.

François smiled.

"Good," said Colin. "And above all, if anyone asks you any questions about yourself, answer without giving any explanations. They don't have to know where you are going. With all these chatterboxes hanging about the town, you'd soon be put down for what you are, rest assured of that!"

"What chatterboxes?"

"The bishop's," said Colin. "He has the streets and the taverns full of them. He's a swine, is Monsignor Thibault d'Aussigny, and worse perhaps, if what they say is true ——"

"Yes, I've been told about that."

"That he loves men?"

"Exactly."

Colin laughed loudly.

"And when all's said and done, the best thing is not to concern yourself with him overmuch, for sooner or later he'd teach you it and you wouldn't get out of it. . . ."

They arrived on the night of the third day and put up

at a hostelry Colin was acquainted with, where Piez Blans, when he came into the town, had his room, which was reckoned for him at three livres.

"Ho!" said François, "what couldn't one buy at that price?"

"The sergeants!" answered Colin. "On every three livres they get one. So there's nothing to fear. It's worth it, you see."

"And are the girls included in the price?"

"The girls!" said Colin. "You aren't going to set about spending your cash, are you?"

"Do you think so?"

"Wait first till you've seen Piez Blans. He'll get you something in that line, and what's more, through him you can provide yourself with such pedlar's trash at an easy price so as to continue your journey. But in God's name, be prudent!"

Piez Blans, in very truth, was at Orléans at the moment. And they met him in the same hostelry, and so grandly and cleanly clad that François was left breathless at the sight. They dined all three together, drank at their ease, and then, as it was getting late, they sallied forth and went to the place which François desired. It was in a house of worthy and peaceable appearance, where the wenches had each her own lodging, properly kept, warm and comforting, like rich bourgeoises in the absence of their husbands.

"Well," thought François, "here is something not at all displeasing."

III

He chose a fair woman, gentle and a trifle plump, and passed his night in her bed, then the whole of the morning, and then ate his midday meal and went away delighted. It was the first time that so commonplace an adventure had befallen him, and it cost him, all in all, only the money of the room, to within half a livre. In the street he put on a lively pace, visited several taverns, strolled about, and then in the evening he rejoined Colin. This time the latter took him to a shop where he could make a purchase of silks and stuff, laces and pictures, which were wrapped up for him in a bundle such as the pedlars carried.

Outside Colin said to him: "Let's see if you know how to sell something?"

"Bah! I'll try all right," answered François. "I'll be taken for a pedlar, and I thank you for that. You are right. It's the way to go everywhere ——"

"And don't forget to proclaim on the price of foodstuffs, you know, and the bad weather, and so on, eh? Except with customers, you should always make yourself out to be rather poor ——"

"Come on now, no need to be teaching me that," answered the poet to this. "Poor — I've been poor quite enough in my time."

And taking Colin by the arm, he went back towards their hostelry, without knowing exactly any longer whether he was blithe or sorry, and whether life, which had already treated him so scurvily, might not still hold fresh disappointments in store for him.

III

But what was he thinking of! Around them the young girls, the sober citizens, children, and serving-maids were walking and hurrying in every direction, just as in Paris, on any evening in the long rue de la Juiverie.

"Have you no regrets?" the poet said to Colin.

"No."

"Are you going to stay here long?"

"I've spoken to Piez Blans," said Colin, "and he will be taking me away with him in three days' time."

"Where will that be?"

"Oh, along the roads, I suppose! Don't you worry. I've played the game, and lost. So much the worse! The goat browses where she's tethered, and it's all the same to me. Provided I've got a purse with something to jingle inside it" — Colin burst out laughing — "I snap my fingers for the rest ——"

There was a moment's silence.

"And you?" he asked.

"Maybe I'd have need to ask from Angers for you to come, eh?"

"For the uncle?"

"Yes," said François.

That night he went out alone and wandered as chance led him, hugging the walls, and turning round when he happened to meet a woman as he went. A dark desire was tormenting him, and driving him on from street to street in search of he knew not what. Was it perhaps that display of vice which in Paris he had so highly cherished for the assuaging of his basest instincts, against the wasted background of hideous and drab misery, amongst the tables and benches of crude wood? Perhaps too it was that regret for Paris which he had felt but an hour or two ago when he had questioned Colin? But Colin made light of it, whilst he, by this town in which he was merely a passer-by, linked himself up with all that still recalled his tastes to him. It left him with his heart aching and his throat dry, and he went on, picking up a scent sometimes in some villainous alley, a scent with which he was familiar, which he followed up with the true zest of the dissolute. Twenty times, turning the corner of some cluster of houses, he told himself that he must be approaching the places he yearned for, and as many times he found himself, a stranger in a strange land, at the same deserted corners where the melting snow dripped noisily from the roofs on to the window-shutters. At last, shamefacedly, unable to withstand longer, he applied to a drunken man he came upon, and was shown, quite close on his left, certain walls which had been newly rough-cast, whence some rays of light were glittering at the height of the windows.

François was there in one bound, pushed his way into the main room, with a floor of trampled earth and an arched ceiling, and discovered, seated amidst some men, three wretched women, not one of whom stirred.

"I'll get them to rise," the keeper of the house assured him. "Hi there! Berthe! Catault! Perrette! What are you waiting for? It isn't your time yet! Are you coming, Catault? Yes, you!"

She came, went over to François and took her place beside him, and, not knowing what to say, took his hand and asked him if he would stay the night.

"And to drink?" inquired the landlady.

He ordered some Anjou wine, which Catault preferred should be served up in the room. He felt no desire for anything, but nevertheless he pulled himself to his feet, followed the girl, and paid the reckoning. Suddenly he felt himself so far away from everything that he stopped still in front of a large picture fixed to the partition and stood staring at it vacantly.

"It's the girl from Lorraine," said Catault.

François stood back from the picture. It showed Jeanne d'Arc on horseback, in a splendid suit of armour, pointing her sword in the direction of Orléans.

"There are some here who can remember seeing her," Catault went on. "Men and women both. It doesn't make one old: ten years and seven."

"True."

"The landlady, now; you can hear Madam talking of the siege. She hasn't forgotten it. At the time she was a maid, if you can believe her story, and the English took her, it seems, and kept her with them in their camp."

François was silent. He was not listening to what this creature was saying, pouring out water into a basin as she spoke. He wanted to go away, but Catault came up to him and began to caress him.

"What's the matter?" she asked, surprised at his silence. "Do you want to drink?"

Mechanically he drained the glass that she held out to him. And then Catault sat down on the bed and drew him towards her. How odd he was with his sulking airs! Had he anything against her? Yes? No? That was of no importance. She was accustomed to that. She was ready to fall in with everyone's way. And yet he surprised her: he was not like the people from hereabouts. No. So dark and so thin. Ah, he came from Paris? Or further still perhaps, from Flanders? From Spain? What! he wouldn't answer? What a man!

"Stop!" said François. "I don't know."

Whereupon Catault broke into a loud laugh and fell back suddenly, dragging François with her. And though he struggled to free himself, he had none the less to submit to her. For she was practised in her art, and sturdy and firm beneath her clothes, as his taste demanded.

"And now do you know where you come from?" she mocked him as he got down from her bed.

But François set his clothes to rights with never a word, put on his hat, and was at the door with one step. He opened it, went straight across the main room, and set off down the street outside with headlong steps.

He left Orléans behind him towards noon on the next day, after providing himself at a merchant's with a large stock of the picture of Jeanne d'Arc, a woodcut printed in colour. With those which he had in his pack, they formed a small collection which, as he passed through the villages, he pinned on to his coat and displayed to the humble folk.

"Come, look at this 'Last Judgment,'" he would say. "You see Christ holding a flaming sword in his right hand and a lily in the other. I got it in Germany. What? Does Saint Christopher take your fancy more? Or Queen Blanche? Or Héloïse?"

And at the same time, to a plaintive air, he would declaim the lines, pointing to the persons named as the lines came round:

" Où est la très sage Helloïs,
Pour qui fut chastré et puis moyne
Pierre Esbaillart à Saint Denis ? "

"There he is. We see him," answered the worthy folk, dumbfounded by his way of speaking the verses.

But François continued. He asked each if they knew what had become of these great names:

La royne Blanche comme lis
Qui chantoit à voix de seraine,
Et Jehanne la bonne Lorraine
Qu'Englois brûlèrent à Rouan . . .

And in a loud voice he added his cry:

Où sont-ilz, où, Vierge souvraine ?
Mais où sont les neiges d'antan ?

Following the livid floods of the Loire, he made Blois one stage, Tours, and Saumur, and arrived next at Ponts-de-Cé. He had sold hardly anything except some silk to the women, for no one could make head or tail of all these cuts which he offered as he declaimed his ballade.

"And you yourself?" they used to ask. "Can you answer your question?"

"Yes, of course I can." François would reply. "They've been carried away into nothingness."

And the people crossed themselves, whilst he, vexed that no one grasped the sense of his words, gazed at the stupid peasants, and felt himself so lonely in the world that he almost felt tempted to turn on his tracks.

However, he was drawing near now. He covered the distance from Ponts-de-Cé to Angers in a couple of hours. Very soon the heavy towers of the château and the spires of the churches rose into view, and then, at the foot of the fortifications, the sheet of water spread over the meadows by the overflowing stream of the Maine. As he was quickening his pace, he suddenly heard two men talking to each other in thieves' cant. He observed them for a moment or two, and then, using the same language, asked them if they had lived in Angers.

"Who may you be, first of all?" they asked him.

François gave them a name that was not his own, and told them that, being one of the Coquille, he hoped they would take him into the town along with them.

His new companions led him along under the enormous and menacing mass of towers of King René, into a kind of tavern where, at the sight of him, several individuals paused in their dicing and asked for explanations. François provided them without compromising himself too deeply, drank and dined with them, went off to sleep — and changed his lodging the next day, for during the night he had been robbed of his pack, his purse, and his cloak.

"Of course I would choose the most rascally place," he reflected sadly.

But as he was rich, he took it as quits that his friends had fleeced him, discovered a safe hostelry, and prepared to pay the visit to his uncle for which he had come thither.

He thought of the proverbial saying about Angers:

> High towers and low town,
> Rich for a whore, poor for a gown.

And François, the poor scholar, did not doubt it. As he passed musing along the back streets, he noticed brothels by the way, and that restored his good humour. A little further on, in two or three houses, women hailed him, knocking at the window-panes.

"I know where to apply," he thought gladly. "But later: I've plenty of time."

He evoked the recollection of Colin to resist temptation, bought a new cloak, and then repaired to the convent where his uncle dwelt. He introduced himself, spoke for a moment with him, and by his excessively fine manners made so bad an impression that he did not receive a hint of an invitation.

"Oh, we'll see things otherwise yet. A fool! I'm a fool!"

III

For a whole month he lived at his ease, undoing the gold crowns stitched in his belt, and scattering them to the wind. A vagabond scholar relieved him of eighteen livres, the wenches of more than thrice the sum. In the end he was beguiled by a shopwoman who cost him so much that he had to be careful and calculate the sum still remaining to him. Thanks be to God! It was still enough for him to go on living this life for a long time yet, and he therefore composed some verses in which, careless of the morrow, he gave rein to his free fancy.

This town was pleasing to him. It was in a state of high animation from the presence of King René, who had come to settle there after the loss of his Kingdom of Naples. François counted neither hours nor coins. In the taverns he became friendly with scholars who, themselves rhyming after the manner of the prince, made him repeat his poems. In a short time this became known. The poet received a command to the château itself, and there, amongst little panelled rooms laid with carpets, carved galleries, corners with the walls covered with tapestries, musical instruments, Turkish quivers, clocks, brass plates, and precious stuffs, he saw the King's chamberlain, who conducted him before his lord.

King René was a robust man with shaven face, short nose, a prominent chin, and small lively eyes. He bade Villon welcome, listened to his reciting, and complimented him. But Villon protested that compared with the King's verses his own were tawdry stuff, and begged him to believe him that he knew them by heart. Whereupon he repeated that pleasing piece, *Regnault et Jehanneton,* in which King René, full of his love for his second wife, called her "sweet shepherdess," and sang the springtime, the fresh grass, the budding flowers, depicting himself gracefully in the guise of a shepherd.

"Do not be too flattering," he was told one day by Jean de Beauveau, who had made a friend of him, and, through his high episcopal functions, kept him in favour. "It would not be forgiven you."

"But I am perfectly sincere," answered François.

"Then be a little less so. '*Il n'est trésor* ——'"

Villon blushed. How could he have claimed that he really liked those over-sweet pastorals when, in direct counter to them, he himself had just written:

Sur mol duvet assis, ung gras chanoine,
Lez ung brasier, en chambre bien natée,
A son côsté gisant dame Sidoine,
Blanche, tendre, polie et attintée,
Boire ypocras, à jour et à nyutée,
Rire, jouer, mignonner et baisier,
Et nu à nu, pour mieulx des corps s'aisier,
Les vy tous deux, par un trou de mortaise:
Lors je congneus que, pour deuil appaisier,
Il n'est trésor que de vivre à son aise.

Did Jean de Beauveau, then, know these verses? No doubt he did. He appeared to know much else, for he smiled and murmured: "Come, come, Master François Villon, he who can do the most can do the least."

"I shall bear your words in mind," said François simply.

III

A few days after this, as he was playing knucklebones in a bawdy-house, a man came and asked for him on behalf of Colin.

"Yes," said Villon, rising and going out with him. "What's the matter?"

"The matter," said the man, in thieves' jargon, "is that the business at the Collège de Navarre has been blabbed."

"Since when?"

"A week or two back. Colin heard of it from Régnier."

"And Régnier?"

"Nothing. Colin bade me tell you," the man went on, "that he is at Montpipeau, hard by Meung. In case you might be in need of him."

"Thanks," breathed François.

He came back in ill humour to his game, lost, won, lost again, and then suddenly and quietly went away, his mind made up, passed the Saint-Michel gate without making pretence of anything, and reached the open country.

The news had struck him hard. But how? Had anyone been talking? François did not know what to say. He sought for explanations, and asked himself scores of questions. Tabary? Oh, no! And yet, if anyone had told the story of the Collège de Navarre, it could only be Tabary, the devil! What an adventure! And now what was to be done? Where was he to go? To Montpipeau? At first François took that into his head, and then set it aside. In these fields he was lost. On the right he discovered vines; on the left, great stretches of tilled land, woods, a road. — He made over towards the road, and struck it: it was only a by-road, and suddenly, after some straw-ricks, it divided into several ill-defined tracks which could not lead anywhere. Should he turn back? Well, he would have to, but darkness was coming on and a thin drizzle was falling which soaked François to the skin, and that was the last straw. Nevertheless, on he walked, bearing this time to the right, towards the vines, for they were on higher ground, and from here he could take his direction. How stupid not to have thought of that sooner! Stupid enough to eat hay! Stupid enough to let himself be caught, yes, he too, like the other, that Tabary, that more than stupid, that ——

"No, no! Not yet!" he growled. "Not too fast! Look out! The moment I was warned ——"

And he halted, for it was so dark that he could hardly see now, peering to see whether some lamps were going to be lit and, from far away, give him a direction.

16

François would willingly have rested at Saumur, but he remembered that two years earlier they had seized some of the Coquillards there, and the reflection lent further strength to his legs. He held straight on his way, bought some dripping and black bread at a farm, devoured them, swallowed a mouthful of wine, and set off again. But not knowing exactly where he was going, he sat down on the edge of a steep bank. The sun, already hot, was shining brilliantly. The earth exhaled a steamy mist which quivered on the line of the horizon, away beyond the coarsely drawn line of the tillage. The air was soft. In the damp grass, here and there, thousands of tiny spiders ran hither and thither, and the crows flapped across the fields, or else, standing motionless, preened their feathers with their beaks, making them glisten, pecking the insects from them.

"Shall I go and find Colin?" Villon wondered.

He hesitated and then came to the opinion that it was better for him to risk his luck alone and to part once and for all with his old friends. What had he been brought to by believing them and helping them in their guilty concerns? To wandering on the high roads, as he was this very day, to flight, to constant apprehension wherever he might be. His drenched and mud-stained clothes made him feel ashamed. He had pains in every limb of his body. He was weary and broken, and the solitude in which he sadly foresaw he must needs live, became hateful to him and drove him to despair.

Some mercers were passing by at that moment, in a band, and they decided him. He was allowed to join company with them, and then, having learnt at a halt that they were bound for Niort, he declared that he too was going to that town, but that on the previous night he had been robbed of the very wonderful pictures which he had been selling on the way. These men let him have his say, but they were mistrustful, and in the end parted company with him. François cared not a whit. On the following days he kept company with pilgrims, with monks, and with townsmen, who, without forbidding him to walk behind them, nevertheless rose early the next day and set off the first. He inspired confidence in nobody. His mien, his looks, his silences, or else, when he tried to engage in conversation, his Parisian accent, had the instant effect of making them quicken their pace, and even, if he persisted, of making them ask him to remove himself. Every time, for all his attempts, it was the same brutal result. Why should he tell a tale of his being a Master of Arts? So much the better: they weren't going to contradict him. As for the rest — "God keep you!" And steps were quickened.

The end of it was that François, rebuffed by all these simpletons, amongst whom he had hoped to find distraction during his long and tedious journey, shut himself up within his own thoughts. And so discomfited did he feel thereby that he began to rhyme verses for his own benefit and to recite them in the jargon of the Coquillards.

" Spelicans
Qui en tous temps,
Avancez dedans le pogois,"

he hummed, walking along to the beat of the measure.

" Gourde piarde
Et sur la tarde
Déboursez les povres nyois
Et pour soustenir vostre pois
Les dupes sone privés de caire
Sans faire haire
Ni hault braire
Mais plantés ils sont comme joncs
Pour les sires qui sont si longs."

"Oho!" said a monk behind him who had heard him murmuring the last lines of the song, and asked: "What are these '*sires*' that are so long?"

"Go on ahead and don't interrupt me," said Villon.

And as the monk opened his eyes wide as saucers, he went on, but in a louder voice:

" Souvent aux arques
A leur marques
Se laissent tous jours desbouser . . ."

"I'll see you later," said the monk. "And you'll teach me all right!"

Villon paid no heed. He did not even notice the other outdistancing him. But in the evening, as he reached Saint-Generou, he caught sight of him waiting for his arrival with an armed man stationed in the midst of the way, and a crowd of men gathered in front of the gates.

"Devil take him!" grumbled François, stopping. "Is that for me?"

He drew back, jumped suddenly through the hedge, crouched in there, listening, and then, as everybody ran towards him with shouts, he took to the open country and made a rapid escape. Barely troubled by stoutness, he made a wide circuit of Saint-Generou, stooping as he ran so as not to be visible, and kept on the run until nightfall and darkness, like a hunted animal.

This annoying incident prevented him, at Niort, from admiring the town and staying there too long. And yet it was chock-a-block with jugglers and mountebanks, pedlars and merchants, who were arriving on horse and on foot for the fair, and creating a great stir in the place. François did not persist. He furnished himself with a number of pictures and small objects for sale as he had done at Orléans, and, over new roads, continued to wander this way and that, traversing the region in every direction, so much so that instead of gaining money he found himself, when winter arrived, almost penniless.

"But who's taken it from me?" he asked himself in consternation.

It was he himself. He had lost it by not having the knack of selling, by letting himself be talked round, by offering gifts of laces to the girls or pictures to the children, and carrying the rest into taverns. What could he do? Money burned holes in his pockets. Even when it was stitched up, he had spent it. And here was a pretty result! To keep himself alive, François had to part with his cloak for a ridiculous sum, although he would have needed it, and then, not knowing what to put his hand to, he held on in the Blois direction, on the short grey days, with the wind tearing the clouds apart and whipping up the even surface of the river like the plumage of a pullet's tail.

He had one hope, and one only: to make an appeal at Blois to Charles d'Orléans, the duke, and win his favour with some piece of verse rhymed for his special benefit. And his hope gave him courage, for Charles was a lover of poetry, and himself practised the art so brilliantly that he was deemed, and not by any false right, the chief poet of all France. In his castle, amid the court whose stipends he paid, this man of sixty-three lived wisely and well, turning grey now and hard of hearing, and clad always in a fur-lined gown of black velvet. He divided his days between the chase, reading, chess, and agreeable discussions in the course of which, on a given subject, everyone had to pay a sacrifice to the Muses, and then hear himself praised or criticized as he had deserved. Why should not François have taken part in these debates? He was no clumsier than another. As for bearing himself well in so noble an assemblage, he had given evidence of that only recently at Angers;

and he had no doubt that, once presented to the Duke's presence, he would at once obtain something to help him in his hour of need.

His arrival at Blois on the very day when the Duke was overjoyed at the good fortune of the birth of a daughter gave François further encouragement in his plans. He composed a long poem for the occasion, had it presented, and awaited an answer. He received three crowns, and also an invitation to appear before Charles d'Orléans, who wished to see him, on the following day.

"I'm playing luck," said Villon to himself.

And luck smiled at him. François was received by the Duke, who treated him with the utmost attention, inquiring as to his work and his life, his poems, and the reasons that brought him to Blois, and proposed that as he was in the town he should be lodged in the castle. François was at no pains to refuse. His name was inscribed in a register, and Charles d'Orléans marked with his own hand in the margin the payment that was to be made to him.

"Do not thank me," he said gently to the poet, "and in my house consider yourself at home. It is the least I can ask."

"But it is also more than ever I expected!" exclaimed François.

He bowed low. Then, led by his patron into a large hall where people were waiting, he was presented to them as he had never been to anyone, and recommended to them in such terms that he found himself immediately the centre of them all.

"And you come from Paris, in good earnest?" asked one of them.

It was Fredet, a small round chatterbox of a man, who cloaked an invariable perfidy beneath his affable exterior.

"Oh, yes, I do —" answered François.

"And tell me," squeaked Master Astesan, who had just lately set down his name in the register of payments, "do you know the Duke?"

"I know him by his verses, which I admire," said François in all sincerity. "As for the man himself ——"

"The man is as good as the poet," declared Master Astesan with a dignified air. "And tell me —" he went on.

But François, fired upon from every hand, did not hear the new question that was put to him.

"You'll help me through, won't you?" he thought it wise to whisper to Fredet when the bell for dinner rang out. "I depend on you."

Fredet took his arm.

"Come along," he murmured. "I'll tell you what's what, for, look you" — he lowered his voice still further — "we are in the midst of monsters here ——"

"How?"

"Monsters and nullities," said Fredet. "The Duke has a queer trick of welcoming beneath his roof the first wretched rhymster who may come along, and imposing him on us. At first he will swear by nobody but by him. But you'll see! He quickly grows tired."

"But of whom are you complaining?" retorted François with some vexation. "You have had your day."

Fredet looked at him.

"Excuse me," he said, freeing himself. "Someone is calling me. Yes, yes — I'm coming, I'm coming ——"

"Go to the devil!" swore François.

And as Master Astesan drew near, he leaned towards him and solemnly mimicked his stupid and pretentious air.

"Tell me —" he began.

Astesan stopped him, seeing that he was being made fun of.

"You are wrong, young man," he said. "Have patience for a few days; we shall speak of this again."

These few days left François stupefied. Never in his life had he met so many poets, never had he had so many to judge. They were all jealous of each other, quick to take offence, full of gall, and vain as peacocks, for all their airs of subtlety. There was none among them so jealous as Fredet in attracting the Duke's attention to himself. Whenever the noble patron showed interest in one of his colleagues, Fredet would declaim very loudly in order to conceal his spite, or else leave the hall with endless grimaces. Yet he was not devoid of talent, and hearing him recite his verses, François was surprised at the turn he gave them. This small, well-fed man, quarrelsome, touchy, and garrulous, had a striking fineness of wit, a delightful gift of expression, and vivacity, colour, and rhythm. François could not but say so. The same morning, however, thanks to Fredet's having promised to rouse him and failing to turn up, François missed hearing mass at the chapel, and the Duke had noticed it. Bah! — he thought no more of it. He had forgotten about it. And yet when François in his turn had to rise and recite some or other of his ballades, Fredet displayed no sign of enthusiasm. So much the worse! What did it matter? He was at liberty not to appreciate his verses, to find him detestable, or common, or gross.

This was precisely Fredet's opinion, and he was about to communicate it in a whisper to his neighbours when the Duke Charles took François by the arm and went out with him. What an occasion for scandal! It was not only Fredet — all were dumbfounded, and there were murmurings. Master Astesan scolded. What? Eh? He could not make it out. It passed all understanding.

"His Grace is too good, too courteous," said Fredet acidly. "After all, he cannot like these verses."

"Exactly, exactly!" breathed Master Astesan. "You share my opinion there?"

"The rhyming is flat and unmusical to the ear," Fredet went on.

"And what carelessness of construction!"

"Yes!"

"What a trivial and displeasing tone in them!"

III

"Tell me," continued Master Astesan, gathering strength, "where can you find in his ballade —"

But François came back. He perceived that they were talking about him, but feigned to notice nothing, and came forward towards Fredet, who turned his back on him.

"Oh, as you please," said the poet gaily.

Then, seeing that the others were avoiding him, he sat down, contemplated them for a moment in silence, and then, amused at their expressions, he suddenly stood up and went away laughing.

If he had not been so sorely in need of money, Villon would doubtless have cleared out, and turned his back on the Duke and Fredet and Astesan and the castle, with the keenest pleasure. For he was not made for the humour of these gentlemen. But where was he to go? He had no choice. It would have been madness, pure and simple, to leave the warm dwelling at Blois in this winter, when an icy wind was whistling under the doors, freezing the water in the fountains, and covering all the country-side with a heavy layer of snow.

One could live there without fear of the bad weather. One could eat there. One was clothed there. One had wages paid there. No, François was not so foolish as all that. Youth was leaving him. Already, at twenty-six, he no longer had that irresistible impulse to follow his own fancy and nothing else, even if he might come to repent of it. A mischievous fairy, some star, or perhaps some planet of malign influence, had taken upon itself to teach him that to hold a bird in the hand is worth more than letting it go and running risks. He had made the experiment, and that sufficed him.

Nevertheless at the thought of Colin scouring the high roads and Régnier hiding in Paris, as no doubt he must be doing since the disclosure of the robbing of the Collège de Navarre, François felt overcome by frequent bursts of nostalgia. Would his old comrades have accepted this bondage of his? Even if they were destitute of everything and brought at last to bay, would they let themselves be constrained to live between an old man with a mania for verses and fifteen puffed-up and pretentious rhymesters? François did not know. One moment he would think no, and reject the ridiculous idea, for with the passage of time Colin and Régnier had become in his eyes paragons of courage, boldness, and tenacity; and the next moment he would be thinking that if they, like himself, had had the gift of poetry, they would perhaps have followed his lead.

But the idea kept recurring, and the life he led at Blois seemed to him so insipid that instead of making himself agreeable to the Duke by taking part in the contests, he passed whole days in the kitchens, warming himself and drinking deep. That at least had some sense in it. And when he was told that his place was not with the servants and that his wage would be docked, he answered that, weighing carefully his words, he preferred to have his belly rather than his soul in a servants' hall.

"Ha! What impudence!" cried Fredet.

In this way time wore on until the early days of March came round. Then, after the showers falling in the sunshine, the spring brought the buds out everywhere in the park, and at the foot of the trees an abundance of sturdy, stout, flowery grass.

" Le temps a quitté son manteau
De vent, de froidure et de pluye
Et s'est vêtu de broderie " —

thus the courtiers confided in each other, when the Duke could hear them, in ecstasies over the verses of their patron, and rolling expressive eyes.

"Ay," said François, "The roads will be better."

"What is this talk of roads, friend Villon? Do you feel the lack of them?" asked Charles d'Orléans.

"I have long been waiting to know that myself, my lord," he made reply.

"And what have you decided?"

"To go away," said Villon quietly.

The Duke looked at him, pained. He received him that evening in his library, and asked as to the reasons which had brought him to think of departure.

"Nothing," said François. "Wherever I go, I have to move on somewhere else. I come and I go. You must pardon me."

"Perhaps it is on account of the wage which was withheld?" asked the Duke.

François said nothing. He looked steadfastly at this old man sitting shivering in his arm-chair, his feet set on the warming-pan, and smiled. Then he sighed and made a vague gesture.

"I understand you," said Charles affectionately. "As for myself, my life is over ——"

"My lord!"

"No. Do not protest. Over long since, and you must live your own life as it may lead you. When all is said and done, that is only natural. All these people who surround me here, and help to distract me, are not living. You are worth far more. — But all the same," he went on, with a touch of melancholy in his tone, "be on your guard — against yourself."

"Yes, I know," murmured François.

"There's something in you that would bring you so far, so low, that you would never be able to catch hold of yourself again. You see: my information about you is full enough, is it not?"

The next day there took place, in the hall of the contests, a great festivity in honour of François, and Charles, anxious to provide him with an opportunity to shine, proposed that everyone should make a ballade based on the line:

Je meurs de seuf en cousté la fontaine.

François placed himself in the corner of a window, from which he could see, over beyond the trees and alleys of the park, the dim blue horizon, the waters of the Loire, the fields that were just turning green, and the sky. And he turned that line over in his mind. It might have been the device of his own life. The pens squeaked on the paper in the silence. Fredet, his mind racing, kept repeating the measure of the line, beating time with his foot:

"Je — meurs — de — seuf. — Je — meurs . . ."

"What!" exclaimed François to himself in astonishment. "He finds it difficult! The fact is that he lacks for nothing, the poor devil! He's as fat as a swine. And as for perishing of thirst — *he* knows where the wine's kept!"

Master Astesan gnawed his nails, and asked whether it was necessary to keep to general ideas, or whether one could, by some allusion or other, trace a picture of his own particular desires.

"Do as you please," was the answer given him.

Villon gathered his wandering thoughts together. Amongst all these rhymesters, he experienced a fantastic impression which was vexing to him, but in a short time he began to express himself, and his first stanza came to him with the utmost facility. He reflected on the falsity of his existence, on his misfortunes, on the cruel necessity which invariably, at the very moment when he thought himself saved, thrust him down as if for the very pleasure of it; and that gave him light, and guidance, and inspiration.

He rapidly turned his second stanza:

Rien ne m'est seur que la chose incertaine . . .

and then continued, following the idea propounded by the Duke, right on to the envoy, in which, addressing himself to Charles, he seized the occasion of asking back his wage. Then he trimmed certain lines, and corrected others, and waited until the rest of the gathering had finished before presenting his poem.

Then the Duke himself announced his reading. Everyone listened to the insipid stuff of which he was the author. From every side there rose cries of "Excellent! Excellent! How perfect that delicacy! How subtle! Exquisite! What grace! How pretty that is!"

They gobbled their delight like so many turkey-cocks. They clapped their hands. They begged the Duke to read it again. François was dumbfounded. All this nonsense disgusted him, disheartened him, wearied him; it seemed tedious to him; he was greatly afraid that his ballade, kept back till the last, would meet with no success. When that of Master Astesan went straight to the company's heart with great effect, he felt ashamed of human stupidity pushed to such an extent, and then, as the Duke called for silence, François lent his ear and felt himself overcome by stupor.

"Ha!" he grumbled. "No? It isn't possible."

Fredet assumed his proudest air. He had gently closed his eyes, and let himself sway to the rhythm of his lines, revelling in them as in some godlike delight.

"My turn," said Villon suddenly, whilst all around him the incense of praise was still being raised for the plump poet, and exclamations poured forth. "Look out! This is a change!"

"Listen, then! Listen!" someone threw out.

Je meurs de seuf auprès de la fontaine
Chault comme feu et tremble dent à dent;
En mon païs, suis en terre loingtaine;
Lez ung brasier frissonne tout ardent;
Nu comme ung ver, vestu en président;
Je ris en pleurs . . .

There was a low murmur of approbation. They turned and looked at François.

. . . et attens sans espoir;
Confort reprens en triste désespoir;
Je m'esjouys et n'ay plaisir aucun;
Puissant je suis sans force et sans povoir,
Bien recueully, débouté de chascun.

"These lines are admirable," said the Duke slowly.

Fredet coughed. The Duke continued the reading, and at the end of each stanza he stopped, observed the effect it had produced in the hall, and then went on. And François, surprised that they should listen without laughing or making fun of him, gave a sigh of relief.

But the Duke reached the envoy, and François was expectant as he came to that touch:

Que sais-je plus? Quoi? Les gaiges ravoir.

He had apprehensions, for Fredet made an exclamation, and said as if in indignation: "Listen to that! To have the wage back, indeed! There — that spoils the whole thing!"

"I do not share that opinion," replied the Duke drily. "François Villon would show you how to set about it."

And then, with these words, he went over to the poet,

and seizing his hand he added: "Leave Fredet to his own ill humour. It is only too legitimate."

"Oh, my lord!" Fredet tried to protest. "Were you not shocked? Not at all?"

"In no way."

"But — but these wages!"

"He shall have them," said Charles. "Master Astesan! Well — Master Astesan — these wages — you shall double them!"

III

17

Of his stay at Blois, Villon preserved only one satisfactory memory: that of the morning when he left the town, with his purse full, setting off with a blithe heart. That dazzled him. He would no longer answer to anybody for his tastes, his whims, his humours, his weaknesses. He felt himself delivered from the Fredets and the Astesans, and from the Duke himself, whose mania for verses and versifying had almost disgusted him with his vocation of poet. — And his folly, which he had repressed too long, filled him with jubilation to overflowing. No. If it was like a chained dog that he would have to gnaw his bone, then he preferred to do without it and to pull his belt tighter round his belly. And what matter? He was accustomed to that, and what was more, he was hampered neither by scruples of conscience nor by stoutness of body.

Once over the Loire, he went up it along the other bank, bore over to the right, plunged deep into the open country, and kept straight on. On the fourth morning he caught sight across the fields of the tall spire of the cathedral of Bourges. It stood out, afar off, against a milky white sky. The road rolled out its ribbon between the fields of fresh corn, the meadows watered by scores of trenches, the hedges and bushes; it was lost for a while and then climbed towards the surrounding walls of the town with their massive towers, and disappeared into it. François remained at Bourges for five days, spent some of his money prudently, earned some more by reciting his verses in taverns, and pursued his way with a contented heart. The summer found him at Nevers, selling pictures to the girls, and this time making them pay with silk and stuffs, and he also sold his poems. He made copies of them for a couple of sous, taught how they should be spoken, and then set off again without any precisely planned route. On his back he carried a pack like the pedlars, undoing it in the wayside inns, and showing off his stock-in-trade; and sometimes, when no one had an eye on him, he seized the opportunity and made off with something.

After the summer, as the vintage season came on, François proceeded along the Saône as far as Lyons, and then along the Rhone as far as Vienne. Then, satisfied with his commerce, he turned on his tracks, struck slantingly across the hills to his left, lost himself, covered an immense distance, and arrived in the end on the Loire just above Sully. The country-side pleased him. He followed the fairs with the Cheap Jacks, the jugglers, the sharpers, the tooth-pullers, and other more or less picturesque characters who drew him along with them as they went and found amusement in his songs. All winter he was to be seen on the high roads, often weary when he was hungry, and often full of spirit and pleasing humour when he had drunk too much. His pack scarcely contained any stuffs now, or silks, or lace, but it held hens and ducks which he had nabbed at night, and then wrung their necks, or hams, or even rabbit-skins. A very queer pedlar, this François Villon! And how carefully he avoided any worthy folk who asked him of an evening to open his pack and display his wares! He answered that he had sold out the whole lot to some rich gentleman, or perhaps he burst into laughter; and then when one of the customers led him over into the corner and asked him in the greatest secrecy the price of his chickens and ducks, François joined him in the stable and made arrangements that suited everybody.

None the less, this existence became stale to the poet's taste, and he was filled with a deep contempt for all these vagabonds who at first had fascinated him and now interested him no longer. Was he going to wander for ever with them from fair to fair, amusing himself and compromising himself? It would have been ludicrous. Here he was, fleeing Paris in fear of the Châtelet, and yet exposing himself here to even graver dangers. Really, he must be mad! The veriest trifle, some mistaken action, a word too much, and the prison doors would be opening in front of him. Heavens above! François Villon felt afraid. In these regions, where he knew nobody to whom he could have appealed, he felt himself already marked down for the hangman, and dragged, barefoot and with the rope round his neck, despite all his excuses, towards the gallows. That terrified him. He abandoned his companions, with all their games and habits, avoided the inns, ran to right and to left, and at last, with nothing at all in his possession except a letter of recommendation from Charles d'Orléans to Monsignor Jean de Bourbon, had no real breathing-space until, having gathered some information, he entered the town of Moulins like a hunted creature towards the end of the year 1459.

"Heigh-ho!" he exclaimed. "There we are! I feel better!"

He reached the château, saying, to any who wished to hear, that he arrived from Blois; and he was far from sorry at seeing so pleasant and inviting a city, with its fine high, crenellated walls, its heavy, iron-bound gates, its drawbridge, and its stone houses, with their weathervanes fashioned into coats of arms. Everything was beautiful, everything gave him a feeling of comfort, and everything, even to the motto of the Duke, which was "*Espérance,*" quickened his heart with joy. It was different still when from Jean de Bourbon, who bade him welcome, he received a purse of six crowns. François set no further bounds to his insensate delight: he declared himself the subject of so noble and charitable a man, recalled that, through his father, he was himself of Burgundian origin, and convinced, it may be, that in this country he had only to let himself live, he paid no heed to anything which might have persuaded him otherwise.

But whether at Blois or at Moulins, life in the houses of the great implied certain obligations to which Villon never bowed with a good grace, and he quickly noticed that in place of the Fredets he would have to put up with the Duke's secretary, Jean Robertet, his bailiff, d'Usson, Guillaume Cadier, clerk of the accounts, and various other wits who treated him in a somewhat lofty way.

"Are you the author of a certain ballade which His Grace has from the Duke d'Orléans?" they asked carelessly.

"Yes," answered François.

Jean de Bourbon sang his praises, but, as he was young and devoted himself to nothing except poetry, Villon's shrinking and artful look, his reserve and dissimulation, were displeasing to him, and he neglected him.

"It is going to be necessary for me to think of my wages," said the poet to himself bitterly.

Alas, he would have liked not to think of them all by himself. For after a long month of bad-tempered reflections, he was scarcely one step further advanced. Of the Duke's six crowns none were left in his purse. A tailor had had three of them for clothing him, an innkeeper two others, and the last had gone to a doubtful creature who had taken François's fancy. How was he going to get on at Moulins without any money? The hapless fellow dared not give the question too much thought. He passed whole days in his room, pacing to and fro, dreaming, and racking his brain, and occasionally piecing together a poem to while away the time.

III

And very paltry distractions these were, in Villon's own estimation. Expecting to be able to indulge his appetites as at Blois, he was on the contrary living badly, and forced himself in the evening to capture the attention of the Duke. In his pocket, for the benefit of His Grace, he had a petition in verse, and he was awaiting a favourable moment for reading it.

" Le mien seigneur . . ."

he began in low tones, his eyes fixed on Jean de Bourbon.

" Le mien seigneur et prince redoubté . . ."

But Jean kept talking of hunting and travels, tournaments and love, and the persons of his court did not know what next to invent to flatter him, to give him the opening to reply, to amuse him, to bring laughter to his lips, when François, his patience exhausted, boldly stepped forward and said: "If you permit, I shall recite a ballade."

"What?" said the Duke. "On what subject?"

"Concerning a certain Villon who is desirous to explain his plight to you."

And he read:

" Le mien seigneur et prince redoubté,
Fleuron de lys, royalle géniture,
Françoys Villon, que Travail a dompté
A coups orbes, par force de bature,
Vous supplie par ceste humble escripture
Que lui faciez quelque gracieux prest."

"Ha! I understand!" said the Duke.

After a moment's hesitation François went on:

and while his voice grew firmer, little by little, and as Jean de Bourbon found this singular request for money had in it something of the finest wit, he set forth the whole of his ballade, bowed, and withdrew.

"Where is he?" asked the ladies. "Has he run away?"

The Duke sent for him to be found.

"Master François Villon," he said, "it gives me pleasure, in return for a ballade so skilfully made and so neatly turned, to come to your aid."

"I am put to shame," murmured François.

"Come, come," said the Duke, "forget the past. I am deaf only to bad verses."

And the next day ten crowns were paid to the poet. He was taken aback, counted them, and counted them again, stuffed them into his purse, and then, pirouetting on his heels, he ran to throw himself at his patron's feet to thank him. Jean de Bourbon raised him, and as François caught hold of his hand and kissed it, he gave him a little fillip on his cheek, and asked: "Will you be content here?"

"My lord," answered François, "the crosses the roads are marked with have not the value of those that are stamped on coins!"

"Maybe!"

"No, no," he said, "give me a trial!"

"We shall see," said the Duke, and added: "I know from my cousin Charles d'Orléans that you can be kept through the winter, but in the spring that is not exactly to be counted on."

"That depends."

"In three months, think of that!"

"Bah!" replied François. "But that's true: it will be April."

"And you will be going away."

"The contrary, I am certain."

"Four months, let's say!" exclaimed the Duke.

And when the fine days came, Villon, tired of cooling his heels at Moulins, did indeed set off for Orléans. There he hoped to meet Piez Blans and get news of Colin. Perhaps he might even see Colin and hear from his own lips if he could get back to Paris. The affair of the Collège de Navarre must surely be forgotten after four years. François desired that most ardently. He had exhausted his patience, and the time that had now gone by seemed enough to him to justify his going back to his friends without danger, and his never leaving them again. Had he not been wrong to separate from them in that way? The uncertainty in which he was made him neglectful of all measures of prudence. He was weakening, he was in a hurry to rub elbows with his old comrades, to pick up threads with them once more and share their lot. What had he accomplished during these four years? He saw his spoiled life stretching behind him, and felt for it only a profound disgust. Out of fear of the Coquille he had become a poor wretch, no more than an obscure marauder, or worse, a sort of courtier, a paid rhymester. And that humiliated him; for if ever Colin asked him how he had been making use of his time, he would have nothing to tell of which he could be proud.

But at Orléans, as he went through the gate, François recovered his heart. He went to Piez Blans's tavern, asked about a room, gave a borrowed name, and then, noticing that the landlord of the place was no longer the same, he felt undecided as to what he should do. In the town he was suddenly overcome by fear, startled at the way he was scrutinized. Several times he thought he was being followed, and did not turn his head. And towards the evening, furious at his scanty courage, he betook himself to the address of the woman with whom he had formerly spent the night.

A man came and opened the door to him.

"What may you want?" he asked politely.

Villon beat a retreat, but the man barred his passage.

"Don't run off! What's the matter?"

"I must have made a mistake," stammered Villon.

"But whom do you want to see?"

"No, no — it's nothing."

"Humph," grunted the man. "It would not be the Jacqueline who lived here last winter, would it?"

"I don't know."

"A fair girl," said the man, laughing. "Eh? Yes? Fair and nice — a bit on the strong side. — Yes, yes. Well, you'll have to be told. She's dead."

"And the others?" asked François in spite of himself.

"The others?" And he whistled.

"Gone away?"

"To prison."

"What? To prison? You're joking?"

"Indeed! They had connexions with queer characters, eh? Rogues. Bandits. Great and important bandits. They were all taken."

Villon stared at the man, shook his head with an air of doubt, and then stumbled silently down the stairs and reached the street again.

"God help me!" he sighed, as he passed along beside the row of shops, not noticing that this time he really was being followed. "I've put my head in a hornets' nest and I've got to get it out."

He dined with a poor appetite at the inn, went early to bed, and slept poorly. When morning came, he had decided to clear out, and after paying his reckoning he made off rapidly. His legs trembled. He seemed to be walking on the brink of an abyss. His gaze did not dare to fasten on anyone, and an intolerable buzzing sounded in his ears.

"The best thing would be to get to Montpipeau," he judged.

He knew the direction, and already, without any hesitation, he had reached the postern, when the man who had told him that Jacqueline was dead met him, as if by chance, and went up to him with outstretched hand. But François avoided him, so clumsily that the other, without saying a word, fell into step with him.

III

"Ah! If I escape this time," the poet thought in his fury, "it will be a miracle!"

The man did not leave him. Villon felt that he was behind, and felt also an abject terror going through his limbs. Nevertheless, once past the bridge and the great damp and oozing archway of the towers, in which the country-side beyond seemed as if it were framed, the high road opened out. But this arch had to be passed, and the bridge too. François shuddered. He went forward in the midst of the women carrying their baskets on their heads, and artisans, and peasants leading their hooded carts, when a sergeant, to whom someone had just signalled, stopped him and asked him where he was bound for.

"For Blois," said François.

"Wait," said a voice that froze Villon with fear.

He turned round. It was the man, and he bade the sergeant follow him, and led François off.

"But I don't want to," protested the luckless man. "You have no right. . . . No, no. . . . What have I done? Look here. — Well, answer me, at least. . . . I've not done anything. . . . Where are you taking me anyway?"

The poultry market with its crowds and benches, and the tall building which flanked one whole side with its threatening look, came into view. And Villon understood. He struggled, he beseeched, he cried out, he let himself stumble. He was dragged along as far as the doorway of the prison, and thrust into a low room. And there, as he did not cease to call out, a couple of jailers seized him and battered him with blows.

"Is he quietened down?" one large devil came in and asked.

"Mercy," beseeched François.

"Mercy for what? I have not touched him. The stupid fool! Go on now: forward march!"

He brought him right down into an underground cell, forced him in, and then, from behind the door, gave him warning that he must keep quiet if he did not want another chastisement.

"For pity's sake," groaned the poet. "Oh, have pity! Speak to me! Tell me why I am here. . . . Eh? . . . Yes, why? What have you got against me? What are you going to do with me?"

For three whole days François bemoaned his lot, for he was ignorant of the reason of his being shut up. But when he had been confronted with the companions of Jacqueline, and both women recognized him at once, declaring that they received him with Piez Blans and another fellow, he felt such deep despair in his heart that he thought his last hour had come.

It was June the nineteenth, 1460. On the following day he was interrogated on the statements of the girls and again confronted with them. They held to their declarations, and met his denials with an absolute silence. As he still denied everything, he was put to the torture, and he confessed. It was true: he had spent the night in their house, and Piez Blans had then left him, as well as the others, whom he did not know at all. He wept hot tears as he revealed these things. He asked for pardon, and the clerk, who wrote by the light of a wretched flame, had to pull him up every instant to go slower in order to set down the act of declaration from his dictation. This act was thereupon read out to him, and François had to sign. But he was pressed again concerning Piez Blans, on June the twenty-third and on July the second, until he had told all that he knew about him.

"I am lost," said the poet sorrowfully to himself. "God has forsaken me. They will hang me. I can't do anything. Oh, François, my little François, you aren't going to weigh very much at the end of a rope! Dead or alive, scarcely any heavier — scarcely any wiser ——"

He had atrocious spasms of fear which left him sweating and trembling with fever for whole nights through, or else he called out, dragged himself up and down, rolled on the ground, sobbed aloud, spoke with invisible persons, was carried away with excitement, awaiting the executioner. At certain moments he prayed to Our Lady to help in the hour of his death, and he was visited by a profound calm. At others he broke out into insults, and whenever the sound of footsteps echoed dully along the narrow gallery that led to the dungeons, he cried out in horror: "Is that for me?"

"Yes," answered the jailer one day. "Come, François Villon. You'll be pleased."

III

"In God's name," said François, "do you know it's wrong to mock like that?"

"Well, come along first."

"What do you mean?"

"You are free," said the turnkey. "Duke Charles d'Orléans, his Duchess, and the little Princess Marie arrived here yesterday, and have remitted the sentences in the prisons."

François was overcome by the news. He had to support himself against the wall. And then he followed the jailer in silence, and during the formalities of his being set at liberty he stood there very pale, not certain if he were not dreaming. Outside he saw the town beflagged, and heard the bells, and was carried along by a jocund crowd crying out: "Noël! Noël!" in honour of the Duke Charles. And still numbed with the chill of his cell he found himself in an open square where young girls were throwing flowers, and archers were marshalling the crowds of people who thronged from all directions in the hope of admiring the procession. Until evening François let himself drift along with the crowd, and on several occasions he caught a glimpse of the little Princess Marie, very solemn and clad in a long robe of silk and gold with a train, throwing kisses. She was a child of three. François remembered that she had been born at Blois on the day he arrived there, and reflected that she had twice saved his life. He grew exultant at the idea, danced, called "Noël" with all the others, and confident that Providence was being made manifest to him by the presence of this child, he wrote a poem in her honour, in which he showed his recognition and asked leave to serve her.

"It is to you," he stammered next day as he bowed low before her, "as well as to my lord your most noble father, that I owe my sight of the light of day, and I beseech you to take me into your service, in whatsoever capacity, for you will have no more devoted servant than myself."

"But I would willingly have kept you, friend Villon," said the Duke.

François rose to his feet and said: "I was mad, my lord. I could not rest where I was."

"And now?"

"And now you see how I am," he answered bitterly.

Charles d'Orléans looked at him, shook his head, and, drawing him aside, gave him five crowns. And then, as François thanked him and respectfully inquired as to his decision, he answered gently: "Go to Blois. We shall be there in a week, and then, if I can keep you, I shall, for it is high time!"

18

Two months later it was not, alas, amidst the courtiers of the Duke, still less in his magnificent dwelling at Blois, that Villon savoured the pleasures of life. It was at Meung, in chains, and on the stone floor of a dungeon. He had not been able to withstand temptation, and had fled to Montpipeau, where Colin, who held that region in his hand, had been the first to recognize him. François remembered how this man, rough as he was, had run to meet him as soon as he saw him, and had given him the news of the death of Régnier. The latter, it seemed, had been captured, tried, and hanged, three years ago, and although his sisters had worked to obtain letters of remission for him, they had not been able to save him. Régnier was swinging from the gallows when they presented themselves; or rather, the authorities had hurried on the delivery of Régnier into the hangman's hands, and when the unhappy women returned on the following day and produced their letters, they were told in answer to go to the new Montigny gibbet and see if their brother were there.

"Ha!" exclaimed Colin malignantly. "It's nothing to die: but when you could get out of it, to be hurried off like that, in that dirty way, from behind — by God!"

And François also recalled the manner in which Colin placed his men in the evenings to attack travellers. He had been present at several ambushes, and had himself proposed one night to carry off two corpses behind a low hedge. After that, wandering across the countryside, he had discovered at Baccon, on the Paris road, a church, and had slipped in. — But — heavens above! — how François cursed that church! Without the lure of its chalices and gold vases, its bowls and copes and well-stuffed coffers, he would never have been flung into this dungeon at Meung, nor, doubtless, would Colin have been caught. It was a dire moment for them when they forced that church door, for although François bolted, he had been certain that he would not escape. During a whole week he had fled, with scarcely any idea of where to take refuge in this region so little known to him. Hunted down from all sides, he had taken to the woods, and did not dare to come out of their cover. But one evening, coming upon one of the men with whom he had operated at Baccon, he stopped him and asked the way.

"That way you go to Meung," said the fellow.

"Well?"

"I've just come from there: the bridge is guarded."

"And after Meung?"

"It's Orléans."

François made a grimace.

"Once past the town," went on his informant, "if you look in the direction of the low road running down towards the Loire, there is — the gallows."

"What? The gallows?"

III

"Colin!"

"What do you mean?"

"Oh, it's Colin; I'm sure! You can go and see for yourself. But be careful, if you care for your own neck. Don't stop there."

Villon had tramped as fast as he could towards Meung. As night was falling, he discovered and recognized Colin, shrivelled and black on the gibbet, his neck broken. There he hung motionless, amongst five or six others, his eyes swollen and tumified, his mouth buzzing with flies, his nostrils dilated, and his belly showing swollen beneath the long shirt. François approached him. He spoke to him, as if he could have heard and touched him. And then suddenly he felt himself seized. Two armed men, whom he had not seen coming up, flung him to the ground, bound and gagged him, and dragged him to the castle.

And how often since that tragic hour Villon had again inwardly lived through the moment when Colin had appeared before his eyes! He thought of it unceasingly. He was stricken by a terrible emotion. Colin hanged, Régnier hanged; he was the last of the three, until his turn should come to perish by the rope. It was fate. Every time the door of the cell opened, François stared at the monk who, every two days, brought him a little loaf of bread and a jug of water, and he asked: "Will it be soon?"

But the monk did not answer. Off he went, shutting a second door, away up the staircase of the tower of the prison, and the light which for a moment had filtered down between the walls vanished. Villon began to eat. Crouching on the chains which clasped his ankles, he slowly chewed his black bread, and thought his thoughts.

He was not afraid of dying. He was ready. He thought of his two friends. And yet —— No, no. That was not fear. It was living in this way, in ignorance, which made him sometimes feel perturbation, lose his courage, and call out to the monk that if Monsignor d'Aussigny wanted to wear him down first, he would not succeed. Ah, he knew what sort of man that was! He had been told, an abject being, a monster, a coward; and when the monk on these occasions bade Villon pray to God to be received into His compassion, he retorted: "Compassion indeed! If God did justice in the world, he would begin with your bishop. It is an evil turn that I depend upon him."

And one morning he was led, with thumb-screws on his fingers, into a great hall, where the *officialis* questioned him concerning the affair of the church at Baccon and his share in that enterprise. François answered loyally. But the functionary asked him whether he did not belong to the Coquille band, and so insistently did he deny the accusation that he was urged to tell the truth if he did not want to injure his own case still further. Villon declared that he knew nothing of what they were speaking about.

"Just reflect now," said the *officialis* quietly. "In

your present situation it is no longer of any great importance. Well?"

"No," said François.

"You are wrong," continued Master Étienne Plaisance, still very quietly. "Remember, you can be obliged to speak."

"But I swear to you that ——"

"Do not swear!"

And suddenly changing his tone, he went on: "Yes or no: will you make up your mind?"

François lowered his eyes.

"If it's a question of confessing in accordance with your intentions," he murmured, "I am ready. But of your charity inform me first what I must answer."

"Now you are reasonable," declared the *officialis,* as he drew out from a bundle of papers a certain declaration made at Orléans in July of the previous year, and signed "Villon." "In any case, in connexion with Piez Blans, here named by you" — and he signalled to the torturers to come nearer — "I must know where we could lay hands on him."

"Master!" stammered François.

"Do you not know him?"

"Oh, mercy, mercy!" groaned the wretched Villon. "You are not going to push me to that! I have never met Piez Blans except at Orléans one evening, with Colin. It was in an inn mentioned in that declaration, and then he took us to a house which is likewise mentioned there. — That is all! Oh, oh, I beg you! In God's name, send away those men! I don't know — I can't tell you anything at all ——"

He was on the point of flinging himself at the feet of Master Étienne Plaisance, such was his horror of what was in store for him. But already, at a sign from the functionary, François was brutally seized and laid out on a framework. His arms and legs were bound. He was hoisted up.

"In God's name, Master —" he appealed. "In God's name!"

His frame cracked, stretched out, was drawn longer and longer. He cried out loud. It was abominable. The higher he rose, the more it seemed to him that everything within him was rending and breaking. The muscles — the bones. There was a weight on his feet which held him from beneath, and yet this weight, which no longer touched the ground, rose little by little along with him.

"It hurts me!" he sobbed. "It hurts me! Oh! Oh! Hurts! Help! Help!"

His wrists, attached to the cord which was slowly pulling him upwards, burned as if with fire. He felt his ten fingers swelling as if about to burst, and his head likewise. His head sank between his shoulders, and he had the impression that the blood was flooding it to the point of splitting it. He was choking; a veil floated before his eyes; in his ears a dull hammering that was ever quickening; on his tongue the taste of earth. Did he know? He was howling with the pain, without interruption, in every part of his poor body, hoisted by the pulley, dislocated fibre by fibre and nerve by nerve. He was no more than torture, flesh torn and tried and powdered to its uttermost fragments, terribly, minutely. And he flung out one last atrocious cry, fainted away, and recovered his senses to find himself back in his cell with somebody at his side.

"There — who are you?"

It was the monk.

"I'm thirsty," said François feebly.

He had to drink from the jug, and then, suddenly remembering what had happened, he looked at his hands one after the other for a long moment, felt himself, and, shutting his eyes, fell back upon the straw.

"If you had answered the question of Master Étienne Plaisance, you would have come better out of it," said the monk tranquilly.

"No — leave me ——"

"It was not very serious, however. But look you: they put you to the torture of the pulley, and it will be necessary to start again, because you haven't told anything ——"

"It is cold," whimpered Villon.

"Very well, as you please," scolded the monk. "You'll be left for this week; but after that you'll be taken up again, you see?"

"Go away!" said François. "Go away! Be off with you!"

Two days later, when the monk brought him his

bread and fresh water, Villon abruptly asked him if it was fine weather outside.

"You do better to occupy your mind with Master Étienne Plaisance," advised the monk with a surly air.

"Oh, he'll torture me, no doubt," said François.

"Well, you could avoid it if you chose."

Villon's only reply was to turn against the wall, and counting that he had four days still before his summons to attend the functionary, he told himself that at least he would live till then. Since this great suffering of his a complete reversal of mind had taken place within him. No longer did he think of death. On the contrary, a vague hope sustained him. He thought that by undergoing this examination he would perhaps succeed, from one week to the next, in avoiding the gallows-rope, provided that these gentlemen displayed a certain obstinacy. It would suffice if he did not yield to them, and then, by force of endurance, obtained his liberty from them in order to discover the whereabouts of Piez Blans. Wild ideas vexed his reason and obsessed him, but when he was brought back a second time from the ordeal, the blood was pouring from his ears and nose and mouth, and he thought himself on the verge of death. The third time he remained in a swoon for more than nine hours, alone in the darkness of his frightful dungeon, palsied with fever, his body shattered, half dead. He was no longer recognizable. Stretched out on the stone floor, he wept all night long, full of hatred and despair. But then an end was made of these useless punishments. They seemed to have forgotten him. He was left for five days without nourishment, and without a word of any sort. And he, who was miraculously still alive, thanked heaven for having sustained him. Soon he was but the shadow of himself, but the shadow moved, dragged itself along, breathed. This shadow refused to die. It struggled, it clutched on to life, and when at certain moments he was madly exalted by hope, he exclaimed in a poem:

"Aiez pitié, aiez pitié de moy!"

Never yet, not even at Orléans, where he had known the worst agonies, had he felt more wretched. And yet here, in this underground cell where Master Étienne Plaisance had relegated him in order some day to extract the precious information he was held capable of giving, Villon recovered his mastery. The kind of delirium produced by hunger and fever and privations inspired in him verses which he recited aloud to himself, ten or twenty times on end in order to fix them firmly in his memory. A strange fact. This delirium showed itself in a mocking, capricious, unbridled humour which dictated to him, as answer to the gloomy query:

D'où vient ce mal?

the fanciful answer:

— Il vient de mon maleur.
Quand Saturne me feist mon fardelet
Ces maulx y meist, je le croy.
— C'est foleur;

and his soul was angered, and found expression in that curious debate between spirit and matter, imagined by the poet under the form of a ballade:

Son seigneur es et te tiens son varlet
Voy que Salmon escript en son rolet:
" Homme sage, ce dit-il, a puissance
Sur planetes et sur leur influence."
— Je n'en croy rien; tel qu'ilz m'ont fait seray.
— Que dis-tu?
— Dea! Certes, c'est ma créance.
— Plus ne t'en dis.
— Et je m'en passeray.

The mordant touch, the exactness of the words, the freshness of the retorts, the rhythm, the character — all were there. Everything in the verses bore the mark of François Villon, and sometimes in the midst of his woes he was warned of it, as if by some subtle fire that spread through his veins and tore him away from reality. Yes, it was himself, with no feint and no dissimulation, prompt in repartee, jeering at any advice which might be given him, and invariably replying at the end of each stanza:

Et je m'en passeray!

Nevertheless, was he sure of nothing? The scaffold was awaiting its victim, and François was always brought back to telling himself bitterly that, one day or another, he would have to offer his neck to the hideous noose, and then, thrust forward into space by the hangman's cares, he would have to kick in the air like so many others, jerking there before the final contraction. God above! It was to escape this that he longed above all things! He feared nothing else on a certain morning when he was roused from his rest by the sound of footsteps. He pricked his ears and shuddered. Doors were being opened in neighbouring cells and chains were being loosened. The noises made the hair bristle all over his body, and he knelt down, listening to the coming and going of the monk, who cried out in a loud voice for someone to come forward.

"Make haste!" he grumbled, calling out the prisoners by name and guiding them towards the way out. "Firmin Mahaut! Antoine and Nicolas Camuse! Lemercier!"

François began to moan.

"And you too," the monk said to him, coming into his dungeon. "Up you get! God shows mercy on you!"

"How?"

"He has brought the King of France to Meung."

"King Charles?"

"No, no! Louis the Eleventh," said the monk. "For King Charles is dead and Louis succeeds him. Come along now. Give thanks to Heaven."

François reached the courtyard where the sergeants were marshalling in one corner the hapless wretches thus restored to the light of day. Not daring yet to rejoice too much, they were gazing at each other without exchanging a word.

"God is good!" said one of the prisoners then.

And all together repeated the phrase mechanically,

and then, as the monk had cleared the underground cells and had reappeared, reading over again the list in his hand, they moved forward and lined up awaiting their being set at liberty.

Villon stood in the middle of the courtyard. He was choking for breath. His eyes rested upon two towers, squat and circular, a tall, pointed tower, spiked at its four corners with bell-turrets, the bare walls of the enclosure, the gateway, the drawbridge lowered on the walls of the moat, and one of the sergeants, stupefied at the sight of him, had to go across to him and say: "Well, fellow, what are you waiting for?"

III

19

Thoroughly scared, François set off. It was true. He was free. A letter attesting this fact had been handed to him, and allowed him, without fear of the *officialis*, to proceed, to go slowly forward like an old man along the road, to whimper to himself, to stop and watch the sky and the trees, the thickets and the birds. The weather was fine. A clear autumn sun gilded the branches, gilded too the half-bare tree-tops, and the atmosphere was impregnated with the savour of moss and lichen and mouldering leaves. Sometimes a leaf would come falling down, or perhaps a chestnut would suddenly strike the ground like a stone, and bound up, afar off.

Villon went along beside a wood, passed beyond it; and in the fields he saw the peasants already beginning their toil of tilling. But how ill he was! His wretched feet, bound up and protected by some miserable rags found in a rut, bore him along; but at the cost of what agony! His stiffened joints cracked as they moved. Ay, it was high time for an end to be put to his punishment! What generosity! Three months had passed since he was taken, strong and sound of body, and now he was thrust forth again, worn out, finished, broken down, weak with fever. What was he good for? He was coughing. He felt hot and cold. He sweated. His teeth chattered. And the idea of Paris, which ought to have given him new life, caused him neither joy nor distaste, but struck him solely in terms of the distance he was removed from the city.

However, it was towards Paris that he bent his steps. His sole exertions were painfully directed to that goal, and each new and long day of tramping left him utterly worn out at night with hunger and fatigue. Without the charity of men he would have perished. In such distress was he that even before he held out his hand in the villages, women would often hand him a slice of bread or a small coin, asking where he was going, and shaking their heads.

"You've got a good bit to go yet!" they would think.

Some women of which François asked the way pointed to it with a wave of the hand, in silence, and then stood frightened as they watched him move off, for he alarmed them. At night he slept in barns when he was allowed to, under the porches of houses, in holes that he saw in the hayricks where vagabonds had passed the night. It was warm there, in the straw. François felt unutterably happy in there, and the next morning he woke to the trilling of the lark, took to the road again, and was astonished to feel himself less downcast.

It was Paris, he reflected, that was acting on him. Not a moment went by without his thinking of it as his only refuge; and indeed, little by little, he was regaining his strength. In the course of seven days he traversed a distance which he would never have supposed himself capable of. That restored his high spirits. He smiled to people along the country roads, greeted them, and then, when he had received alms from them, he thanked them and called out: "God preserve you from ever having dealings with my lord d'Aussigny! Mark my words! He would not let you forget it!"

And without any further explanation he held on his way, talking to himself, breaking forth into sighs and groans, and then forgetting suddenly all memories of his woes and reflecting that — God be praised! — they were all over and done with.

"Ha! François, François!" he said to himself. "You're thirty years old, and you're wiser with folly and sin than others are with their book-learning. You are a scholar by experience. Go easy, my friend. Go prudently."

Soliloquizing thus one evening, he felt profound grief at the thought that he was nothing, that he had nothing, that Colin and Régnier were dead. The idea filled him with despair. Without friends what pleasure could henceforth be his? Nay, what reason for going on living? He remembered the gallows at Meung, and Colin with his bloated belly, the dungeon in the keep, the *officialis*, the tortures he had endured. And from deeming his fortune in being still alive a happy one, he fell into the utmost dejection. What was the good of returning to Paris, where the existence which lay before him pained him in prospect? What could he hope for? His uncle would receive him with mixed feelings. His mother, poor old soul, would reproach him with his conduct. She would leave him. Was it worth while hurrying on for their sake? François bemoaned his lot. And what would he be bringing back, after four years' absence? Nothing. Skin and bones. And his skin was cheap enough, too. He would have liked to return with some sort of reputation, if nothing else: but he had not a shred of it, not even in his own eyes. There, alas, was his punishment. All his faults, all his mistakes and weaknesses, rose up before him, accusing him as before some judge, reproaching him for having always yielded to his evil nature. And deep within himself he acknowledged that they were right.

It was then that Villon, to justify himself and to prove that he had not tramped the high roads of the land in vain, had not suffered, loved, wept, groaned, sniffed the rope in vain, to prove that he really deserved forgiveness, conceived the idea of composing a long poem which should excuse his existence. The *Lais* were no more than so much fancy, and probably nobody remembered them.

"I shall do better," he promised himself. "And with my blood and my flesh. Just as I really am, remembering everything, everything ——"

And immediately he began, seeking for the words and the cadence:

En l'an trentiesme de mon aage,
Que toutes mes hontes j'eus beues,
Ne du tout fol, ne du tout sage,

III

Nonobstant maintes peines eues,
Lesquelles j'ay toutes receues
Soubz la main Thibault d'Aussigny . . .
S'evesque il est, seignant les rues,
Qu'il soit le mien, je le regny.

The lines sang, hurrying to his lips, and found their own rhymes. They took on their proper forms in a sudden flight, a measured and calculated flight, as if they had been awaiting this marvellous moment to call out to each other, to answer each other, to feel their heart beat in the realm of dream, and to signal from afar, one to another, that they were akin and knew it.

"Ah!" François went on, "that miserable Thibault!"

Mon seigneur n'est ne mon evesque,
Soubz luy ne tiens, s'il n'est en friche;
Foy ne luy doy, n'hommage avecque,
Je ne suis son serf ne sa biche.
Peu m'a d'une petite miche
Et de froide eau tout ung esté;
Large ou estroit, moult me fut chiche:
Tel luy soit Dieu qu'il m'a esté!

The poem modelled itself, took on bodily form. A secret rhythm flowed through it, like the fresh sound of the sea in the hollow of a shell, and gave it life. And François imprinted it with the subtle movement which he felt quivering in his heart, gave it stress and measure, and then, himself carried along from stanza to stanza by the conception of the whole work, determined its scope and distributed its parts.

III

However, he pursued his way, and, in contrast with that Thibault d'Aussigny who had soused him with cold water in the underground cell at Meung, the image of a drinker, free and full, came into his memory. It was that of Jean Cottard, deceased. François evoked his memory, and exalted it to hold up wine against water, and felt himself suddenly gay at heart once more. But where the devil was he? As far as the eye could see, there stretched an expanse of country-side cut up by small woods, meadows, and tilled land. Evening was coming on. In the hollow a mist was weaving its soft cobwebs, and in the sky a single star, the first of the fine autumn nights, was glittering. Villon quickened his pace. He was merry. He experienced a sense of happy relaxation, and his head was, as it were, slightly on fire.

"I shall write down that beginning shortly," he said to himself. "It isn't bad."

En l'an trentiesme de mon aage
Que toutes mes hontes j'eus beues.

At night he arrived at an inn of no very promising appearance, where he was kept standing before the door because there was a stout nobleman at table, eating amidst his followers.

"Everyone according to his purse," François was forced to note, watching the victuals with an envious eye and sniffing the fumes. "If there's anything left over, my turn will be then. . . ."

In this way he waited without complaining for more

than an hour, and then the innkeeper bundled some bread and dripping and cheese into a bowl and threw it down to him as if to a dog. He insisted on payment and the poet sat down.

"May I have this drop of wine?" he asked, seeing that one of the diners had not finished his glass.

The glass was pushed to him without a single word of answer.

"Thanks, thanks! Many, many thanks!" said François.

What a windfall! It was more than he had hoped for. That wine! That bowlful of scraps! He had had something for his money, and God had not utterly forsaken him. Did not François owe to Him that opening of the poem which he was meditating, here, leaning his elbow on the table, now that he felt his strength returned, and now that a flame was flickering in the lofty fireplace and flinging up its fiery glow on the ceiling? He was a poet, and he could find no more complete satisfaction than in the fine turning of verses. And he was tasting this satisfaction to the very utmost. It was almost as if he were intoxicated by it, although in himself, thinking of this nobleman whose crumbs he had just finished, he reflected that if perhaps the great ones of the earth did not set so great a gulf between their own precious persons and starving vagabonds, the latter would not often be reduced to the use of force for securing their nourishment. An anecdote he had once heard related of Alexander the Great giving succour to a pirate, making an honest man of him by enabling him to live like other men, plunged him into many reflections. He commented upon it in three stanzas, and then, his eyes gleaming in the fire-light, he murmured:

Si Dieu m'eust donné rencontrer
Ung autre piteux Alixandre
Qui m'eust fait en bon eur entrer,
Et lors qui m'eust veu condescendre
A mal, estre ars et mis en cendre
Jugié me feusse de ma voix.
Nécessité fait gens mesprendre
Et faim saillir le loup du bois.

It was true. Having always counted only on chance, and having too often helped chance to deign to succour him, he was not really evil at bottom. Surely not! He sighed. He remembered the days of his youth and the wasted years, the bad company he had kept, which had drawn him into evil courses, and he went on with melancholy:

Je plaings le temps de ma jeunesse,
Ouquel j'ay plus qu'autre gallé
Jusques à l'entrée de vieillesse
Que son partement m'a célé.
Il ne s'en est à pié allé
N'a cheval: hélas! comment don?
Soudainement s'en est vollé
Et ne m'a laissié quelque don.

Allé s'en est, et je demeure,
Povre de sens et de savoir,
Triste, failly, plus noir que meure . . .

III

Yes, and whose fault was it, he asked, that he was left now poor in sense and knowledge, and sorry and derelict? All he could do was to declare the heart-rending result of his countless follies, and to repent them. François had forgotten nothing, but he was not hard of heart, for after a long pause, while his past appeared to him, he went on:

Hé! Dieu, si j'eusse estudié
Ou temps de ma jeunesse folle,
Et à bonnes mœurs dédié,
J'eusse maison et couche molle.
Mais quoy? je fuyoie l'escolle,
Comme fait le mauvais enfant.
En escripvant cette parolle,
A peu que le cuer ne me fent.

He had asked for paper and ink, and, left alone at the table while a servant-woman was clearing, he sat, with his pen squeaking as it ran.

"Enough of that," said the innkeeper. "What are you writing?"

"Nothing," answered François.

"Well, go somewhere else to do it!"

The poet stuffed into his pocket the sheets he had just covered, and rose. He went out, and reached the open country, and there, filled with a great need for relaxation and for filling his lungs full of the pure air, he walked on through part of the night, in a happy shade, set free from bodily weight, light as air, and inspired. Everything had words for him: the obscure expanses alongside the road, the clumps of trees standing slender and erect against the sky, the low tiled roofs gleaming in the milky, gentle, cold light of the moon, and, far above, the swarm of stars filling the heavenly vault, in which one's gaze was lost. François did not know. He listened, and away beyond the black horizon, he plunged so far beyond the realities around him that he heard an inward voice replying to the deep and undisturbed harmony of the universe, and at the same time saw his own vanished and lamented years, and a thousand others too, effaced before his day, scattered, broken into fragments, and for ever destroyed. And then he remembered the ballade which he had made up to sell prints to the peasant folk, and he declaimed it, seized with a great thrill. To the stones and the stars he cried it, as he had done to those creatures, and just as before, nobody breathed a word. Nevertheless it was from the very bottom of his heart, of all his poor fragile self, that he asked:

Dictes moy où, n'en quel pays,
Est Flora, la belle Rommaine,
Archipiades ne Thaïs,
Qui fut sa cousine germaine;
Écho, parlant quant bruyt on maine
Dessus rivière ou sus estan,
Qui beautté ot trop plus qu'humaine,
Mais où sont les neiges d'antan?

Who could tell? Where indeed? In what places? He thought he knew the places, but the voice within him answered "No" when he asked it, and all these things around him, which the moment before had seemed to him to be revealing the mystery of their existence, now turned silent, became deaf, distant, impenetrable. Ah, he was feverish! Why was that? Why did they not make answer? Was it madness? He stopped short, bowed his head, and waited. And then at last, tired out and depressed, he sat down in the shelter of a hedge and fell asleep on a heap of dead leaves, reflecting that they too, for a time, enjoyed some repose, but that to-morrow the wind would send them running as it willed, in fantastic, protesting swirlings.

It was the common lot. He himself, resuming his road at dawn, was chased from point to point — was he not? — by this restless spirit in him which was his undoing. Of course he was! And he could do nothing to help it. He was forced to yield to its most troublesome whims, to leap and run and fall and clamber up again — God knows in what sort of plight as often as not! — and then to leap again, run again, fall again, fall over and over again! Oof! What a wretched business! He was in consternation at the thought, but he reproached himself for tormenting himself in this way, smiled, made a gambol where he stood, and broke into an abrupt and noisy laughter. He had arrived at Chartres.

"Now I am getting on," he said to himself.

Poor devil! At Chartres he was forced to take payment from a public writer to earn a few sous, and this held him for a week in the town. And there in the evening, by ill fortune, he saw girls at their door-steps signing to him to listen to them. In vain did Villon struggle. He was consumed by a mysterious evil, which forced him to slow down his pace and give a shameful answer to those appeals, addressed to the first chance passer-by, and then to tell himself that perhaps, for all his appearance, he was not so displeasing. What was he thinking of! Was he mad? In the end he stopped, and asked of one of these prostitutes whether she would care to have him.

"Oh, come in any time you like!" she chuckled.

He entered. The woman pushed the door to, and Villon looked all round, as if the scene within this room had restored him in a flash to his former exploits. He explained that he was from Paris, and that in Paris he had had his day and was well known.

"I dare say," said his companion. "Have you got any money?"

"Oh, afterwards," he grumbled.

He came nearer and caught hold of the girl, pushing her towards the bed. But she struggled to free herself, and insisted on his paying in advance, for he was hardly one to inspire confidence, with his tattered clothes.

"What! Go to others for that!" exclaimed François.

And then, as the poor creature threatened to call out for help if he did not let her go, he grasped her tighter still, clapped a hand on her mouth, and, heedless of God or devil, set upon the girl until she bit him so that the blood came. He gave a loud cry.

"Now will you stop?" she said to him then. "Brute that you are! Scoundrel! Help! Help! Murder!"

François lifted his arm.

"I'll smash your face in!" he said between his teeth. "You just wait, you whore! You'll know what I am!"

But the girl called out all the more lustily and, slipping from between his arms, opened the door and dashed out headlong, startling everybody as she went. François pursued her. He was in a wild rage, panting and growling, and he was on the point of overtaking the creature, when an individual stepped out suddenly in front of him.

"What do you want with me?" François snapped at him. "That slut!"

"She is mine," said the man.

And backing him into a corner, he brutally gave him several blows, so violent that Villon staggered, struggled to keep his balance, and crashed to the ground half stunned.

"There!" said the man. "Don't you come back here! Take my word for it, you'd best not!"

François did not insist. He raised himself to his feet as best as he could, amidst general laughter. And he took himself off with bowed head, beaten and humiliated; and on the next day, having got the public writer to pay him the minute sum owing to him, he went off without furnishing the slightest explanation.

"God has punished you," he said to himself bitterly. "Ah, François, you are crazy! Old and wretched and made as you are, you should not be playing with girls! You ought to have seen yourself, beforehand! It's all over, you've passed the age."

Stooping and dragging one leg, he walked all day long, irritated, and grumbling obscure words. And from time to time he remembered that from women, except for Margot, he had never received anything but mockery and ill treatment. Marion had laughed at him, in the old days. Catherine had had him beaten. And Marthe, on his return from Bourg-la-Reine, had been at such pains to get rid of him that he had broken his heart over it. What could he do? It was his vice which had brought him such disillusionments. He was too fond of women. All the time they had had an inexplicable power over him. Even the lowest and the most vile he desired with his flesh. He had a need for them. He could not do without them.

"Lord, who am I? Tell me that!" he prayed. "I do not know myself. I suffer and I am ashamed, and yet I must needs offend you."

But these complaints did not appease him, and he saw himself beset by those vices of his which, whatever he might do, had always seduced him and swept him off his feet. There was his gluttony, there was his lying, his violence, his lusts of the flesh, his idleness. In vain did he turn away from them. Here was the voice of Gluttony, saying: "Always you have cherished me as is fitting. Drinking and eating — nay, more than drinking: drunkenness. Remember!" And his Lying spoke:

"I helped you when your uncle asked you where you spent your nights, François, and when you answered your mother's questions. Why reproach me to-day with the services I have rendered you?"

"But I don't know —" protested François. "You took me as a child —— No, no — have mercy!"

"And what of me," said Violence. "I lived in your heart and ran to help you at your slightest summons. Is it not so? When you were spying upon Sermoise in the evenings when you were pursuing Catherine and little Noël Jolis, was I not your friend?"

Villon covered his ears and his eyes. He was silent. He calculated the depth of the abyss of his sins, and then came Lust in her turn, preceded by a thousand smiles, and, appearing on the soft couch of his first mistress, Lust, that nude female body, freely offering itself, quivering with desire, warm, already half a-swoon.

"You have had your joy of me," she sighed with a mournful, satiated air. "Beneath my robe, what joys! What ecstasies upon my lips! Ah! you cannot deny me. I am always the same. Look!"

And she displayed her bosom with its round breasts heaving with her sighs, her strong and lissom waist, her belly with its secret fold, her great thighs ready to hold him still, and the firm white arms, whose embrace was his delight.

"François, I am the chosen queen of all your appetites, the one you rejoice most to celebrate. Come back. Let me console you for your petty chagrins; they are as nothing when I give myself. And you know it. You belong to me!"

The wretched man drew back. He was afraid of this monstrous female, with the whites of her eyes showing, and her narrow, twitching nostrils, her pale and tragic face. She troubled him more deeply than his worst apprehensions, and, stiffening himself against her, he felt as if he were about to die when at last Idleness murmured in her low voice, saying: "Was it not you who slept all day instead of studying, who wandered idly about the streets, who caressed the girls, who woke up yawning in their rooms? Let fools bestir themselves. You have time enough. They make me laugh, all those who never have recourse to me, or who despise me! What wind drives them on? Believe me, nothing will ever be equal to my long hours of rest, my dubious dreams in the mornings, nor yet that pleasure of exhaustion, ever seeking itself, yet never able to find itself."

All his vices at once, like the girls at Margot's long ago crowding round a customer, came calling him and flattering him, and called him and flattered him again. But he refused to see them, to hearken to them. He fled before them. He forced himself to keep them at their proper distance, and as his distraction grew the greater, he prayed to Our Lady to help him to overcome his own weakness, for left to his own resources, he knew that he would be lost.

The further he went, almost at a run now, the more he felt that his strength was giving out. But then he said to himself that he must resist none the less, and he thought of that poor old woman, his mother, with so deep a surge of feeling that he had an instant's respite. He called up the picture of her, a lonely little figure, there, at the Cordeliers, awaiting him with tears in her eyes. He remembered his childhood, and that low and melancholy room in which he had grown up, the street too, and the convent where he had prayed to the Holy Virgin. He felt his heart-strings tighten. He imagined himself a tiny boy, beside that poor woman who had reared him and rocked him to sleep, who had guarded him from the wolves, in that winter of 1438 when all the little children of Paris had the same air of suffering, so universal was the distress. It softened his heart. He would have liked to fall dead there, in his distress, with that picture before his eyes. To die like a man accursed, who had done wrong, who would do it again, forced by a fatality which would not let him go! It was too much. Yes, to die there alone, abandoned by all, hating himself, loathing himself, and at the same time pitying himself so acutely that burning tears poured down his cheeks, so odious did his fate seem to him.

And he was sincere. And he cried thanks to the good and the bad in that cold twilight which, little by little, was creeping over the fields, when suddenly, torn from his agonies by an inexpressible intervention, he raised to Our Lady this prayer, in which his mother seemed to be moaning and borrowing his voice:

Dame des cieulx, régente terrienne,
Emperière des infernaux palus,
Recevez-moy, vostre humble chrestienne,
Que comprinse soye entre vos esleus,
Ce nonobstant qu'oncques rien ne valus.
Les biens de vous, Ma Dame et Ma Maîtresse,
Sont trop plus grans que ne suis pécheresse,
Sans lesquelz biens âme ne peut merir
N'avoir les cieulx, je n'en suis jangleresse.
En ceste foy je vueil vivre et mourir.

A votre Filz, dictes que je suis sienne;
De luy soyent mes péchés absolus:
Pardonnez-moy comme à l'Égipcienne,
Ou comme il feist au clerc Theophilus,
Lequel par vous fut quitte et absolus,
Combien qu'il eust au deable fait promesse.
Preservez-moy, que face jamais ce,
Vierge portant, sans rompure encourir,
Le sacrement qu'on célèbre à la messe.
En ceste foy je vueil vivre et mourir.

Femme je suis povrette et ancïenne,
Qui riens ne sçay; oncques lettres ne leus.
Au moustier voy dont suis paroissienne
Paradis paint, où sont harpes et lus,
Et ung enfer où dampnés sont boullus:
L'ung me fait paour, l'autre joye et liesse.
La joye avoir me fay, haulte Déesse,
A qui pécheurs, doivent tous recourir,
Comblez de foy, sans fainte ne paresse.
En ceste foy je vueil vivre et mourir.

There François lost himself in the immensity of his fervour, and, composing the envoy on the acrostic of his own name, he completed this ballade, the most lovely, perhaps, that he had ever penned:

V ous portastes, digne Vierge, princesse,
I ésus regnant qui n'a ne fin ne cesse.
L e Tout Puissant, prenant nostre foiblesse,
L aissa les cieulx et nous vint secourir,
O ffrit à mort sa très chière jeunesse;
N ostre Seigneur, tel est, tel le confesse,
En ceste foy je vueil vivre et mourir.

Title-page of the First Edition of "Les Poésies de Villon", published at Paris by Pierre Levet in 1489

IV

1

EPILOGUE

Once back in Paris, Villon lived at his mother's, or, rather, took hiding there, for the business of the Collège de Navarre was still far from being finished with. Master Guillaume came one morning to inform him about it. François listened to him, and suddenly, at the mention of Tabary, he exclaimed: "Ah! That fellow deserves to have his tongue torn out!"

"Like enough," said the chaplain, "but for the love of God do not let yourself do it!"

"Good," said François with an oath. "I said that he *deserved* to have his tongue torn out, not that I was going to tear it out myself."

"I understand all right," answered Master Guillaume.

"Nevertheless, he sold us all — Colin, Régnier."

"All."

"The vermin!" swore François.

"How could you expect him not to betray you? They put him to the torture twice. Once the small rack, and then on the big one. It was no good his denying it. They knew he would speak. And didn't you say something yourself in that poem of which he made several copies:

"Adieu, je m'en vais à Angiers"?

"Come, uncle, we must not confound!"

IV

"I don't want to pain and vex you, my child," Master Guillaume continued gently. "What has been done, alas, had been done — and thoroughly. The deposition which Guy Tabary had to dictate before Master Estienne de Montigny, who brought it to me, François Ferrebouc, and various other venerable persons, amounts to an overwhelming accusation against you."

"All the same," protested the poet, "Tabary managed to get out of it."

The chaplain nodded his head.

"He got out of it by paying."

"He did?"

"His family," replied Master Guillaume, "had to put down a sum of fifty gold crowns in two instalments. Fifty crowns! We haven't got them!"

"That's so. Oh, I'd have done better to stay where I was. All that money!"

"And prison too, don't forget! Prison —— You know what it's like there? Think it over, my son. All that is required is for someone to meet you and recognize you and denounce you to the police: then nobody could do anything for you."

At these words his uncle rose to his feet and tenderly embraced his nephew.

"Be easy in your mind," said François in a low voice. "Nobody's going to recognize me in the streets just now. I give you my word for it. Come! As for being locked up, well, I prefer that that should be here, where I am."

IV

For two whole months he remained at the Cordeliers, lying on a mattress on the ground, never going out of doors, and passing his time, while his mother went off to the washing-place or to the family who employed her, in continuing his long poem. Villon wrote at a small table, with his back to the fire, turned towards a wicket which looked out on to the street. And his lot seemed pleasant enough to him. He extracted what profit he could from it, and when the bad cough which he had contracted at Meung forced him frequently to lay down his pen, he reflected that, outside, the rain was falling in sheets; that comforted him.

"Oho!" he exclaimed inwardly. "Quite enough water for me! Thibault d'Aussigny has taken away my taste for it."

But that cough racked him through and through, and he had to make efforts to resume his task. He saw himself so weakened in his room, with its absolutely bare walls, low ceiling, and floor of trodden earth, that a strange uneasiness filled him. But still François stood firm. And one day he imagined, as a stratagem against his difficulties, that he was rich and was dictating his poem to a scribe, as he had seen the Duke Charles doing at Blois. This amused him. He wrote with application:

Je sens mon cuer qui s'affoiblit
Et plus je ne puis papier.
Frémin, sié toy près de mon lit . . .

But François was his own scribe, and he waited with docility to speak his verses aloud before copying them, reading them again, stroking out, starting again, until his satisfaction with them was complete.

"Come, Frémin, don't weary yourself," he decided. "Write on a bit yet."

And little by little, carried on by this fancy of his, he could not prevent himself from furnishing to his *Lais* a kind of reply, for there, he found, he had neglected a great number of his friends.

" Premier, je donne ma povre âme,"

he murmured,

" A la benoiste Trinité.

"Go on, Frémin. Have you got that? That's the soul provided for. Now for the body: wait! As it has to be bequeathed, here you are:

"Item, mon corps j'ordonne et laisse
A nostre grant' mère la terre;
Les vers n'y trouveront grant gresse,
Trop luy a fait faim dure guerre.

And well you know it! You can vouch for that yourself, Frémin! Look. It's a pity. No, I'm not lying —

"De terre vint, en terre tourne.

That's it. Earth to earth. Into a hole in the earth, it's bound to be. Come what may, everything is rounded off for everybody in the selfsame way. Big and little, handsome or hideous, a hole — but let's get on to other things."

Speaking thus and suddenly kindling himself, he conceived the idea of what his poem ought to be. And he called it *The Testament.* And why not? He saw it printed in capital letters and set forth according to the formulas of his time. Yes. That took on a meaning. *The Testament of Françoys Villon,* or perhaps *The Great Testament.* He possessed nothing in the world except the dearly bought experience of his countless follies, but he could enrich, and greatly, those who were pleasing in his eyes. It was his right. He burst out laughing, shook himself, and then, summoning up his memories, he seized the pen and, after a legacy to his worthy uncle, transcribed his ballade to the Holy Virgin under the title: *The Ballade made by Villon at his Mother's Behest, praying to Our Lady.*

But then his good humour left him. For he called to mind Catherine, and the verses he had written for her long ago, when he was at Bourg-la-Reine. Was he to overlook her? He could not do that. The woman had filled too great a part in his life for him to make no allusion to her. And yet François hesitated, deep in his thoughts. He did not know what line to take up, when suddenly he decided, and engrossed the words:

Item, m'amour, ma chière rose,
Ne luy laisse ne cher ne foye:
Elle aymeroit mieulx autre chose . . .

and went on until, freed of this false and cruel creature, he came on to his own companions. He named them, recovered his verve, and gave himself up to it. There, God be praised! he was at his ease. There he had no fear of being saddened overmuch. Oh, no! Each of them had something from him: Régnier, Turgis, the sergeants of the *prévôté,* Casin Cholet, Brother Baude, Margot — blithely he cited them all and distributed the queer gifts amongst them.

"This will please them," he said to himself as he wrote. "Whatever I have is theirs — and even what I have not. All's well meant. Take it and carry it off. I give it you — really."

When his mother returned that evening, he was still at his task, and in such a state of excitement that the poor old soul was alarmed.

"Bah! It's nothing," he explained. "I've worked a lot to-day. Look! And very pleased I am too."

"Woe's me!" said the good woman.

François caught her in his arms and kissed her, and then, tidying up his papers, he helped her to make ready the table for the meal. He supped with an excellent appetite and told scores of stories. But suddenly about eight o'clock, just as the curfew-bells were ringing, he felt himself ill at ease, and started pacing to and fro in the room instead of going to bed.

"What's wrong then?" asked the old woman.

François looked her straight in the eyes, pointed towards the door, and said brutally: "I — well, I'm stifling in here!"

"François!"

"Yes, stifling," he threw out. "Good-night!"

And off he went, banging the door before his mother in her stunned surprise could prevent him. And it was true enough! After all the time he had been living there, without ever taking the air, he could resist it no longer. What! There was no risk at such an hour, outside, at night. Who was to see him? Who would recognize him? Nobody. He wasn't going to walk into a trap for the pleasure of it! His uncle thought him so stupid! François tittered.

"Poor man!" he said to himself, shrugging his shoulders. "Always trembling on my account: it's stupid!"

And the poet crossed the river, bore to the left, and made in the direction of the cloister of Notre-Dame, attracted thither by Margot's hostelry. A strange force led him on. He walked with long strides, not knowing exactly why he was hurrying thus, nor even seeking to know. It was something stronger than himself. He was forced to rush to this woman's, to show himself, to discover what had become of her. And as soon as he caught sight from afar of the one-storeyed white housefront and the steps of the entrance, he felt himself so imperiously pushed forward that not for one second had he any notion of his behaviour being like that of a madman.

"Hullo!" he called out from the threshold. "Margot!"

"Closing-time," said Antoine. "You're late in arriving."

"What's that? Late? But I'm François Villon. Don't you recognize me?"

"I do."

IV

"Well, then?"

Margot came out from the end of the room, and asked with a crabbed air: "What's all this noise?"

"Hark to that!" retorted François. "Are you making mock of me?"

"Easy there," said Antoine. "Don't shout. What manners! He's coming in. He thinks he can do anything. What do you want?"

"Nothing."

"Come, come!"

"No. Nothing," François went on. "I came here thinking you would welcome me with pleasure. But I was mistaken."

Margot was watching him, very attentively.

"That's no reason for making all that din," she said to him. "Look now, you must be reasonable. If you promise to behave quietly, Antoine will serve you."

"And if I don't?"

"If not," declared a pale individual who had come up to them, "if not, it will be me. And I take pleasure in warning you: you'll get good measure."

Of this meeting François kept a profound sense of deception, but he could no longer prevent himself from sallying out in the evenings and wandering about the streets. He came back at an early hour, however, and his mother, who was on the look-out for his return, did not dare to say a word to him. Villon heard her weeping, and turning over and over in her bed. He felt a great pity for her. He reproached himself for his conduct.

And then he developed the habit of remaining longer out of doors, and, as it were, passing his nights there. At the "Chariot," in the rue de la Harpe, where nobody knew him, he had formed a friendship with several young men who, playing and losing, paid for the tankards without putting a bad face on it. There was Robin Dogis, who lived in the rue de la Parcheminerie, and Hutin du Moustier, and especially a certain Pichart, whose violence, astuteness, and courage had earned him some reputation.

And very pleasing this Pichart was to François. He feared nothing, played about with women, turning their heads with his talk, and in the end robbing them of their money. In the rue Michel-le-Comte this astonishing youth had free access everywhere, and Villon, who bore him company, made him a model. But he lacked decision. If sometimes he got his hands on some trifling coin, it was only one that had fallen on the ground, or one that some drunkard had left lying on a table. And Pichart would say to his friend, disdainfully: "Pick that up."

This was hardly to his taste, however, and he conceived a very simple plan, which consisted in picking a girl to pass the night with, and then robbing her when she was asleep. The chosen night came. Villon had made his choice after the most careful inquiries. He remained in the rue Michel-le-Comte and went upstairs to bed. He was resolved to act without any scruples, and sure enough, just before dawn, he rose, searched the room, and discovered fourteen crowns put away at the bottom of a coffer. He took them, and without further ado went downstairs. But the dog gave the alarm just as he reached the street-door, and François had to go upstairs again hurriedly.

"What's that? Eh?" grumbled the landlord, appearing suddenly and catching sight of Villon. "Where were you off to?"

"I was just going away," stammered the poet.

At that moment the girl came running down with loud cries. She had woken up, noticed that her coffer had been opened, and that she had been robbed.

"Hold him!" she called, pointing to François. "I want my money back from him!"

"From whom? From me?"

"Oh, he'll give me it back."

François struggled to be free. He was held back by force, and two sergeants, sent for instantly, dragged him off to the Châtelet, for the coins were still in his pocket.

At the Châtelet François gave himself up for lost. In vain did he keep back his name. He was put out of countenance, and Master Laurens Poutrel questioned him. The affair of the rue Michel-le-Comte was dispatched in less than twenty minutes, and then the long declaration signed by Tabary was read over to the poet and he was asked to answer, yes or no.

"Yes," replied the hapless man. "But have mercy — the share that Tabary assigns — he's wrong about that. I did not have ——"

IV

"Enough," Master Laurens Poutrel cut him short. "What's more, you are lying."

He had Villon put in isolation, and caused his uncle to be informed. Then he interrogated the unfortunate man a second time, drew certain admissions from him, and decided that he would send him back if he agreed to refund the sum of one hundred and twenty gold crowns in the course of three years, this being the amount which he had actually taken possession of, that night of the robbery at the Collège de Navarre.

"How could I do that?" the poet moaned. "Forty crowns a year!"

"Bind yourself to the engagement at least," said Master Poutrel. "Your uncle has some property."

And as François was unwilling to sign, Master Guillaume was summoned. He went surety in his stead for the sum demanded.

"Oh, uncle!" sobbed François. "Help me altogether! Take me back under your roof, or I know not what will befall me! I am afraid. Protect me!"

Alas! It was too late. Master Guillaume sold a few vines which he possessed over near Notre-Dame-des-Champs, and a wretched little hovel situated in Paris, not far from Saint-Benoît. But in vain: nothing could save François. Once again he allowed himself to be led away by Pichart. He slept away from home, he got drunk, he haunted the taverns. Pernet de la Barre, the only one of his friends who had had no success, sought him out, and spoke to him of Marthe in the most contemptuous terms. She also had fallen into a life of professional gallantry, even as Catherine had done, and Pernet, who had been minded to marry her, had had to break with her. Such was life. It gave François a bitter pang. One afternoon he met Marthe, and followed her as far as the Innocents, where he saw her accosted by a man; and they went off together. An abomination! Villon remained all alone. He wandered round the cemetery amongst the tombs, until nightfall. He was overwhelmed, shame-ridden, discouraged. Then he began to come back regularly to the Innocents, in the hope of perhaps finding Marthe there again. But he waited in vain, and to kill time he strolled under the arches of the cloister, where the paintings of the "Dance of Death" inspired him with the gloomiest reflections. He gazed on the characters painted along the wall, caught in the infernal circling led all around them by skeletons bearing scythes on their shoulders, and laughing and gambolling. Death, then, was everywhere? He saw death, felt it, prowling like a dog after a scent, sniffing him and fawning on him. And he did not resist it. What was the good? He wrote these lines:

Repos éternel donne à cil,
Sire, et repos perpétuel . . .

as if his last hour had come. And he inserted them into his poem after the epitaph:

Cy gist et dort en ce sollier,
Qu'amours occist de son raillon,
Ung povre petit escollier,
Qui fut nommé Françoys Villon.

IV

Nevertheless, he had moments when his old madness seized him, and then he stupefied Pichart by the old tales he told him of Colin de Cayeux, who could have shown the pair of them so many tricks, as he did to others. But this gaiety did not last, and Villon, lost in his memories, recited to anyone who wanted it that stanza in which he conjured up his unlucky friend:

Beaulx enfans, vous perdez la plus
Belle rose de vo chappeau;
Mes clers pres prenant comme glus,
Se vous allez à Montpipeau
Ou à Rueil, gardez la peau
Car, pour s'esbatre en ces deux lieux,
Cuidant que vaulsist le rappeau,
La perdit Colin de Cayeux.

He had to be given drink if he was to be more or less tolerable. The further he went, the oftener he experienced those abrupt starts of humour which were so ill understood. He kept on coughing. His thinness of body was startling, and when he delivered one of his ballades at the "Chariot," his voice was often so husky that he could barely be heard at all.

"You ought to keep your room," said Robin Dogis one night, who had asked him to supper. "Believe me. We'd come and see you. You would read your *Testament.*"

"Bah!" was all Villon's answer.

But Pichart and Hutin du Moustier declared that Dogis was right and that they would bear François company if he went to bed early that night, whether he liked it or no.

"I'll put you to bed myself," declared Pichart, "and keep you there! If need be, we'll all three go."

"That's it. Come along," said Dogis at once.

They went over to the rue Saint-Jacques, went up it, and reached the "Mule." Finding a light showing at Master Ferrebouc's, the pontifical notary's, Pichart went over to the window and laughed at the scribes.

"Look at them!" he said to the friends. "Poor devils! They'll wear their eyes out."

And he tapped on the window until one of the scribes raised his head, opened the window a little, and asked what they wanted.

"To sell you some flutes," said Pichart, bursting into a laugh.

"You wait," cried the clerk, "and I'll pay you for them!"

"What with?"

"Come on," grumbled François.

But Pichart was too much amused to leave his game, and he spat through the window while François moved off.

"Where are you going to?" Dogis reproached him. "Wait a bit — François!"

There was an uproar. The clerks had hurled themselves all together on Pichart, and were trying to bind him. But he struggled to be free, his dagger raised aloft, when Moustier, who intervened, was seized and dragged towards the house, uttering loud cries.

IV

Then Master Ferrebouc appeared in person, and vented his anger so brutally on the unlucky man that he sent him rolling to the ground.

"Oh, that's too much!" said Pichart.

He dashed forward, crying out: "Murder! I'm being killed!" And Hutin du Moustier rose in fury, rushed up to Master Ferrebouc, and struck him several times with his knife. Then they made off at top speed, both disappearing, whilst Dogis took frenzied flight down the narrow lane of the Mathurins.

"This is a ridiculous affair," groaned the poet, "and here I am mixed up in it. What will happen to me now? I'll be caught."

Of course he was. Caught and led off to the Châtelet, where this time he had to undergo abominable wrongs, for he was taken before Master Pierre de la Dehors, who put him without any questions to the torture by water. Villon was condemned. The sentence was read out to him, and he gathered from it that he was to be "hanged and strangled at the gibbet of Paris," and that troubled him not at all.

"I must resign myself to it," he kept saying stoically. "One day or another it was bound to come, and I knew it."

And as the jailer looked at him in surprise, François recited to him these lines which he had composed as a kind of funeral oration for himself:

" Je suis Françoys, dont ce me poise,
Né de Paris emprès Pontoise,

Qui, d'une corde d'une toise,
Sçaura mon col que mon cul poise."

"Amen!" said the jailer.

But François changed his way of thinking. He appealed against the sentence before the Parlement, and on the fifth of January 1463 the court quashed the judgment in so far as the sentence was concerned, but maintained that, on account of the poet's "evil mode of life," he should be banished for a period of ten years.

"By God!" swore Villon. "This is stepping back to spring better!"

But he danced with joy because, in spite of everything, his life was safe. His uncle, whom he ran to embrace, and his mother also, were in despair. He comforted them, borrowed a little money from them, and set off early next day by the road he had formerly gone with Colin. It was almost the same time of year, but it was not snowing. An icy drizzle driven by the wind was falling. It ceased, and then came on again, and the misty clouds galloping across the sky seemed to be rearing like vast white horses, or like the foam of enormous waves suddenly falling back. From the earth there rose a cold, harsh odour. The trees, dripping with water, waved their bare branches, and a liquid mud splashed the foot-passengers as the carts rolled by, their hoods flapping and swelling in the wind.

Villon went slowly forward; his hood pulled well down, his gown drawn up round his waist, he walked alone, his face to the wind, with never a look for any of the travellers making for Bourg-la-Reine, who, from time to time, outstripped him. He went as chance led him, saying to himself that at Pourras the abbess would perhaps take him in, or that at Blois the Duke Charles would not refuse to hear him or to give him shelter. They were the only people in the world on whom he could count. But what had become of the abbess? He did not know, and was reflecting on that when, from behind him, he heard his name called by somebody.

"Stop, is that you, Perrot Girard?" answered François as he turned round.

"None other," said the barber.

"Are you going back to Bourg-la-Reine?"

"Yes."

They walked along without talking to each other, but the barber gazed at Villon with curiosity, and asked him whither he was bound.

"I've got ten years' banishment from Paris," said the poet. "For nothing. For being present at a quarrel between Ferrebouc and some friends of mine. Good measure I was given."

"I know," murmured the barber.

François was silent. He remembered that this man owed his safety only to the services he had rendered to the police at the time of the Coquillards' affair, and he felt some uneasiness at the thought.

"If Colin had been here," he reflected with disgust, "the cowardly devil would never have hailed me."

But the barber divined the poet's thought, for he

said to him very suddenly and directly: "What would you? A man makes his living where he can find it. Well or ill."

"God judges us," answered François.

"Hey!" exclaimed the other, "God? Hey! Hey! Hey!"

"What is it?"

"Yes, of course," said the barber. "You're right there."

At Bourg-la-Reine, as François did not stop, he seized him sharply by the sleeve and drew him over in the direction of his house, proposing that he should at least come in to dry himself and drink a glass of wine.

"What are you afraid of?" he asked. "Just long enough for me to find some wood and fill a pot, and then you'll be off again. Are you afraid?"

"Oh, I'm all in order," said François.

"Well, come on," continued the barber. "You'll see somebody at my place you know very well. But poor devil, he's no longer the man he was."

"Somebody?"

"Come in then!" said Perrot Girard, pushing François before him. "Straight forward. Go right into the kitchen."

"Well!" exclaimed the poet in surprise.

It was Piez Blans, seated beside the fire and plastered with mud from head to foot. He turned his gaze towards the new-comer, stared at him, and then, without betraying the slightest astonishment, burst out in his harsh voice: "Villon! Well, what's up then?"

"Not much to tell you."

"Nor have I," said Piez Blans.

He was fleeing from Orléans and from his own men, who knew that he had gold stitched into his jacket and had constrained him to take refuge with his worst enemy. For forty-eight hours now they were spying on him outside, keeping watch on the roads out of the village, and fully resolved to strip him of all he had, dead or alive. And here he was in this kitchen, vanquished but still redoubtable, on guard against everybody, with his knife in his hand, and from time to time picking his teeth with it or scraping his shoes with an air of disillusionment.

"I'm cornered," he explained. "You see. Ever since I've been hunted by order of Bishop d'Aussigny in his territory, I've held on as best I could. But up to now I've been losing the game."

"Ay," said François. "One after the other."

"God's body!" grunted Piez Blans. "To get me they'll have to put a price."

Perrot Girard came back from the cellar and flung an armful of faggots on the fire. Then, with a forced laugh, he exclaimed, playing the jovial host: "Well, here's the wine!"

François did not sitr. He gazed at the fire on the hearth, leaping and twisting its tongues of flame, and an inexpressible distress stabbed at his heart. His damp clothes smoked. He coughed, and sadly he took the glass which Girard held out to him, drank, and wiped his mouth.

IV

"I'm going," he said. "Evening's coming on."

"Oh, you've plenty of time," grumbled the barber. "Wait till to-morrow. I've room for you to sleep."

"No," answered François.

He went over to Piez Blans and grasped him by the hand. Piez Blans was suddenly seized with the idea that the poet was sent by heaven to save him. He rose, kept Villon for a good minute or two talking of Colin, of Régnier, of the short cut to take in order to reach the Abbey of Pourras, and then, as night was falling, he took off his cloak, saying: "Here, take this with you. I give it you. You can't refuse me."

"And what about yourself?"

"Me? Oh, don't worry about me. I've no need of it."

"But — it's raining."

"Go on, now," Piez Blans ordered him. "Go quickly! You must go! And God preserve you!"

And he stood waiting on the threshold, until a loud cry rang out in the darkness. It was followed by the noise of a sudden, savage struggle, which warned him that he could slip off unnoticed. But suddenly, only twenty paces away, Piez Blans himself was seized, disarmed, and bound fast by three sergeants whom Girard the barber, in great secrecy, had brought back from Paris.

APPENDIX

In the following pages are printed translations of all the verses by Villon quoted in the text. Some of these translations are by John Payne; others by John Heron Lepper. For the use of the latter, taken from *The Complete Poems of François Villon,* we are indebted to the kind permission of Boni and Liveright, Inc. In every case the initials of the translator follow the poem.

Page 96 BALLADE

OF VILLON & FAT MARGOT

If I do serve my love, nor ask for hire,
Must that be termed a vile or foolish trade?
For she possesses all that men desire.
I don for her the buckler and the blade.
When folks come in, with pot in hand displayed
I fetch the wine as silent as the dead,
Fruit, water, cheese, loaf, on the table spread,
And, if they pay well, show politeness great:
"Revisit us, when looking for a bed,
Within this brothel where we keep our state!"

But other times the fat is in the fire,
Margot *comes home without a penny made;*
I hate her sight; my heart is filled with ire;
And swear her finery shall be conveyed
To pawn, since giving credit I forbade.
At that in scorn she tosses high her head
And, arms akimbo, swears in language dread,
By Christ *I shan't! To finish the debate*
A sudden slap upon her mouth is shed
Within this brothel where we keep our state. . . .

Page 97 *Come wind, come hail, come frost, I've baked my bread!*
A brawling bully to a baggage wed.
Each worthy of the other be it said.
Like follows like; the beast must find its mate.
We sought the mire, and mire befouls our tread.
We fled from honour, honour now is fled,
Within this brothel where we keep our state.

J. H. L.

Page 202 BALLADE OF VILLON TO HIS LOVE

F alse beauty, costing me so very dear,
R ight harsh in deeds and yet dissembling fair;
A h love, more sharp of wound than sword or spear.
N o deadlier these, whose name I could declare;

C harm stained with crime, my heart in twain to tear;
I ndocile pride, whence many wounded are;
S pare, eyes so pitiless, your rigour spare;
A poor man's fortune mend, and never mar.

My better hap had been to seek, I fear,
Another's grace. . . ."

J. H. L.

Page 218 EPITAPH IN BALLAD FORM

Brothers, that after us on life remain,
Harden your hearts against us not as stone;
For, if to pity us poor wights you're fain,
God shall the rather grant you benison.
You see us six, the gibbet hereupon:

As for the flesh that we too well have fed,
'Tis all devoured and rotted, shred by shred.
Let none make merry of our piteous case,
Whose crumbling bones the life long since hath fled:
The rather pray, God grant us of His grace! . . .

J. P.

THE LITTLE TESTAMENT

Page 229 *This year of fourteen fifty-six*
I Francis Villon, *man of letters,*
With might and main, full speed, prefix
Advice to all in Fortune's fetters,
To take the judgment of your betters
About your work, the truth to know;
Vegece *has made us all his debtors,*
The sage of Rome, by saying so.

This winter, as was said before,
Near Christmas, season deathly old,
When wolves eat wind and nothing more,
And men are held indoors by cold
Where hearthstones glowing faggots hold,
The will I won to break a way
From Love's sweet gaol, whose walls enfold
My breaking heart this many a day. . . .

Page 230 *Then first, in His our Father dear,*
The Son, and Holy Spirit's name,
Our Lady's too, whom we revere,
Whose grace keeps all of us from shame,
I leave, God helping me, my fame
To Guillaume Villon, *foster sire,*
My goods and chattels, and proclaim
The honour that those names inspire. . . .

René de Montigny, three hounds,
As nobly born, I dedicate. . . .

Page 231 *Then to the* Wolf *and* Chollet *falls*
As legacy the ducklings which
Are snatched at dusk, beneath the walls,
As is their custom, from a ditch;
A mantle long and wide to hitch
About their prey, nor aught disclose,
Wood, charcoal, peas and gammon-flitch,
And my old waders lacking toes. . . .

Page 233 *At last, while sitting at my writing*
To-night, alone, in humour prime,
This lay composing and enditing,
I heard the Sorbonne *belfry chime*
At nine o'clock, its proper time,
The Angelus rang through the air;
And so an end was made, for I'm
Accustomed then to say a prayer.

Thereat, I fell into a doze,
But not from wine I swear to you,
My wits went wandering, I suppose;
I saw Dame Memory review
Her shelves, collect in order due
Concurrent mental operations,
Opinions either false or true,
And other psychic ideations. . . .

Page 234 *By* Francis Villon, *name renowned,*
On date aforesaid made and writ,

No figs or dates with him abound.
Of all his chattels not one whit,
Though black as scrubbing-brush with grit,
But for some special friend is meant;
Some coppers make his only bit
Of cash, and they will soon be spent.

J. H. L.

Page 243 BALLADE OF THE LADIES OF BYEGONE TIMES

What land afar, ah tell me where,
Doth Flora, Rome's *delight, retain,*
Archipiade, *or* Thais, *ne'er*
Were cousins a more lovesome twain;
Or Echo, answering again
Where mere lies still or river flows,
Whose beauty knew no human stain?
But where, ah where be last year's snows?

Where's Eloise, *of wisdom rare,*
Whose passion brought her lover pain?
For gelding Abelard *must bear*
And then in cloister monk remain.
And where the queen who did ordain
A sack should Buridan *enclose*
Before they dropped him in the Seine?
But where, ah where be last year's snows?

Queen Blanche, *as lily pure and fair,*
In voice so siren-sweet of strain,
With Bietris, Bertha *debonair,*
Alicia, Eremburge *of* Maine,
And Joan, *the valour of Lorraine,*
At Rouen *burnt by English foes;*
Where, Lady Blest, be all the train?
But where, ah where be last year's snows?

Prince, all enquiry will be vain
Of weeks or years where they repose;
No answer comes but this refrain:
But where, ah where be last year's snows?

J. H. L.

Page 247

BALLADE

ENTITLED:

FRANC-GONTIER REFUTED

A jolly canon on down cushions laid
Beside a stove in room both neat and gay,
Dame Lovesome *lying at his side displayed,*
Fair, tender, smooth, and tricked in rare array:
A-drinking wine from dawn to eve were they,
Rejoicing, kissing, toying, full of glee,
And both all bared the easier to be,
I saw them through the keyhole on my knees:
Then knew, that if from care we would be free
No treasure is like living at our ease. . . .

J. H. L.

Page 265

BALLAD

WRITTEN BY VILLON UPON A SUBJECT
PROPOSED BY CHARLES DUC D'ORLÉANS

I

I die of thirst, although the spring's at hand;
Hot as a fire, my teeth with cold do shake:
In my own town, I'm in a foreign land;
Hard by a burning brazier do I quake;
Clad like a king, yet naked as a snake.
I laugh through tears, expect sans hope soe'er
And comfort take amiddleward despair;
Glad, though I joy in nought beneath the sun,
Potent am I, and yet as weak as air;
Well entertained, rebuffed of every one.

II

Nought's dim to me save what I understand;
Uncertain things alone for sure I take;
I doubt but facts that all unquestioned stand;
I'm only wise by chance for a whim's sake;
"Give you good-night!" I say, whenas I wake;
Lying at my length, of falling I beware;

I've goods enough, yet not a crown to spare!
Leave off a loser, though I still have won;
Await bequests, although to none I'm heir;
Well entertained, rebuffed of every one.

III

I care for nought, yet all my life I've planned
Goods to acquire, although I've none at stake;
They speak me fairest, by whom most I'm banned,
And truest, who most mock of me do make:
He is my friend, who causes me mistake
Black ravens for white swans and foul for fair;
Who doth me hurt, I hold him debonair;
'Twixt truth and lying difference see I none;
Nought I conceive, yet all in mind I bear;
Well entertained, rebuffed of every one.

Envoi

Most clement Prince, I'd have you be aware
That I'm like all and yet apart and rare;
Much understand, yet wit and knowledge shun:
To have my wage again is all my care;
Well entertained, rebuffed of every one.

J. P.

Page 272 BALLAD OF VILLON'S REQUEST TO THE DUC DE BOURBON

Gracious my lord and prince of mickle dread,
Flower of the Lily, Royal progeny,
François Villon, whom dule and teen have led
To the blind strokes of Fate to bend the knee,
Sues by this humble writing unto thee,
That thou wilt of thy grace to him make loan.
Before all courts his debit he will own:
Doubt not but he thy right will satisfy,
With interest thereunder due and grown:
Nothing but waiting shalt thou lose thereby. . . .

J. P.

Page 290 BALLAD OF THE DEBATE OF THE HEART AND BODY OF VILLON

I

What is't I hear? — 'Tis I, thy heart; 'tis I
That hold but by a thread for frailty,
I have nor force nor substance, all drained dry,
Since thee thus lonely and forlorn I see,
Like a poor cur, curled up all shiveringly.
How comes it thus? — Of thine unwise liesse. —
What irks it thee? — I *suffer the distress.*
Leave me in peace. — Why? — I will cast about. —
When will that be? — When I'm past childishness. —
I say no more. — And I can do without.

II

What deemest thou? — To mend before I die. —
At thirty years? — 'Tis a mule's age, perdie. —
Is't childhood? — Nay. — 'Tis madness, then, doth ply
And grip thee? — Where? — By the nape. — Seemeth me
Nothing I know? — Yes, flies in milk, maybe:
Thou canst tell black from white yet at a press. —
Is't all? — What words can all *thy faults express? —*
If't's not enough, we'll have another bout. —
Thou'rt lost. — I'll make a fight for't none the less. —
I say no more. — And I can do without.

III

Dule have I, pain and misery thou thereby:
If thou wert some poor idiot, happily
Thou mightst have some excuse thy heart anigh.
Lo, foul and fair are all alike to thee.
Or harder is thy head than stone by sea
Or more than honour likes thee this duresse.
Canst thou say aught in answer? Come, confess. —
I shall be quit on't when I die, no doubt.
God! what a comfort 'gainst a present stress!
I say no more. — And I can do without.

IV

Whence comes this evil? — Surely, from on high:
When Saturn made me up my fardel, he
Put all these ills in. — 'Tis a foolish lie:
Thou art Fate's master, yet its slave wilt be.
Thereof see Solomon his homily;
The wise, he says, no planets can oppress:
They and their influence own his mightiness. —
Nay, as they've made me, so shall it fall out. —
What sayst thou? — 'Tis the faith that I profess. —
I say no more. — And I can do without.

Envoi

Wilt thou live long? — So God vouchsafe me, yes. —
Then must thou — What? — Repent; forswear idlesse
And study — What? — The lore of righteousness. —
I'll not forget. — Forsake the motley rout
And to amendment straightway thee address:
Delay not till thou come to hopelessness.
I say no more. — And I can do without.

J. P.

THE GREAT TESTAMENT

Page 297 *Not wholly fool nor wise man quite*
I've come to this my thirtieth year
And drunk up all my shame outright,
In spite of many pains severe
Thibault d'Aussigny, *as is clear,*
Inflicted on me of design;
Although a spiritual peer
He certainly is none of mine.

Page 298 *As lord or bishop he from me*
Shall neither faith nor homage find;
No land of his I hold in fee;
And I am not his hart or hind.
A summer's tide on crusts I pined
And water cold by his decree.

He starved me sorely, harsh or kind
God be to him as he to me. . . .

Page 301 *Had* Heaven *in my great distress*
A pitying Alexander *sent*
To bring me into happiness
And had my life been still misspent,
For such a sinner's punishment
To burn to ashes were too good!
'Tis need drives men to devilment
And hungry wolves to leave the wood.

How I regret my time of May*,*
My days of riot, now no more,
That unperceived stole away
Till age was knocking at the door.
No sluggard foot nor charger bore
Them off. How then? As quick as thought
On eagle wings away did soar
My youth, and I am left with nought.

Yes, it is gone and I remain
Right poor of learning and of sense,
But rotted fruit and blighted grain;
Devoid of power, or place, or pence;
And object of the most intense
Dislike from every relative.
The humblest even takes offence
Because I lack the means to live. . . .

Page 302 *Had I but studied hard, in truth,*
When I was young, nor played the fool,
But been a very virtuous youth,
I'd have a house and lie in wool.
But ah! I ran away from school,
A way that naughty children take.
The words are written; with the dule
Indeed my heart is like to break.

BALLADE THAT VILLON MADE
AT THE REQUEST OF HIS MOTHER
TO INVOKE OUR LADY

Page 311 *Lady of heaven, Queen of earth below,*
And Empress of the dread infernal shore,
Receive me your most humble Christian, so
That I with the elect may you adore,
Although I ne'er was worthy heretofore.
Your bounties, oh my Lady and my Queen,
Are greater far than all my sins have been;
No souls without this bounty merit buy
Or heaven have, no quibbling here I mean.
And in this faith I wish to live and die.

Say to your Son I'm His for weal or woe;
Through him be cancelled my offences sore:
As pardoned was Saint Mary *long ago,*
Or clerk Theophilus, *absolved of yore*
And freed from debt, you did to grace restore,
Though pact was made him and the fiend between.
'Twixt me and all such doings intervene,
Oh Virgin, in whose spotless breast did lie
The sacrament that at the mass is seen.
And in this faith I wish to live and die.

A woman old and poor I nothing know,
Unlearned, and ne'er on printed page did pore,
But at my parish church I see the show
Of heaven, with lutes and harps all painted o'er,
And hell where damned souls flame for evermore:
This frights me, that gives joy and pleasure keen.
Grant, Goddess *high, such joys I too may glean,*
Oh you to whom all sinful folk must fly
With faith endowed, of sloth and feigning clean.
And in this faith I wish to live and die.

Page 312 *V irgin and princess rare, you bore I ween*
I esus *who rules for aye each earthly scene.*
L ord of all power He took our human screen,

L ike man to help us came from heaven high;
O ffered to death in beauteous youthful mien;
N o lord but Him, on no one else I lean.
And in this faith I wish to live and die.

Page 315 *My heart grows weak and weaker still;*
The power to draw my breath has fled.
Come, Fremin, *paper ink and quill*
And take thy seat beside my bed. . . .

First, to the holy Three-in-One
I do bequeath my wretched soul. . . .

Page 316 *Item, my body's carrion*
I leave to our great mother Earth;
The worms will not wax fat thereon,
For famine has reduced my girth.
Make haste: from dust it drew its birth
And unto dust it shall return. . . .

Page 317 *Item, to my beloved* Rose
Nor spleen nor heart of mine shall go:
She craves for something else than those. . . .

Page 324 *Eternal rest be his for aye*
In clear and everlasting light. . . .

Here lies and sleeps within this tomb
A scholar poor and never tall,
Slain by Love's fatal arrow, whom
Men's tongues did Francis Villon call. . . .

Page 325 *Dear lads, beware of letting fall*
The fairest rose you own to-day;
My clerks, like bird-lime gripping all,
When out upon the prigging lay
Or robbing, watch your skins I pray:
For following these pastimes twain,
Colin de Cayeulx *had to pay,*
Relying on appeals in vain. . . .

J. H. L.

Page 328 THE QUATRAIN THAT VILLON MADE WHEN HE WAS DOOMED TO DIE

François am I, — woe worth it me!
At Paris born, near Pontoise citie,
Whose neck, in the bight of a rope of three,
Must prove how heavy my buttocks be.

J. P.